JACK & JILL

ARTS AND LOVERS

RACHEL CAREY

OLIVER HEBER BOOKS

HE LOOKS HANDSOME AND KIND, so he must be married. That is one of the fundamental rules of dating over the age of thirty-five, at least in my experience. The more he looks like a menswear model and listens like a therapist, the more likely it is that someone has already claimed him for the expanding empire of minivans and home mortgages. If a man is thoughtful, warm, and mature, then you can bet that he is jointly filing taxes in the land of the happily married. I used to live there myself, or at least on its fragmented borderlands. Now I'm exiled from that nation, with no way back in. "Borders closed," the signs say. "All territories spoken for."

My sense of isolation isn't helped by the fact that I'm watching the man through the glass wall of my company's conference room. He paces in front of a large group of children, talking to them with the enthusiasm of an overcaffeinated kindergarten teacher. It's 'Take Your Child to Work' Day, the yearly event in late April when parents at my accounting firm get the chance to show our children the wonders of our jobs, which mostly involve book-keeping, financial services, and tax advice. Our office tries to spice up the day with fun activities for the kids, so various employees always sign up to take turns entertaining their coworkers' children for an hour or two while their parents desperately try to get work done.

I didn't commit myself to a time slot this year, even though one of the kids in the conference room is mine. I honestly have no idea how to entertain more than one child at a time; I would probably have bought the kids golden retriever puppies and cans of Silly String out of sheer desperation.

This handsome, auburn-haired man is somehow managing it, though: eight children are standing against the wall behind the conference table, clutching papers in their hands and bouncing up and down enthusiastically. The table near them is littered with discarded cupcake wrappers, which may explain why the kids look so excited; their charming Pied Piper created an invisible bouncy castle out of sugar instead of air.

The bounciest of all is my own daughter, Hannah. She is six, with dark curly hair and an amusingly world-weary way of speaking that she picked up from her Aunt Abby, who babysits her after school for four days a week and helped teach her a pint-sized version of New York City cynicism. As I watch, Hannah starts jumping from one leg to the other while explaining something to the man, waving both hands for emphasis like a lawyer making closing arguments in a courtroom drama. The man in the suit nods in agreement, and I watch as she sways back and forth, giddy from all the attention.

Of course she's glowing, I think; she isn't used to having a reliable male presence in her life. Her father, my ex-husband, is a lot of fun—don't get me wrong. He has taken Hannah to waterslides and outdoor movies. He knows how to mimic motorcycle sounds and stomp his feet like a dinosaur. But he is also a musician, and a few years ago he went to Los Angeles to pursue his dreams, insisting that we would join him as soon as he hit it big. His refusal to return when he didn't hit it big was one of the triggers of our divorce. Ever since then, he tends to pop in and out of our lives at unpredictable intervals, like a 'guest star' on a tv show who never quite turns into a 'series regular.' Even before we split up, you could never count on Nick to show up exactly when and where he said he would.

Right now, I'm watching this nice married man spend more time with Hannah in an hour than her father has in the last three months.

I assume he is married, anyway: my firm is too large for me to know everyone by name, but I'm pretty sure he is one of the tax attorneys from the fourth floor. He has red-brown hair, just long enough to be combed back, and his friendly face is framed by a short beard and dark, thoughtful eyebrows. He is also wearing a green-grey tweed three-piece suit, which seems like further proof that he's in the legal department: the lawyers are usually the sharpest dressers in our business-casual financial accounting firm. I personally gravitate toward men in tattoos and jeans, but I can recognize good fashion sense when I see it; this guy looks like he should be cataloguing manuscripts in a library in Scotland.

"Are you ready for your parents?" he calls loudly enough to be audible through the doors. He has the faint trace of an accent: Cockney, maybe? Welsh? I haven't watched enough British television shows to place it.

"Yes!" The children are fully jumping now.

The man opens the glass door with a flourish, letting in the other parents who have lined up behind me to come see their kids. He glances at me and blinks once.

"Come in," he says after a second, casting his gaze to the ground.

Well, at least he thinks I'm cute, too. That's something. Not that I would ever hit on a married man; I've barely been on a date since my divorce, but it is nice to think that I am still capable of causing the occasional double-take. I used to be considered pretty back in high school, when I spent hours curling my dark brown hair into shampoo-commercial waves. Now that I'm nearing forty, I rarely bother with more than minimal make-up, and my hair is usually in a bun at work and a ponytail the rest of the time. The best I can manage these days is 'hot accountant.'

I pause at the man's side as the other parents file in around us.

"Okay, confess. What's your dirty secret?" I ask.

He blinks. "My uh...?"

"Are you some kind of ringer? Did they hire a schoolteacher for the day? How did you get them all to listen to you?"

He chuckles lightly. "Ha. No. I teach sometimes. Not kids, but..."

"You're amazing with them."

"Nah." He blushes a little and runs his hand through his hair, messing it up a bit. He reminds me of a celebrity on late night television, ruefully giving an aw-shucks look at the floor, pretending he doesn't know that he's handsome and charming.

"Which one is yours?" I ask as I look around the room.

"Oh." He shrugs, embarrassed. "None of them. I'm covering for my co-worker who was out sick today."

My heart misses a single beat.

"But my wife is pregnant with our first, so I'm preparing myself for the chaos," he adds with a grin.

And there it is. Of course he is married. Of course he is about to become the perfect father to some lucky offspring in an upscale corner of Westchester or North Jersey. The single popu-lation of New York would never have allowed him to remain on the market for longer than the length of a subway ride. He is too attractive, too likable.

I remind myself that I am happy being single. My daughter

Hannah, my sister Abby, and I function pretty well as a little family unit. I'm *happy*, I say to myself. Happy and just a tiny bit sexually frustrated.

The children ready themselves in front of the room while their parents find seats around the conference table. I grab one myself, not too far from the door. It's irritating how well I can imagine this man's life: the wife who does Pilates, the color-coded nursery, the house with its artfully weathered front porch and climbing roses. In my mind, this man has already bought his unborn child a pony and built a two-story playhouse in his backyard.

"Everyone ready?" he calls from his place near the door. "Let's show them what we rehearsed!"

The children nod and then begin reading from the pages in their hands.

"Oh no! What shall I do?" cries a slender girl with the vocal commitment of a Disney channel starlet. "Our finances are a mess!"

"You need the greatest h-h-hero the world has ever seen!" cries another child, stumbling a bit over the words.

"Superman?" asks my daughter Hannah, her eyes shining.

"No," says a small boy, stepping forward. "An accountant!"

Everyone laughs as the tiny 'accountant' strides forward.

"These numbers are all messed up. We need a tax attorney, too!"

Right then, the red-haired man's cell phone rings. He glances at it, puzzled.

"Sorry," he says quietly as he heads to the door. "I think I grabbed my wife's cell phone this morning. Keep going! You're doing great!"

The play continues, but my eyes follow him out into the hallway. I glance between Hannah's performance and the man I can still see through the glass wall. He is staring at the phone.

He hasn't answered the call, but his expression grows darker as he scrolls through notifications. Then his face shifts like he's been punched. I try to look away, but it is hard to ignore how upset he is, leaning against the wall, pulling his hand slowly over his face. I tear my gaze back to my daughter.

Hannah grins at me as she clutches a paper with our company's Murano Accounting logo printed on it, and I smile back encouragingly. She loves being on stage, just like I did at her age. I used to tap-dance and sing even though my mother could never afford to get us lessons. I copied whatever I saw on television, and I thought that meant I was a great performer until I got old enough to compare myself with the other girls whose mothers had bought them real lessons at local dance studios. It was one step on my path to realizing that our family wasn't like other families, that our life with my mother was a slow-moving trainwreck.

Does Hannah need dance class? I wonder. It's one of a long line of doubts I have about whether I'm sufficiently enriching my child's future. The constant worry hums in the back of my mind, a whispering voice that says I am not being a good enough parent.

She grins again, and I smile back. I can't help but feel grateful to the man who pulled this silliness together, especially if he is having a bad day. I want to tell him that much, at least, whenever this is over—that he did something special for these kids.

But when I turn around to look for him, he is gone.

"IT CAN'T HAVE BEEN *that* bad."

"Think 'twenty car wreck on the BQE. Home perm with bleach highlights.'"

I'm sitting in the courtyard near my office building with Vivian, my best work buddy. We always eat outside on nice days; it is cheaper than going to a restaurant but less stultifying than having a meal inside the Murano offices. Whenever the weather isn't openly hostile, we grab a spot at the scattered tables clustered across the street from our thirty-story high-rise, watching pigeons filching potato chips from stoned teenagers and buttoned-up office workers.

"Okay," she continues. "What was the worst part of the date?"

"Well, first he says to me, 'You have pretty lips. Like my mother's.'"

"Oh, no." Vivi shakes her head. "No, no, no." Vivi has enviously straight, thick black hair, and it swings back and forth to emphasize her disapproval.

"He says, 'My mom had curvy lips like yours. Want to see a

photo?' And he shows me a photo and then zooms in on his mother's lips."

"And then you walked out."

I shrug. "No. I figured, okay, that was weird, but a lot of people are awkward on a first date, you know? And then he starts talking about his home business."

"He was some kind of entrepreneur, right?" This is my fourth date in as many months, and Vivi enjoys keeping track of the details. She is a happily married mother of twin boys who seems to get a vicarious thrill from her friends' terrible love lives.

"Oh, that part was true," I agree. "His business turns out to be selling essential oils, which he mostly advertises on porn sites."

"So he's basically selling oils to make men's junk…"

"Smell like patchouli, yes."

Vivi starts laughing. "Oh, honey. How do you find these guys?"

"They're all that's out there, Viv. This is why I tried so hard to make things work with Nick. He's unreliable, but at least he's sane."

"I thought you liked Nick because he was a bad boy."

"I'm over bad boys. I'm over *all* boys." My voice sounds pathetic even to me. "But the *men* are all taken."

"Well, you gave Nick his shot, so you have to move on from that dream."

"I know." She gives me a hard look. "I know, Vivi."

The previous summer, when Hannah was seven, I spent almost two months living with my ex-husband Nick in his current city of Atlanta. The decision came after he insisted he had found a steady gig as a musician, and I should give him one more chance to patch things up. We would buy a cute little house together down there, and he would pick Hannah up from school every day, and we would turn into a real family at last. It was a roller-coaster ride for all three of us: four weeks of Hannah and me learning to live with her dad again...four weeks of romance, and family dinners, and the hope that Nick was finally going to put us first...and then three weeks of realizing he was exactly the same as he'd always been. He wanted Hannah and me in his life, but only on his schedule, and only when he was available. I ended up taking Hannah back to New York again and begging for my old job back.

Hannah is now eight and still hasn't forgiven either of her parents for disrupting her life like that, only to return to New York a couple of months later. Not long after that, my sister Abby left the city to move in with her fiancé in Newfoundland, breaking up our little family even further. My daughter has gotten her revenge by making a precocious transformation into a sarcastic tween.

Nick isn't entirely out of our lives, though. He says he is going to come to New York to watch Hannah during her upcoming April vacation, a break that lands right in the middle of peak tax season when it is impossible for an accountant like me to take time off. That is only a week or so from now, which means I will be dealing with my bad-boy ex-husband soon enough.

If he shows up.

I really want him to show up.

"There are good men out there, you know," Vivi says, packing up the remains of her salad. "I married one of them."

"And when you are killed by an asteroid, I will sweep in and ask out Peter."

"Just wait until the day after my funeral. Otherwise it's tacky."

"Well, of course. Twenty-four hours. But only because we're friends."

"You know how they toss a bouquet at a wedding?" Vivi

says thoughtfully. "They should toss the flowers off the caskets of people who leave behind a good spouse. All the single people can line up to grab it."

This dark joking is why Vivi and I are friends. "Funerals would be so much more lively if we included a speed-dating round," I agree. Then I take in the city, the restless traffic, the buildings sweeping endlessly above me. All these people and no one ever seems to meet anyone. How is that possible? "Honestly, I'm so pessimistic I think I should give up on dating entirely."

And that is when I spot him: the auburn-haired man from two years ago, stepping out of our building across the street in another nice tweed suit.

"It's that guy!" The words pop out of me. I haven't seen him since he left the conference room on 'Take Your Child to Work' Day, but I've thought about him a few times since, wondering what his horrified expression was about.

"Which guy?" Vivi's sharp eyes scan the area like she's a bird of prey.

"The red-haired guy. I thought he left the company."

Vivi's gaze locks on him. "Oh yeah. Oliver something? I thought they moved him to the Toronto office, didn't they? Maybe he's back."

"He was going to have a baby, right?"

"Ooooooh. Yeah." Vivi's voice is full of insider information. Trust her to have the dirt on everybody in an office of two hundred people. "I remember *that* story."

"There was a story?"

Vivi smiles, delighted, which means it must be very bad news indeed. "So you know Katy who works in the legal department?"

"Maybe by sight?"

"She and I were part of an infertility support group a few years back. So apparently, she knows that guy. Ollie, I think? And a couple of years ago, he was telling everyone that his wife was expecting a baby, and they had a shower at the office because Katy was also friends with the wife. But then…"

"Oh, no." My heart hurts. "Not the baby."

"No, the baby is fine. But the baby is not his. The baby was his brother's. And then the wife left him for the brother."

"Ouch." I feel the story in my gut, watching the man as he lines up at the high-end food cart that sells espresso and fancy pressed sandwiches. "And Katy was sure about that, or was that a rumor?"

"She went to college with the wife. She was friends with them both before he got the job at Murano. But I think we can guess why he wanted out of New York for a while."

I watch him for a moment. He still reminds me of a librarian, polite and thoughtful. It's the way he's dressed, but also the way he is listening to the cart owner intensely, his head tilted as the man tells some long, elaborate story. Vivi follows my gaze.

"Laura," she says. "Are you staring?"

I pull my eyes away. "No. I'm done with dating. I told you."

"Uh-huh," she says. "Well, I'm going to ask Katy about him, find out how heartbroken he is these days."

"No, please. If he is single, then he won't want a forty-one-year-old divorcée who is aging out of the possibility of more kids."

"I have two words for you," Vivi says. "Essential oils."

I put my face in my hands. "Please never mention that date again."

"Let me see if there's a chance. Come on. I feel guilty about how much enjoyment I've gotten from your horrible love life. This is my chance to repay you."

I watch him from across the street. He has moved aside to make room for the people in line behind him to order as he keeps talking to the cart owner. There is something about the scene that holds my attention: the way Oliver treats the cart owner like a real person, the way he moved out of the way so as not to hold up the line, the way he really seems to care about someone besides himself.

"Alright, fine," I say. "But do not tell him I'm interested."

NICK'S VOICE on the phone is deep and warm. He sounds the way he always does: gravelly, apologetic, like I'm the only woman in the world for him. I probably am, too. Cheating was never the issue between us.

"Hey, Laura." My heart speeds up, but I'm not sure whether it's from lingering attraction or the anticipation of bad news.

"Hey." I'm trying not to sound nervous or angry. He's due in New York first thing Saturday morning, in three days, and I don't want to start his visit with a fight. My house growing up was full of my mother screaming after men on their way out the door. It's one reason I try to stay calm; I know the bitter harpy who lives just under my surface, and I refuse to let her out. "Did you find a place to stay yet?"

I am determined not to offer Nick my sofa. Staying under the same roof with him is too much of a temptation, even now. His voice still gives me shivers.

"Not yet." There's a pause.

"Well, it's coming up soon..." My voice is gentle. Not whining. Not threatening.

"I know, but here's the thing..." And before he says it, I know.

"Oh, come on, Nick."

"I *want* to be there," he replies.

"It's not about wanting or not wanting. Hannah needs someone to watch her while she's out of school this week, and I have work. These are some of the busiest days of the year for me."

"I can make it to New York by Wednesday," he offers, like we're negotiating.

"Wednesday," I say flatly.

"And then you'd only need childcare for Monday and Tuesday and maybe Wednesday morning."

"What am I supposed to do, Nick?"

"I'll pay for a sitter. Anything you need. Look, the money for this gig is really good. It's a good band, and the pay is on a whole different level for me, and that means—I know I'm still a month or two behind on child support, but I could pay you back all that, too. And this could lead to a tour. I'm doing this for all of us."

That's what he has always said, every time he let me down. And I know it's sincere, on some level. He is always right on the verge of getting the job that's going to allow Hannah and me to live a life of luxury, if he just takes this One...Last...Gig.

"I don't even know if I can find one of our usual sitters at this point," I tell him. "And I don't want her to be with a total stranger all day."

He sighs, like I'm the one being illogical. "Well, other people in New York must have this problem with school vacation, right? Aren't there camps or something? I'm sure we can figure something out. Look, I'm really sorry, okay? I need to take this because it's basically an audition for joining the band, but I'll come up as soon as I can. And I could be there for the entirety of the week after."

"She'll have school then."

"Then I'll come for a weekend."

"You know what's really sad about this?" I let the words hang there for a moment, almost not wanting to say them. "I didn't even tell her you were coming."

I can hear the quiet on the other end of the phone. Finally, something has managed to sink in.

"I'm sorry." His voice is low.

It is my turn to sigh. I'm done with him, and it's breaking my heart a little. "I'll try to find a sitter, and I'll tell you how much it costs."

Then I hang up the phone and look out the window. Calm. Stay *calm*, Laura.

Three days later, the doorbell rings.

"You can get it, Hannah!" I say as I exit the kitchen, making it clear that just this once, she is allowed to open our apartment door. Hannah glances at me and then runs to the door of our apartment and throws it wide.

"Tabby!"

Hannah throws her arms around my sister's shoulders, and Abby lifts her up and spins her around.

"You came here from *Canada?*"

Abby is grinning. "Well, I heard there was some kind of New York holiday called 'Take Hannah to Museums' week, and I wanted to be here for it."

I want to hug her, but it's hard to make myself step closer. It's hard to go through this again—Abby swooping in to help me when my ex-husband bails. It makes me feel like an idiot every single time, although in this case, it was completely her idea. I called her to brainstorm what I should do, but it didn't even occur to me to ask her.

"Hey," I say, more coldly than I mean to, because I feel so

humiliated. She's had Nick's number since the first time she met him; that makes one of us.

She walks over, leaving Hannah fiddling with the handle of her rolling suitcase. "What's wrong?"

"I hate this," I say, my voice sounding like I'm near tears.

"What? Me shamelessly assuaging my guilt for abandoning you guys?"

I shake my head, unable to get more words out.

"It'll be fine. It'll be great." Abby gives me a hug and smiles. "I'm here for as long as you need me. You should go on a date or something. Make the most of this."

My sister Abby is a financial writer, so she can work from anywhere. This is one reason it was so easy for her to leave New York for Canada, and one reason why it hurt so much to see her go. I love that she's happy, but she has stopped being my daily emotional support and my most reliable babysitter, and it's made things a lot harder. Not impossible, exactly: I managed to get Hannah into an after-school program that runs until six every day, so my child-care costs are manageable. It's just shifted the entire rhythm of our lives.

"I'm not doing anything but work before the fifteenth," I murmur quietly in her ear. "And then Nick may get here."

"Okay. But plan something fun for next weekend," Abby whispers. Then her eyes light up with a mischievous smile. "If Nick does show up," she murmurs, "he can watch Hannah while you go on a date."

Hannah approaches us and starts pulling Abby by the arm, insisting they return to the sofa to watch her show. I know Hannah watches too much TV; it's another one of the penalties I pay as a single mom—not striking the perfect balance between wholesome activities and brain rotting screen time or home-cooked meals and take-out dinners.

"Come on," Hannah insists as Abby follows her to the sofa. "We're missing the best part."

"Okay, okay, kid. When did you get taller than me?"

"I'm not *taller* than you." Hannah rolls her eyes.

They sit down and then Hannah leans one elbow right into Abby's lap, resting her head as she gets absorbed back into her show.

"I'll get you a ginger ale," I say, my heart wrenching at the sight of them back together like a little team.

"Perfect," Abby says with a grin. "I'm going to dribble it all over this kid's hair."

"Hey!" Hannah cries.

"Okay, fine, I won't," Abby groans. "Maybe just a little dribble?"

"No!" Hannah wails.

It occurs to me, not for the first time, that Abby always has more fun with my kid than I do. It's not that I don't adore Hannah. There's just a constant thrumming worry when I look at my daughter, a sense that I'm forgetting something like setting up a doctor's appointment or filling out forms for school. I rarely think about having fun with her; it's too far down the list of responsibilities.

As I pour Abby's ginger ale in the kitchen, I feel an ancient impulse to pour myself a drink. I haven't touched alcohol in years, but I still miss that immediate sense of relief I got from sipping something and then staring into space, waiting to feel less of whatever I was feeling right then. I inherited substance-abuse tendencies from my mom, so I can't go halfway on alcohol, unfortunately, which means there is none in my apartment. I still miss it, though, even with occasional AA meetings. Even with help.

That was always part of the appeal of Nick when I was with him. He supported my sobriety, but he also felt like his own addiction. Being in his arms was like being on the back of a motorcycle or sipping strong whiskey: dangerous and exciting. You could forget everything in the world except his hands around your waist, his voice in your ear suggesting some dangerous plan that you were both going to enjoy. Being with him felt like flying. We just never found a solid place to land.

3

A COMPANY PARTY

VIVI TEXTS me first thing in the morning: *Did you get that meeting request for today?*

I write back: *tragically yes*

The entire New York office is being called in to the large meeting room on Murano's second floor, a sloping space that feels like one of those big lecture halls where I caught up on sleep during my statistics courses in college. We haven't been given any information about the purpose of the meeting, which is never a good sign. This could mean layoffs, or leadership changes, or just an irritating piece of software we all have to learn. It could mean anything, and it's coming the day after April 15th, Tax Day... right when those of us who work as individual and small business accountants are coming off a stretch of frantic phone calls from desperate clients.

I arrive early at the meeting so Viv and I can sit in our favorite spot: the second-to-last row. It doesn't single us out visibly as slackers, but it allows us to sit next to each other and write occasional amusing notes on legal notepads. It's a strategy we worked out early in our work friendship: it helps us blow off steam in the various torture sessions held by a rotating cast of managers and V.P.s who always have a 'vision' for the new direction of the company, usually involving something that has been tried before and failed spectacularly.

The meeting starts with general information about trainings that are being rolled out across the company in our seven worldwide offices, and Vivi draws a picture on her legal pad of someone rolling their eyes, and then writes a little arrow showing the direction of the eyeroll whenever the presenter talks about how *useful and engaging* we're going to find the sixteen-hour training module that we have to do on top of our regular work over the next five weeks.

Then there is a brief discussion about benefits changes, which translates, as always, to the company charging us a little more money for a little less service while spinning it as offering us more choice.

Unionize! I write to Vivi on my notepad.

She writes back: *Can you imagine this crowd agreeing on anything, let alone a union?*

Next up is a woman named Destiny, one of the department's Human Resources Directors who was hired three years ago and has shot up the org chart like a blazing meteor or a childless, competent woman who doesn't mind answering weekend emails. She wears a structured cream linen suit, her cropped grey hairstyle flattering against her warm brown skin.

"So." Destiny takes in the room with the look of someone about to deliver bad news. "Some of you may be aware that an employee in our Dallas office was investigated for sexual harassment last year after a relationship with a subordinate. I can't speak to the details of that, but part of our settlement was that we will be reviewing our policy about inter-office dating and making sure that it is as clear as possible. We have asked each manager to suggest trustworthy and impartial people to serve on this committee."

I write to Vivi: *note to self: stop being trustworthy and impartial.* I flip up the notepad to she can see it.

There is a brief, muffled chuckle behind us, and I turn around to see Oliver, my office crush, lowering his eyes to his laptop from the seat behind me. Apparently Vivi and I were not being as subtle as we thought.

When he glances back at me, I give him a shocked, scolding expression to try to shame him for reading our notes, and he raises his hands in a gesture of apology before returning to his laptop.

Destiny continues. "If you are asked to serve, I hope you will take it very seriously. It is an important and legally mandated task that the office needs to fulfill within the next few months."

Vivi watches my expression and then smirks a little as she looks down.

I haven't asked Katy about Mr. Redhead, she writes to me in tiny, barely readable letters at the top of the notepad.

What about him? I write back in equally small letters.

She points back to her drawing of someone rolling their eyes.

When I get back to my desk, my co-worker Brant is waiting at my desk. He is tall and muscular with a nearly shaved head, the kind of guy who was ruggedly handsome in college but now has a sharp, disaffected air, like life and his hairline have both disappointed him. He and I used to be decent work friends during my first couple of years at Murano. We were hired at the same time, and we became buddies during the initial endless training sessions. Then he received the promotion that I missed out on when I left to try things again with Nick last summer, and now he is essentially my manager. I need to keep on Brant's good side if I want a promotion, but this has grown trickier since his divorce two years ago. He has developed a tendency to share deeply bitter sentiments about love and marriage with me on the assumption that I will agree, when what I usually want to tell him is that it sounds like he needs therapy. There are only so many times you can say that to someone who has the power to fire you, though.

"So, Laura," he says with a dry tone, "I promise this is work-related, but you're not dating anyone in the office at the moment, are you?"

"Uh...no?"

He gives a dry half-smile. "Great, because I volunteered both of us for that committee on workplace relationships. I thought it would be good for you to get some face time with people from other departments. Show folks you're here to stay after your thing last summer."

He is referring to my disappearing act when I moved to Atlanta, of course, and I nod with my best appreciative smile. I can never tell whether Brant is trying to help me or just remind me of how close the company came to firing me so that he can keep me on my toes.

"Yeah, of course. I can do that."

"They asked me to try not to recommend someone who was already in the middle of an office romance, since that might undermine the committee's credibility."

"Well, I am safely single."

"That's because you're smart," he says. "Who needs the misery?"

"Yep!" I try to give him as little fuel for his smoldering pile of pessimism as possible, even though I secretly share it. He hangs out at my desk for another few minutes, asking me about my weekend plans and whether I'll make it to the company's yearly office party.

"I hope so," I say. "But we'll see. Childcare and all that."

"Yeah, Kara has the girls this weekend, so that's not a

worry." He frowns. "She's introducing them to the new *boyfriend*."

"Oh, dear." Kara is his ex, and I hear more about her from Brant than about anything work-related.

"No doubt that means four people are soon going to be living off half my salary, so good for him I guess."

"Right. Well, I should..." I gesture feebly to my computer.

"Right. See you at the committee. We should just tell everyone not to date anyone, period."

"Ha. Yep."

He laughs once and then turns to go.

When I open my work email, the notification is already there. I have been selected for the "Policy Revision" team on office relationships, which is going to start up in a couple of weeks. I sigh. I am not looking forward to spending hours in a room with Brant, listening to his opinions on workplace romance. He is right, though; I'm still on thin ice after last summer, and this is definitely not the time to refuse any special requests.

Then I notice another name near the top of the list of six people who have been asked to serve on the committee: Oliver MacCormack. My heart lifts a little even though I'm not sure he's *my* Oliver. I search through the company directory for any other Olivers, then write Vivi a quick text: *Emergency. Will be serving on that new committee with office crush.*

Vivi texts me back on my way home from work: *Definitely write a policy that says that you can have sex with members of that committee anytime you want.*

I reply: *Can you find out from your friend if he's got some live-in yoga instructor girlfriend before I put in that request?*

Vivi replies, *Will check on yoga instructor gf.*

. . .

Nᴉᴄᴋ ꜰɪɴᴀʟʟʏ ᴀʀʀɪᴠᴇs in the city on the Thursday night of Abby's school vacation week. I have told this to Abby ahead of time so she can book her flight home on Friday, but I don't tell Hannah until Nick is literally on the elevator coming up to our apartment. You have to be careful, when it comes to Nick. He could land a gig on his taxi ride from the airport.

"Daddy!" Hannah shouts when she sees him, and Nick throws his arms around her and spins her in a circle, saying, "Baby, baby, baby."

Abby watches from my sofa with raised eyebrows.

"You and Tabby are both here!" Hannah cries.

"Yeah, crazy coincidence, right?" Abby drawls.

Nick has the grace to look abashed, but only for about three seconds. "Abby," he says, "good to see you," walking forward to give her a brotherly hug, which she accepts with the facial expression of someone picking up a used tissue from the sidewalk.

"Nick." Her tone is as sharp as a pen knife.

"Listen," he says, "you stepped in to be a superhero. But it worked out this time. I'll tell you over dinner, maybe? Laur?" He glances over at me.

"It's a bit late for dinner around here," I say.

"I'm sorry it took me so long to get here. There was a delay on the runway."

And there it is, the brief apology, as if none of this is within his control. I glance at Hannah, not sure if I should cover for him again. "Things worked out," I reply quietly, "thanks to Abby."

"Well, now that you're here, Nick," Abby says briskly, "I'm going to go out and try to catch up with a couple of friends. Not that dinner wouldn't be fun." She glances at Hannah. "Have a great time with your dad, sweetie. I'll kiss you good-bye in the morning before I go to the airport, okay babe?"

Hannah's face falls. "You're leaving?"

"Tomorrow. I have to get back to Newfoundland, but I was waiting for your dad to get here first. You'll come visit me for three whole weeks this summer, okay? That's only a few weeks away. I can't wait." Abby clearly didn't tell Hannah about her departure plans, either; she also wasn't sure Nick would turn up.

"You have your dad here to watch you," I add, "so that should be fun, right?"

Hannah nods. She senses a tension in the air but can't be sure of the source of it. That is one of the big downsides of my covering for Nick's absences. It hurts Hannah less to believe that her dad isn't at fault when he doesn't show up, but then she blames me for the hostility that's lingering between us. Someone has to be the bad guy, and when I let Nick duck the responsibility, there's only one parent left.

"So where's your hotel, Nick?" Abby asks pointedly. Bless her.

Nick looks between us, rubbing the back of his head. "Yeah, I have to book something. I was so caught up in trying to get here..."

"Yep. Sounds like you have to," Abby agrees, nodding.

I step forward, bolstered by Abby's firmness. "I'm sure we can find something nearby. Let's let Nick order some dinner and I can do a quick search for hotels." Abby shoots me a grin, proud of me for not offering him my couch to stay on.

The next morning, while Abby packs her bag and then strips her sheets from the sofa, she reminds me that I should go to my work cocktail party on Saturday. More quietly, she tells me that I better "have sex with someone in the bathroom."

"That's how I met Nick," I tell her.

"Ugh, then forget it."

Hugging Abby good-bye feels like losing the stable foundation in my universe yet again. I have to get better at accepting that she's always there for me but no longer here for me.

It's a good idea to go to the party, though. I confirm with Nick that he can watch Hannah while I go to a work event; I suggest that he take her to the aquarium and then to dinner so that I can slip out without them noticing that I'm dressed for a party.

No such luck, though. Hannah isn't feeling well on Saturday, which means that Nick and Hannah are sitting on my sofa watching a slightly problematic 1980s action film when I head out the door a little before 5 p.m., my hair in a French twist and my wine-red cocktail dress clinging to my body.

"Sorry about this. Professional obligation," I tell Nick as I tuck my lipstick in my purse.

He looks me over, a strange heat in his eyes, and then nods once. "Sure. Have a good time."

I feel unsteady as I walk down the hallway. We are divorced, I remind myself, and he is spending time with his own child. He is a grown man, and he can handle the realities of what being divorced means.

Why do I feel guilty?

The company cocktail party is being held in an elegant atrium room and outdoor patio that have been reserved for the evening in the conservatory of the New York Botanical Garden. We are surrounded on all sides by trailing walls of flowers and dangling vines, the room decorated with sparkling lights and attractive servers proffering wandering trays of canapes and crostini. A DJ plays a collection of instrumental versions of the old jazz standards. As I step into the space, I left myself drift on the current of magic for a few moments. This is my glamorous life as a New Yorker, I tell myself—nights out, warm breezes, elegant people in expensive shoes. I let myself feel sophisticated, polished, confident.

Then the first person I spot is Brant, predictably, approaching me with a glass of wine in hand.

"Doing the making an appearance thing?" he asks.

I nod. "Looks like it."

He glances at my red dress. "Quite an appearance." I can't tell if he means it as a compliment or an insult.

"Well, I don't get out to grown-up functions that often, so I probably overcompensated."

He smirks. "Kara is probably out on the town in stilettos every time I have the kids for a weekend, but I try not to think about it."

"Mmm."

He casts his eyes around. "Well, I guess I'll go circulate, see if I can get a little more info from the V.P.s about the outlook for next year. There was buzz last quarter about layoffs, but if that comes up, I will make sure they know you're an employee of seven years, not a new hire."

"Thanks, Brant."

I move away as quickly as I can while trying to look like I'm casually wandering, not subtly slipping away from him. The glass conservatory looks staggeringly romantic in the last glow of sunset...or so I gather from the three separate couples I see making out behind different vines. It makes me wonder what the new inter-office dating policy should look like. The current rule is that you can date anyone, as long as they aren't a direct supervisor, but the company will act like your grumpy old aunt who doesn't particularly approve. Several marriages have started by disappointing the delicate sensibilities of Murano H.R., as Vivi likes to point out.

I'm making a sharp right-hand turn to avoid another couple when Vivian appears from behind me.

"He likes you."

I spin around to face her. Vivi looks gorgeous, as always, in a sleek black dress and with her hair in a fresh cut that swings just below her chin. "Brant?"

"Oliver. I asked him about you, and he said—"

"I told you not to tell him I was interested!"

"And he said..." She pauses dramatically, one finger poised in the air like an orchestra conductor. "He said he knew who you were, and you were gorgeous."

"Oh my God." I cover my face. "This is like high school."

"No, it is like eighteenth-century England, where your married friends take control of your love life and you communicate with suitors by flipping your fan. But my point is that right now, at this very moment, he is waiting in the courtyard for you, and you are going to take a turn around the garden with him while I watch from an appropriate distance as chaperone."

"Chaperone? I have four tattoos."

"Really?" Her eyes scan my shoulder to where a small Japanese dragon tattoo peeks out from under my dress. "I only know of three. Please tell me the other one is a tramp stamp of an Eagles quote."

"It's Tweety Bird holding a bong."

She snorts as she takes my arm. "He's waiting." She gives me a little shove.

I step out of the conservatory and into the breezy open-air courtyard, my heels wobbling on the uneven paving stones. Sure enough, Ollie stands all alone near a tinkling fountain, his hair glowing redder than usual in the last touches of sunset, his eyes staring into his drink like there's a goldfish swimming in it. He has dressed down from his usual three-piece suit and is in a crisp white shirt and blazer and he looks…not sexy, exactly—he's a little too buttoned-up for that—but deeply appealing.

I take a breath and walk forward. He catches my eye and then takes in my dress, and his eyes widen a little.

"Hello," he says with a half-smile.

"Hi." I hope my cheerful tone acknowledges how weird this all is. "I'm Laura." I thrust out my hand. "I'm one of the accountants. And you are…"

"Ollie. Tax law."

"Hot," I say, jokingly imitating a gum-snapping teen on TikTok, and then I immediately regret it. What if he thinks I actually talk like that? But he's smiling.

"Yeah, I always tell people it's a very sexy field," he says, "but I'm not sure they buy it." He smiles a little more. His eyes catch my tattoo, widening slightly.

"So what are you—"

"So how are you—"

We both stop talking.

"So," I say.

"So," he says. This really is like high school. Neither of us seems to remember how to talk. He continues after a moment. "I guess we'll be serving on that committee together. I read the list of invitees and saw you on there."

"Oh, that's exciting," I say, like I hadn't noticed it myself. Exciting?

"Nothing like committee work to make you feel alive."

"Get enough accountants in a room and it's basically an orgy."

He coughs on a laugh, and I panic.

"Sorry, I just meant—"

"I'll try to prepare myself for that," he says.

"Were you away for a while?" I try desperately to switch topics. "Someone said that you were in the Toronto office?"

"London, then Toronto." An emotion crosses his eyes and then is gone.

"Are you from there? I thought you might have an accent."

"Australia. My family moved here when I was sixteen. And you have a daughter, right?"

I'm touched that he remembers after two years. "Hannah," I say, nodding. "She's eight. I'm divorced, and my ex-husband is... he's not in the picture... I mean he's watching her today, but only because he managed to finally show up halfway into her school vacation after promising he'd watch her the whole time. He lives in Atlanta."

Ollie nods, taking this in. Wrong topic, I sense.

"But you were so amazing with the kids," I say, desperate for a topic change. "You were like Mr. Rogers if he handed out recreational party drugs."

He chuckles. "I prefer to think I was spurring their natural enthusiasm for accounting. I mean, who wants your parents to have a boring job like police officer or firefighter?"

"Someone has to inspire the next generation of office drones."

"Yeah, that day was..." He trails off. Of course he does, because I brought up probably the worst day of his life. Nice work, Laura.

"So are you back permanently—"

"Would you like to..."

We both stop talking.

"...get coffee sometime?" he asks.

"I...I mean yeah, sure. If you..."

"Because I..."

"Sure. Yes. Yes."

"Great." He is smiling. It's a nice smile. There may even be dimples under the beard, which feels chronically unfair. We stare at each other for another moment.

"Would you be willing to give me your phone number?" he asks.

"...Sure. Right." I blink at him like phone numbers are a foreign concept I am just beginning to grasp.

He takes his phone out of his pocket and hands it to me.

What is my problem? I wonder as I type my phone number. I used to be good at flirting. People have slammed tequila shots off my stomach. I used to be *cool.*

My problem is that I never do this anymore. And when I did do it, I did it at bars and frat parties, or in the back of someone's van on the way to a rave, or on a bus hired for a bachelorette night in Vegas. By the time I was thirty, I was already with Nick, and sober, and since then I haven't dated much at all. Occasional patchouli entrepreneurs notwithstanding, I don't really know how to date as sober Laura.

This feels different. He feels different. This can't be right, can it?

I hand back his phone, and he pockets it.

"Well..." he says. He glances over, and I'm pretty sure he notices Vivi watching us.

"Well!" I respond cheerfully. "So what do you think of—" I begin.

"So I'll give you a call?"

I nod. "Great. Yeah."

He nods once, and then walks away, and I can feel myself melting into the paving stones from embarrassment.

Why was I so completely out of my depth? Was he shy, or was I...? *What* was I? Vivi has indeed been watching the whole thing, because she has the nerve to wave at me cheerfully as I walk back toward her.

"That looked like it went well!"

I make a small groaning noise. He didn't even talk to me. I couldn't even talk to him.

"I think he's shy," I say finally. "I hope so, anyway. It's either that or we have no chemistry at all."

"He's probably shy. Come on. There's dancing. Maybe you can ask him to dance."

"I guess."

Vivi pulls me, a little dazed, back toward the main courtyard where we watch the dance floor for a minute or two. The DJ has switched to playing pop hits, and a few couples are attempting a corporate version of getting down to the beat. I love dancing, but I am always amazed by people who can do it at work events like this. It's like dancing at a wedding where everyone on the guest list has the power to fire you.

Brant catches my gaze and tips a glass toward me, and I only then wonder if I've already gotten in trouble in terms of that committee assignment and his questions about not dating anyone in the company. Should I not have said yes to Ollie?

Well, it's certainly not anything serious, if Ollie and I can barely manage to speak to each other. I figure that I will give Ollie and me a date or two and find out if it's even a real issue before I come clean to my manager.

"Let's get you a drink," Vivi says.

"I could use a ginger ale."

"We'll get in the line with the server who looks like a hot Viking."

"As a former bartender, I want to remind you that you are not allowed to flirt with servers at work, young lady."

Vivi grins. "I would never. I have a strict ogling-only policy."

We get into one of the long double-lines for drinks. I notice that Brant has insinuated himself into a group of people from the legal department and looks like he is telling another one of his cynical jokes.

"You okay?" Vivi asks, leaning toward me.

"Yeah, it's just... I don't know." I shake my head. I think of

Nick, back home on my sofa, and how much easier it would be to crawl into his arms and forget about dating, even if I knew he'd be disappearing again within a few days.

"You don't know about what?"

"Dating, or…" I keep thinking about staring into Ollie's eyes. How handsome he was and how it felt like we had nothing to talk about. He was a stranger to me. A warm, kind stranger. When I met Nick, it felt like we understood each other instantly, but that may just have been because we were on a dance floor and I knew I wanted to have sex with him, and then ten minutes later we were backstage in a tiny club doing exactly that.

"So you had no chemistry with Ollie?" she asks.

That isn't exactly it, I think. I'm just worried that the chemistry was entirely one-sided and he was just being polite.

"Well, maybe it's what I need right now," I say, trying to sound flip. "I mean, I had tons of chemistry with Nick, so maybe I need a boring, safe tax attorney who I will have literally nothing to talk to about with."

I'm mostly kidding, but Vivi winces, and I know—even before I turn around—that she has spotted Ollie near us. Sure enough, I turn to see Mr. Tax Attorney standing not three feet away in the other line. His gaze meets mine, his expression flashing with something like hurt, then blankness. My eyes close for a second, trying to block out what I've just done, and then I open them and force myself to step toward him.

"I'm sorry," I begin.

"It's okay." He shrugs, his mouth twisted slightly into an unreadable line. "Not a problem."

He nods once more, then turns and walks out of the line to get away from me. When I glance back at Vivi, her expression mirrors mine.

"I don't think he's calling me."

"No," she agrees. "Probably not."

Something inside my chest twinges. Apparently, my obsession with Nick is still managing to mess me up. When a nice guy shows interest, I immediately find a way to ruin it.

What am I doing? After a moment, I smile apologetically at Vivi and then step out of the line to go find Ollie. It feels like there's more to say. I can't have had a secret crush on this guy for two years, just to have things end so quickly, especially when I didn't even mean what I said. I was just trying to prepare myself for when he didn't call, or disappeared, or ended up wanting someone younger.

When I spot him, he is on the dance floor, dancing with a woman who I'm pretty sure is Katy, the attorney that Vivi is friends with, the one who used to go to college with Ollie's wife. I've seen Ollie and Katy chatting on the elevator once or twice, and she is very pretty, but that's not the part that makes my heart sink.

It turns out that Ollie is a very good dancer. Ridiculously good. He is dipping her and spinning her around in what looks like a polished routine, but I know that it can't be. It's not like he would have made a special request to the DJ to play this 1990s R & B song, and he definitely couldn't have choreographed this ahead of time. He just knows how to dance, and I don't mean that he can move well. I mean he moves like a professional dancer. And on top of that, there's a chivalry to his dancing, a willingness to let his partner shine.

I feel the sharp regret that comes from a realization made too late. Ollie is sexy. Extremely so. Katy isn't as good a dancer as he is, but he's guiding her through steps smoothly, pulling her close and then back again, landing her after every spin or turn.

The song ends, and he whispers something to Katy and turns to go, just as Vivi leans toward me.

"What the hell was that?" Vivi hands me a ginger ale, her eyes on Ollie.

"West Coast Swing," says a woman next to us. We both glance over at her. "He teaches it in the evenings. He used to be a top-ten national competitor or something." She shrugs. "He works in my department. We're all *obsessed* with him."

"I mean, why wouldn't you be?" Vivi says, to cover for my shock.

I glance back at Ollie, who is moving back through the crowds toward the line where people can get drinks, clearly having decided to return only when he was sure not to run into me again.

I shake my head. "I thought swing dancing was something you did to like, the Brian Setzer Orchestra."

"Not that style," the woman says. "West Coast is the slower version. They do it to pop songs a lot of the time. You should look up his videos online. He's amazing."

I think about walking up and asking him to dance, but now I'm too intimidated.

"Can we go home?"

Vivi nods once.

She and I share a taxi back to our neighborhood in Brooklyn. She lives only a few blocks from me in Cobble Hill, and we spend the whole ride on our phones, looking up West Coast Swing videos on YouTube. Apparently if you look up "Oliver MacCormack dancer," you can find over twenty videos of him, most of them from six or seven years ago, dancing at competitions and doing what are known as 'Jack & Jill' dances, improvisational dances where two random dancers are partnered together, given a surprise song, and have to make up a dance on the spot.

Ollie is exceptional at the improvised dances, and his videos have hundreds of 'likes.' When he's matched with a partner who knows what she's doing, he is the most elegant man I've ever seen. Somehow his dancing matches with his nice suits and carefully styled hair: all charm, desire, and restraint.

Right as the taxi pulls up to my place, Vivi gives me a quick hug and says cheerfully, "Well, maybe he'll still call you." I can tell she doesn't believe it any more than I do.

I take the elevator up to my apartment, my heart sinking with every floor. Though it's only eight-thirty, Nick has already fallen asleep on the sofa with Hannah. I stand there watching them as they lean against each other in front of the muted television, an empty bowl for popcorn precariously balanced nearby. Hannah is in her pajamas, and Nick looks as handsome as ever, with his dark curly hair and perennial five o'clock-shadow. He's in a grey t-shirt and dark jeans, and his old, scuffed cowboy boots lean against one side of the sofa.

Two years ago, if I'd found them like this, I would have let Nick crash here for the night. I would have hoped that it was the beginning of something different, a new phase in which he returned to our lives as a real father and husband.

Now I carefully slide Hannah into my arms and carry her back to her bedroom, slipping her under the covers as she stirs awake. She is almost too big to carry, but not quite yet. I can still manage it. When she is settled, I tiptoe away to close her bedroom door as quietly as I can.

"Is Daddy gone?" Hannah's voice stops me just as I'm slipping out.

"He's going back to his hotel now," I say. "He'll be back in the morning."

"How long is he staying?" Her voice sounds small.

I hesitate, not wanting to get it wrong. With Nick, you always end up getting it wrong. "I'm not sure, sweetie, but I know he's staying for as long as he can. We'll talk to him about it more tomorrow."

When I return to the living room, I lean over and shake Nick's knee until he opens his eyes.

"Hey, I'm back," I say. "You can go back to your hotel now."

He sleepily blinks at me and then rises, glancing at my dress again. I watch as he slips on his boots and worn leather jacket and gives me a lopsided, tired smile.

"I'll call in the morning," he says in his sexy, gravelly voice. "I'll come by and see you both tomorrow."

"Sure."

"Did you have fun?" he asks pointedly.

A moment of regret passes my eyes, because tonight was a disaster. I know he catches my disappointed expression because he grins.

"You look good, Laur."

"Yeah, yeah."

As he walks past me, I sense that he is stepping a little closer than is absolutely necessary, close enough that I can feel the heat of his body moving past. I put some distance between us as I hold open the door for him.

"Goodnight," he says with his lopsided smile.

"Goodnight, Nick."

Once I've closed the door and locked it, I walk to my bedroom and imagine a conversation with my mother. She passed away a couple of years ago, but I sometimes talk to her anyway. Not for help or advice... I just like to remind myself how much worse she would have handled things.

"Hey," I say in my head. "If you'd been there tonight, you would have tried to undress Ollie on the dance floor and then gotten trashed and hit on your boss. And after you ended up getting fired, you would have come home and slept with Nick."

"It would have been fun, though," she says back to me.

These silent conversations always make me feel both better and worse. I feel better, because at least I'm not as bad as she was. She's the low bar that makes me feel like I'm doing okay at life. But I'm still so angry at her, and that always hurts, now that she's not alive to hold up her end of an argument.

It's like Abby said to me a week after the funeral. "Mom could at least have slipped in one apology at the end, right? Just on her dying breath, like, 'Hey, sorry I sucked as a parent. Your therapy costs are my fault.'" Abby imitated a dying groan as she said it.

We never got that apology from my mother, even after the years we spent taking care of her hospital bills and sending her money whenever she was about to lose her housing. We never got an apology for the time we spent taking care of her, instead of her taking care of us.

I'm not repeating her mistakes. That's something. But I still managed to ruin my chance with a great guy. A nice, well-dressed, sexy, stupidly handsome man. I lie down, put on head-phones, and punish myself by watching another one of Ollie's videos. As I do, a text comes in from my sister Abby.

How was the guy?

I consider her message for a long moment and then write back: *I think I messed up.*

4

THE AWAY CONNECTION

"ARE YOU HERE FOR A LESSON?"

Unfortunately, I probably am, I think as I nod at the young woman with bright pink hair who is seated at a desk in front of me.

Manhattan Swing Workshop is one of the larger swing-dancing schools in New York City, and they offer a lot of introductory one-hour classes designed to convince people to try out the various swing dance styles they teach. On the first Saturday of every month, one of those classes is taught by Oliver MacCormack. The class description promises to teach newcomers the basic steps of West Coast Swing, including right and left-hand passes and a sugar push and sugar-tuck (I'm dying to know what those are), all in an hour.

For most people, this one-hour class is a way to decide whether to sign up for one of the studio's four-week classes, which start at the beginning of the month...but in my case, it's a way to attempt to throw myself back into Ollie's path, where he probably doesn't want me.

'No partner required!' was what the website claimed—but I can already tell, as I wait outside the classroom door, that several people are here with their significant others. There are several cheerful young women clutching the hands of much less enthusiastic young men, two gay couples joking with each other, and a few single women like me, staring at our cell phones and trying to look like we're not here to steal anyone's man.

"Yeah, totally same for us," I hear one of the young women say to another as the gorgeous twenty-somethings admire each other's engagement rings. "I saw a video, and I was like, 'Okay, we are not learning the waltz. I want our first dance to be to *Disturbia* by Rihanna.'"

I try not to smile. Some part of me wishes I was twenty-five again and capable of unironically choosing a song about dark torment as the first dance with my new husband. Is it even a wedding if you don't hint at your bedroom fetishes in front of your new in-laws?

"We're doing *All of Me* by John Legend," replies her new best friend, searching on her phone for a video of the dance that she's hoping to copy.

I text my sister: *abby what the hell am I doing here?*

She was the one who convinced me to hire a babysitter in the middle of a Saturday afternoon so I could throw myself on Ollie's mercy. She writes back a moment later: *you're humiliating yourself to woo him back. worked for me!*

Abby claims she fell in love with her fiancé over improv comedy, but I've never quite believed her. In her case, I think her fiancé liked her from the start and invited her to his improv group as a way to spend more time with her, which is exactly the opposite of what I'm attempting.

The elevator doors swoosh open, and I contemplate whether I can leap the fifteen feet and jump inside before they close again. Just as I decide that I can probably make it, the classroom door swings wide and a stream of dancers pile out from an earlier class, tired and smiling. They have the comfortable optimism of an advanced class, and they are chatting like they all know each other. They seem to have gotten a fairly intense workout, too, judging by the glow on their foreheads and the sweat stains on some t-shirts. I mentally sigh as I follow our intro group inside the room, where a tiny female teacher is shoving her stuff into a giant tote bag as she prepares to leave. I stand awkwardly near the door, waiting for Ollie to come in so I can give him my little speech and ask him if it's okay to stay. He walks inside a moment later, wearing soft linen pants and a simple grey t-shirt. He doesn't even notice me as he greets the other teacher with a quick hug. The woman is slender and gorgeous, and they seem to know each other very well. I feel a brief, futile flash of jealousy like I'm a freshman in high school watching my senior crush chat with a cheerleader across the cafeteria.

Suddenly, I can't seem to find the courage to approach him with my weak apology speech in front of the twenty people who are quietly standing around waiting for class to start. I should just leave now.

"Welcome!" Ollie says cheerfully, glancing down at his phone like he's trying to connect it to the classroom speakers. "Give me a second and we'll get started. I need followers to get into a circle facing the outside of the room, and leaders to get in a circle facing your partners. If you're new to partner dances, you may want to know that followers are traditionally the women and leaders are traditionally the men, but it is entirely up to you. If you like being the one to make the decisions, feel free to learn the leader role. And don't worry if you don't have a…"

His eyes meet mine, and he stops for a second before continuing. I can't read anything in his expression aside from surprise.

"Don't worry if you don't have a partner," he continues,

with raised eyebrows, staring straight at me. "We will be switching in a rotating pattern."

The young woman with the Rihanna wedding plans groans audibly.

"And if you came here as a couple," Ollie continues in a placid voice, his eyes swinging to her, "I understand why you may not want to switch partners, but trust me, it is very healthy to do so. It makes you a much better dancer because you learn different styles of leading and following, and you don't fall into bad habits by relying on each other too much. Most importantly, it prevents a lot of fights." Ollie gives the young woman a charming smile, then redirects it around the room to a few other couples. "Every time I see a couple starting to argue about which one of them is doing something wrong, we rotate, and they learn that it was both of them." There are a few chuckles. "Or else, by the time they've rotated back to their partner, they are so overjoyed to see them again that all mistakes are forgiven."

Another chuckle ripples across the room, and the various couples look somewhat appeased.

"Alright, so let's get into those circles, then. Followers, stand in the middle of the room and face outwards."

As he gives more instructions, I gather my courage and step into the inner circle with the rest of the followers. Ollie walks right up and stands in front of me, meeting my gaze. There is no point in trying to play innocent; his name was prominently displayed on the sign-up link for the class.

"Hello," he says.

"Hi." We're back to our favorite form of conversation. "I um... wanted to learn West Coast Swing..." I begin. My mind is trying to recall the charming speech that I had planned and coming up totally blank. "And I thought...maybe I messed things up a bit? With you?"

"Hmm." A slow smile is growing on his face. There is a long pause. He opens his mouth to say something else, then closes it again. He gives me an irritatingly smug grin and walks to the middle of the room.

"Okay, everyone," he says, his voice sounding faintly amused, "let's get started. I'm going to explain first about the concept of connection. Connection is about the handhold, the grip that you have on your partner. There are different ways for a couple to be connected in West Coast Swing, and the first one you're going to learn is the *away connection*. Leaders, I want you to put your right arm in front of you, with one finger out, like you're pointing a gun. And the followers should rest your fingers on the leader's hand. And for those followers without a partner..."

He looks right at me, damn him.

"If you don't have anyone to dance with yet," he says with a smirk, "just put out your hand and pretend."

I'm glaring at him by now. He is having way too much fun at my expense. I spend the next couple of minutes doing a somewhat humiliating 'air guitar' version of pretending to have a dance partner, tapping my feet in place as I count under my breath . No music is playing yet, which makes it all feel even more awkward. Ollie is calling out counts from the middle of the room and occasionally lining up with the rest of the leaders to show them how to do something, then lining up with the followers to do the same. He doesn't return to me once, nor even glance in my direction. He is very good at teaching, and I remember the 'Take Your Child to Work' Day event. I never would have imagined that his charm with the kids came from teaching unsteady adults how to do romantically charged dance moves.

Soon enough, the leaders all rotate, and now I am dancing with a deeply earnest young man with sandy blond hair whose eyebrows are knitted together in fierce concentration as he tries desperately not to step on my foot. And then he does so. And then he does so again.

"I'm so, so sorry."

"It's fine!" I say brightly.

I genuinely don't mind; I recognize him as the fiancé of the Rihanna-loving bride. I spent the last few minutes listening to her giving him an earful, so I'm rooting for him to sort out his toe-stepping problems before he works his way around the circle and back to her. I notice his bride-to-be giving me a vaguely insulting once-over, like she is assessing whether I'm a devious homewrecker, and then I watch her mentally dismiss me, which is somehow even more insulting.

After a moment, we both start counting out loud to ourselves. It's a relief to be dancing with someone who is as clueless as I am.

"I think I'm getting it!" the young man says with a smile and then steps on my foot again.

"Okay. Time to rotate!" comes Ollie's voice.

Now I'm dancing with a young man who keeps looking longingly at his fiancée over his shoulder. They are the John Legend couple, and he can't seem to believe that they've been separated for six whole minutes already. He looks like his heart can't take it anymore, and I keep apologizing for minor errors when I'm really apologizing for being part of his one-man version of *Brigadoon*. Will he ever be back in her arms again? Or will fate, and a few other dance partners, toss them upon separate paths for eternity?

Ollie tells us to switch again, and now I am dancing with a very assertive woman who is clearly an experienced dancer already, although perhaps not in West Coast Swing.

"You're a great leader," I tell her.

"Yeah," she says. "I date women, and I didn't really see the point of learning the follower position."

"Why does there have to be a leader and follower?" I ask.

"Is this your first dance class?"

I shrug. "I mean, I took hip-hop in college. And a pole-dancing class at the insistence of my college boyfriend."

She snorts.

"Oh I know. I stayed with that guy for two years," I continue. "Two incredibly stupid years. My early twenties were serial monogamy with idiots."

She laughs. "So, the way the leader-follower thing was explained to me is that the dance turns into chaos if nobody is making the decisions. But it's not like one person just tells the other what to do. It's more like the leader introduces the topic of conversation, and the follower gets to respond. Like the leader says, 'What if you do this turn?' and the follower says, 'How about like this?'"

"So it's a conversation where the man introduces all the topics? Sounds like dates I've been on."

"You could learn leader," she replies with a shrug.

"I think I'll focus on learning not to trip over myself before I start making any decisions for someone else."

"I'm Jody, by the way," she says.

"Laura."

"Nice to meet you," she says. "Always a pleasure to dance with someone who's not destined to quit as soon as she's back from her honeymoon in St. Barts."

We have moved on from the sugar push to the left-side pass, and she confidently guides me around her, giving me a few pointers on my foot position. A sugar push, I was a little disappointed to discover, is just a simple step that keeps your partner not too far away from you. The left-side pass involves switching position with your partner, and it is the first one that makes it look like you are doing something fancy.

"Why West Coast Swing?" she asks after we try another pass. "You saw a dance on TikTok, right?"

I am about to lie and say that I caught a video of some viral dance and fell in love with it, but I decide to be honest. "I have a crush on the instructor," I reply.

She glances over and shrugs. "Well, looks like you'll be dancing with him soon."

I glance over and see that Ollie has been stepping in and out of the rotation at a certain point in the circle, dancing with various followers as he demonstrates certain moves. I'm next.

"Okay, time to rotate," he calls.

He smiles when he notices me standing right in front of him.

"Hello," he says again in that amused voice.

He puts out a hand, and I take it. My hands are probably a little sweaty at this point, but I'm beyond caring, especially because he still looks like he is laughing at me. We haven't started to dance yet, but his fingers feel warm as they hold my hand. He feels safe somehow, in spite of my embarrassment. I want to believe we have natural chemistry, but it's more likely that he's just a very experienced dance partner. He knows how to hold someone without clutching too tight.

We are about to start dancing when he stops.

"You know what?" he says to the class. "Let's do something else first." He gently pulls his hands away, and it feels like a perfectly timed piece of humiliation, like he is making a point that he couldn't possibly want to dance with me. Then he adds, "Let's put on some music for this one."

He takes his cell phone from his pocket.

I glance at it, knowing that somewhere on his phone is probably my phone number, stored away never to be used. He presses a button, and as romantic, slow jazz begins to play, he takes my hands again, looking straight at me.

"You ready?" It sounds like a dare.

"Of course." I keep my chin up, meeting his eyes.

"Sugar push, left-side pass," he calls out to the class, "And keep it going."

He begins to send me gentle signals through his hands, and I feel another thrill, like we're meant to be holding each other. It's gone a moment later, though, as I realize I have to focus on the steps. The music is a perfect match for the steps we're learning... slow enough to allow a room full of awkward newcomers to keep up, fast enough that we can sense how the dance is supposed to work. Ollie calls out moves occasionally, but most of his attention is on me. He is surprisingly gentle and patient as I make mistakes. He keeps murmuring advice to me, telling me how to change the position of my hands.

"You can tighten your grip a little," he says, putting his hand on my wrist. I can feel his fingertips setting my wrist on fire, and suddenly it is hard to meet his eyes. "There needs to be more tension in your arms. Not stiff, but like a firm spring. You remember what I said about frame?"

"Possibly?" It's hard to focus on anything while he holds my elbows gently.

"Your body position keeps a basic framework." He tugs lightly on my hands. "You want to hold position like you're an elastic band. You may be pushed away, but you always want to come back to your partner. Partner dance is about tension."

My heart physically reacts to the word 'tension.' I can't believe I thought there was no sexual chemistry with him, because right now there seems to be nothing else.

"So I should try to pull away?" I ask lightly, my voice a little uneven.

"It's more like you're pulling away to come back again." A

mischievous light comes into his eyes when I finally meet his gaze. He gestures between our chests. "It's like there's a string between us that keeps pulling us back together no matter how much we try to pull apart."

Is he flirting? Or messing with me? I bite my tongue on a reply. There is a twinkle in his eye as he gently swings me around and back into place again. This time I start to feel it: the balanced tension that allows everything else to work.

"Hold on a little tighter," he says. "But you don't have to grip hard. Just commit to how much you don't want to let me go."

Now I'm definitely blushing. Even the faint smell of his sweat is pleasantly warm, and there's a woodsy, cedar scent to his aftershave. He keeps dancing with me just a little longer than he's danced with anyone else, but that may be my imagination. It may be my imagination that it takes him just a half-second longer than it should to let go of my hand when we have completed a few turns.

When we've reached a stop, he gazes at me, his lips parted and his eyebrows raised like he's considering me seriously.

"How'd I do?" I try to display more confidence than I have. "Amazingly good for my first day, right?"

He opens his mouth to answer, then smiles again and looks at the class. "Alright, everyone, rotate!"

I am going to kill him.

At the end of the hour, Ollie nods to the class, glances at me, and then walks outside to talk to the pink-haired young woman at the front desk. I say good-bye to my favorite leader Jody and follow everyone outside, where I stand by the elevator to send a text message to Abby.

Update, I text to Abby. *He will probably never speak to me again and I'll get a complaint at my job for sexual harassment. otherwise it went okay.*

As I am about to send the message, I look up to see him approaching me.

He stops an arms-length away, the amused smile hovering around the corners of his mouth again.

"Hey," I begin. "I'm sorry if coming here was inappropriate. I had a whole speech planned about why I was sorry about what I said, and it wasn't true, and that I do think you're..." I end up just trailing off because I can't manage to say the words 'sexy' or 'attractive' with him looking at me like that.

"Let's get some coffee," he says. Then he glances at my phone in my hands. "Unless you need to get back right away?"

I know he's referring to my daughter, which I appreciate. He's right. There's not much leeway in what I told the babysitter. "I have a few minutes."

"We'll get it to-go, then." The elevator doors open and he holds them open for me and the rest of the class, then enters and stands near me wordlessly as people around us chat about the lesson. I *like* him, I think. Shit.

As soon as we are outside the building, he leads the way down the street toward a coffee shop at the corner. "So what did you think of West Coast Swing?" he asks.

"Amazing," I say, surprising myself with how honest my response is. "I've never done partner dancing before. I used to love music, and I wanted to learn tap as a kid, but we never had money for it. In high school I did the musical and stuff, but I never learned how to dance with another person, and this is really fun. I'm rambling now."

"No, you're not. I'm glad you liked it." His smile is sincere and warm.

"You know," I continue, "I saw some videos of you dancing and you're incredible. At the party, too."

"You mean with Katy? That was nothing."

"But you have those improvised dances on YouTube."

"Those are from a few years back." He looks a little embarrassed. Every time he starts to blush it kills me. And he definitely has dimples.

"Why did you stop competing?" I ask. "I mean, *did* you stop, or...?"

He shrugs. "The last couple of years have been tricky."

For you and me both, friend. "My friend Viv said you got divorced."

He nods, his eyes fixed on the sidewalk a few feet ahead of us. "Yeah."

"Was she a dancer, too?"

"Yes," he says, glancing at me again. "She was not my partner when I was competing, but she was part of the scene. She still is, as far as I know, which... She doesn't come to Manhattan Swing Workshop, but if I go to events around the city, there's a good chance she'll be there."

"Ah." I understand that feeling after a divorce, that there are certain places that aren't safe anymore. "So you've been avoiding her?"

"I was avoiding the entirety of New York." He looks a little rueful. "But I love this place. It's nice to be back."

"The city or the dancing?"

"All of it." He holds the door as we enter the coffee shop together.

"So who *did* you dance with when you competed?"

"That was Eliana Macri. I dated her for a while, but she eventually switched to dancing with someone else. About six years ago. They are doing well, too. Probably top five in the country."

"That's impressive."

"Yeah. She picked the better partner, clearly." He shrugs, like it doesn't bother him, but the words give him away. It hits me that his former dance partner left him for someone else, a few years before his wife left him for his brother.

"Clearly she did *not* pick the better partner," I say. "Because you're amazing."

He smiles. "I'm not sure you're experienced enough to judge that, Ms. Marceau."

"You know my last name." It is also Nick's last name; I haven't quite gotten myself organized to change it yet.

"It didn't require masterly detection skills. I looked you up on the company website."

I smile. "When did you do that?"

His eyes are twinkling again. "I don't think I'll tell you that."

We stand there for a moment together in line, scanning the menu. After a moment, I get my courage to say what I planned to tell him when I first arrived.

"I just..." I look at the floor. I'm not sure why this is so hard to say to him. "I came today because I wanted to prove that I was serious about being interested in you. What I said to Vivi was... I didn't mean it, and I guess I wanted to show that I was willing to humiliate myself for an hour to make it up to you."

"Just an hour?" There's that smile again.

"Oh, did you want me to humiliate myself for longer?"

He grins and steps forward to give his coffee order and then buys me mine.

We stand together against the wall of the tiny coffee shop waiting for our orders as he looks at me again. His eyes are a complicated hazel color—a warm green with a ring of warm brown in the center—and he has a way of fixing his gaze on me that's both intense and incredibly hard to read.

"How about this?" he says. "I would like to take you out. But if we're going to do that, you have to stick with West Coast Swing. At least for a month. You can't just take a one-hour lesson and quit."

"You want to see me embarrass myself more?"

"I didn't say you had to take *my* class. I just want you to stick with it."

"Why?"

He shrugs. "Maybe I think you're a good dancer."

"I am a terrible dancer."

He smiles. "No. The terrible ones have no rhythm and that is almost impossible to teach. You have a sense of how music works. It's visible in the way you move. You *like* music."

"Well, my ex-husband was a musician." I consider what he's said. I've never thought much about my relationship with music. "I used to love going to shows and dancing around for hours, but then I guess I started to associate music with my ex-husband, who never showed up when he said he would."

"Don't let him take music from you. I let my ex-wife take a lot of stuff that I used to love. It's one reason I came back to the city, to reclaim the stuff that I accidentally gave up in the divorce."

He's right. I used to love bands and rooms full of people before I associated them with a man who dropped in and out of my life like a signal from the world's weakest radio station.

I take a breath. "Okay. I'll stick with it for a month. Maybe I can sign Hannah up for karate classes or something at the same time. She's been hounding me for martial arts lessons."

"She sounds fierce."

"You have no idea. She'll probably be Brooklyn Borough President by the time she's twenty-one. She has opinions on everything."

We grab our coffees and walk to the door.

"I remember your daughter, actually," he replies as he holds the door open for me.

"You do? That was years ago."

"She was funny. Dark, curly hair, right? She reminded me of you."

"You didn't even know me back then."

"I noticed you," he says. "But I was married and I assumed you were, too."

"No, I was already divorced." I consider what to say. "Hannah is a great kid with an unreliable dad, and I try to shield her from that fact, and that makes her hate me."

Ollie nods slowly, taking this in. "Why would she hate you?"

"Because he doesn't show up, and I pretend it wasn't his fault, and then I'm the bad guy who's mad at her perfect dad all the time. Sorry, you don't need to hear about that. Angry ranting about exes is the third date, right? Or is it the fourth? I'm rusty."

He laughs. "You're not ranting, you're telling me about your life."

I smile, charmed in spite of myself. "My subway is that way."

He walks down the street with me and then pauses when we reach the subway entrance. We stand there for a moment, sipping our coffees, looking at each other.

"Laura, may I take you on a date?"

"So formal."

"I stopped asking women if they wanted to 'hang out' when I was a senior in college. Too many misunderstandings. I once showed up to a movie with flowers, and she'd invited her actual boyfriend along."

"Oh no." I laugh. "Just so you know, I'm sober." The words pour out of me, unplanned. "I'm the kind of sober where I count how long I've been sober."

He nods. He doesn't look upset, just thoughtful.

"I count in years, not days, just to be clear. This is not new. But I need to make sure that you're okay with that. It's fine to have a drink around me, and I can go to bars, but I can't be around people who get wasted. And I can't have it in the house. Not that we're talking about moving in together." Now I'm really embarrassed. "I just wanted to warn you, so you could think about whether you're okay with that."

"I have absolutely no problem with that," he says. "It's not a big part of my life at all." I feel a wave of relief, but then he looks away. "I feel like this is where I should confess something to you."

There is a long, ominous pause. "Yes?"

"After my divorce I am not entirely sure I trust women. I'm not entirely sure I trust anybody."

"Oh." The words are not just a flashing red warning sign; they are one of those fifty-foot billboards in Times Square. It's not even that he has that feeling. It's that he feels it enough to need to tell me about it.

"I'm trying," he adds softly. His hazel eyes look serious. "Just promise me one thing, okay? If you want to get back with your ex-husband, that's fine, but—"

"I don't."

"I heard you at the party. And I heard something about you leaving the firm last summer to be with him, and no one knew whether you were coming back. So if you are in some on-again, off-again thing with him..."

I shake my head. "We're definitely off-again. I mean, we're definitely off forever."

He looks a little skeptical, but he nods once. "Okay," he says. "Then we can give this a try."

He takes my hand in his and squeezes it, and I feel a warmth spread from my palm up my arm and all the way into my chest. He looks right in my eyes as his thumb slides gently across my wrist. "And don't be afraid to tighten that grip a little."

5

A GOOD FRAME

OCCASIONALLY, New York City—expensive, challenging, stressful New York City—offers up a bit of kismet, a reason for you to stay. It's like anything else that's not entirely healthy for you: just when you're thinking about leaving, it shows up with flowers and an apology.

In my case, the flowers appear in the form of a piece of perfect synchronicity. The very night after my one-hour introductory lesson with Ollie, I go online and discover that there is a kids' Taekwondo class on Sunday afternoons right down the block from Manhattan Swing Workshop, at almost exactly the same time as an introductory West Coast Swing class. In the next twelve hours, I manage to sign Hannah up for Taekwondo and arrange for one of Hannah's babysitters to keep an eye on her for the next four weeks while I try out the dance class. It's a bit of a financial outlay, but I can swing it, especially since Nick has started paying back some of his delayed child support. The Taekwondo serves another purpose, too: Hannah doesn't do a lot of activities outside of her after-school program because I've rarely had the energy to take her back and forth to piano lessons, art classes, and tennis lessons while solo parenting the rest of the time. Now I can balance my own enrichment activity with one for Hannah, too.

The Four-Week West Coast Swing course is not one of the classes Ollie teaches, though. I tell myself that's a good thing. I don't know if I can handle a full month of staring into his hazel eyes while he teases me about me not having a partner.

When I arrive at Manhattan Swing, which is on the fourth floor of a building in the Flatiron district, I immediately spot Jody from our intro class waiting by the classroom door. Jody has long, light-brown hair that almost reaches her waist and an upturned nose that makes her look like the sarcastic younger sibling on a sitcom, even though she's probably around thirty. Today she is wearing loose yoga pants and a t-shirt from the Sierra Club.

"Hey!" I say, approaching her. "You're doing the whole one-month course?"

"That was always the plan." Jody has a dry way of speaking that can seem a little hostile if it weren't for the undercurrent of humor running constantly beneath it. She reminds me a little of my mother at her best: cynical, funny, a little tired of everything.

I lean against the empty stretch of wall next to her. "You think any of the engaged couples will be back again?"

"Probably not. Most of them have realized it's going to be more efficient to just take a one-hour private lesson with someone who can help them choreograph their wedding dance, and then they don't have to learn how to actually lead and follow."

"I think improvisation is the fun part."

"Because you're not planning a hundred-thousand-dollar wedding with bridesmaids in matching taupe dresses."

I laugh. "Oh, to be young and have disposable income."

"It's a stupid reason to learn to dance." Jody gives me a once-over. "Speaking of, I'm noticing this is not one of the classes taught by Mr. MacCormack."

"No," I say. I decide not to mention that I'm only here because Ollie dared me to stick with it. "I like West Coast Swing, it turns out."

"Very well," says Jody. "I will postpone my decision to dislike you."

"How kind," I reply with a grin.

"I am always incredibly kind. It's shocking that I'm single."

A plump woman in her sixties walks over to us and dumps a large colorful bag on the floor beside her with a huffing sigh. She has iron grey hair cut in a bob and wears a long, flowing batik-dyed shirt and hot pink leggings.

"Beginner West Coast Swing?" she asks.

Jody nods.

"I'm Helen," she says in a rush. "This is my third dance I'm learning. Last month it was salsa. Before that was tango. My husband died and I said fuck it, I'm going to do everything he wouldn't let me do when he was alive."

I think I'm going to like Helen.

As we line up inside the classroom a few minutes later, I am surprised by one other familiar face: the fiancé of the Rihanna-loving bride, with his sandy blond hair and apologetic expression. I find myself lined up opposite him when class starts.

"Is your fiancée sick today?"

"Oh, no..." He looks a little embarrassed. "She kept talking about how bad I was, so I wanted to surprise her by getting better for our wedding. We're doing one of those private lessons to choreograph our dance, but I thought, you know, if I put a little extra time in, then I could actually impress her. She doesn't know I'm here. I told her I'm training at the gym."

"That's really sweet."

He shrugs. "I hope so. I'm sorry I kept stepping on your feet."

"I'm sure I stepped on yours just as often. I'm Laura, by the way." I put out a hand.

"Ben," he says. "So this is definitely a beginner level class, right?"

"Let's hope so."

Ben nods nervously and glances at the teachers who are setting up some music. He takes a deep breath and starts counting out loud.

A LITTLE OVER AN HOUR LATER, I find myself sitting with Jody and Helen in the coffee shop at the corner, killing time while my daughter finishes her Taekwondo lesson. Jody is giving sharp summaries of the different styles of follower that she's had to deal with in her various Lindy Hop, East Coast, and now West Coast Swing classes.

"You two are fine," she says, waving her hand vaguely. "You two are acceptable. But there are people I've danced with who have the weakest possible grips. It's like their wrists are made of Jello."

"Oh no. That's what Ollie said about mine," I say.

"No. You've improved a lot. There are followers where I take a step toward them and their entire frame sort of melts away, like I'm stepping into the mirror dimension. And it's like, you do need to push back against me a little or I will end up pressed against your entire body."

"Well," Helen says, "some of the leaders have a death grip. There's this one guy..."

"I know the one," I agree.

"It's like he's one of those 1950s tin robots with the arms coming out from his elbows." Helen imitates a robot. "He seems to think his job is to push me around like a shopping cart. I mean, I like a decisive man, but not like that."

I laugh. "The ones who bother me are the ones who fling you away like they're tossing a frisbee. And then they snap you back again, and your wrist hurts."

Helen holds up a wrist. "I just say, 'Be careful, dear, I'm old and fragile.' That usually tones them down. I got pushed around enough by my husband."

"I'm sorry to hear that," I say.

"Oh, he wasn't abusive exactly," Helen replies, looking thoughtful. "Just rigid. Very rigid. He was a university professor. Eighteen years older than me. We met when he was teaching my intro philosophy class in college, and I married him the summer before I graduated. And he was one of those people who just... I would say, you know, 'Maybe we should go to Norway for a trip,' and he would have fifteen reasons why we shouldn't go to Norway. He knew everything that was wrong with Norway. Or Florida. I couldn't possibly want to go to Florida. Do you know how humid it is in Florida? And taking a dance class? Never. We weren't going to become professional dancers, were we? What was the point? Exercise? You could get much more efficient exercise at the gym, and we had a paid membership. I gave up so many opportunities because they didn't fit what he thought was logical."

"And now here you are," Jody says with more than her usual warmth.

"Here I am, dancing with men half my age who are scared to break me." Helen sighs and shrugs.

"You," Jody replies, "have excellent connection and a great frame." Helen's face lights up at the compliment.

I shake my head. "I never expected so much of dance would be about holding hands the right way."

"That's the whole thing," agrees Jody. "Well, half of it

anyway. As a leader, I feel like I'm sending out secret messages, hoping the followers read them."

"Put like that, it sounds very sexy," I say.

"It's a mating dance," Jody agrees. "At least in part. I wish there were more lesbians who came to class. But nevertheless, I persist."

"So are we all going to the Friday night social?" Helen asks.

Our intro class is taught by two dancers, the spunky and experienced teacher named Maria who greeted Ollie the other day, and her assistant and teacher-in-training Hank, who is in his early twenties and bouncily enthusiastic. They both spent the first class heavily advocating for us to attend the school's two-hour 'open social dance' on Friday evening. It is a free event where West Coast Swing dancers have the chance to practice their steps in an informal atmosphere.

I shrug. I'm not sure whether my date with Ollie will be on Friday night. I'm not sure whether my date with Ollie will happen at all, to be honest, because he still hasn't called me. It's only been twenty-four hours since my intro lesson with him, I remind myself.

"If I'm free, I'll try to be there," I tell Helen. I do want to get more practice with dancing. In the back of my mind, though, I wonder why I am bothering. I'm certainly not going to dazzle Ollie, who has already danced with someone who is basically a national champion.

"I'll probably be there," Jody replies, sounding a little weary. "I might as well get the practice in."

Outside the window, I watch a young woman stride by us wearing a punk rock t-shirt, her hair in an untamed wave, her ears triple-pierced. That was my look for a few years in my mid-twenties. I used to dress like Joan Jett, with an I-dare-you atti-tude and copious amounts of black eyeliner. I listened to metal bands and went to dubstep raves and snuck into parties where I didn't bother to learn anyone's name.

Now I have a crush on a guy who wears tweed vests, and I'm learning a dance with neatly assigned leader/follower roles and carefully counted steps.

"Well, I hope you both come," Helen replies, "because I have a feeling most people will bring their partners, and no one will ask us singles to dance."

"That's the best thing about us three," Jody replies, glancing between Helen and me. "We're all alone."

I MEET up with Hannah and her babysitter a few minutes later at the Taekwondo studio and reimburse the babysitter for the white uniform that she hastily had to buy for Hannah before class started.

"How did it go?" I ask Hannah as we wave goodbye to the babysitter. Hannah demonstrates her new moves to me all the way down the street and then on the entire subway ride back to our neighborhood in Brooklyn. Fortunately, the subway is nearly empty, so I don't have to steer her away from starting an accidental street fight.

"Hann," I say, as she practices her posture in the middle of the subway car, "why did you want to learn some kind of martial arts? Was a friend at school learning it?"

"I have to learn because Marshall said he could beat me up."

"He said that at school?" Marshall is one of the boys I hear about a lot, and never in a good way.

She shrugs. "Nina says he can't beat me up if I know martial arts." Nina is her best friend, a tall, dark-haired girl with natural confidence and a tendency to egg on Hannah's worst instincts.

"You're not going to do that, right?" I ask gently. "Get in a fight with him?"

Hannah shrugs. "The best defense is a good offense. That's what Nina says."

Maybe we should just move out to a suburb, I think for the hundredth time, but then I would have an even longer commute and less time to spend with my daughter. As if she can read my mind, she looks over at me. "Are we going to move back to Atlanta?"

She does this sometimes: articulates the thoughts I am thinking right after I've decided not to say them aloud.

"No, sweetie."

"Is Daddy going to move here?" The question feels like its own Taekwondo kick in the chest.

"I'm sure he wants to be closer, but he has to go where his job takes him. Musicians have to tour, and his gigs are changing, so it's not easy for him to stay in one place."

"Does he have to be a musician?"

She has never asked me that before. It saddens me that she's finally old enough to understand that maybe Nick is a bit selfish. I pick my words carefully. "Some people have only one job that makes them happy. I think your father is one of those people. But I know he misses you."

"Do you miss him?"

I force a smile. "He and I will always care about each other."

Recognizing this is a dodge, Hannah turns and lets another kick fly toward the middle of the empty subway. "Right," she says pointedly.

I remember what Ollie said about the elastic band that is supposed to exist between the leader and the follower in dancing, the invisible string that connects your chests, always pulling you back to each other.

The thing is, if one of you doesn't care enough about the string, and keeps pulling farther and farther away, then the string can snap, and then the connection is broken. You aren't pulled back together anymore. That's how I feel about Nick. We were pulled farther and farther apart until something inside me broke permanently.

Ollie calls me that evening at a little after eight o'clock.

"Are you free this Friday night?"

"I can be." I am already mentally filing through babysitter options.

"I'd really like to take you out to dinner."

Something in his tone makes me fall backwards onto my bed like a teenager. *That's not good*, I tell myself. *I can't be this mushy already.*

"Sure," I say, keeping my voice steady with effort. "That sounds nice."

I remember something Brant said last summer when I called him and asked him to put in a good word so I could get my old job back. I told him about the mess with Nick, and he listened with surprising sympathy and finally replied, "As soon as people know that you'll do anything for them, that is when they really have you over a barrel."

Ollie and I meet at a chic little restaurant on Friday evening at the decidedly un-chic hour of 6:30. I asked him to find a restaurant close enough to my neighborhood and a time early enough that I can still get home to start Hannah's bedtime. If he wants to date a single mom, this is the reality: no tumbling into bed together after the first date. Not much tumbling into bed at all. I might as well make that obvious from the beginning; it would be worse to watch him slowly pull away as he learns what he's in for.

Ollie lives on the Upper West Side, so I appreciate that he's making the trek to Brooklyn just to make my evening a little easier. He has chosen an upscale, quiet restaurant with seating under skylights in a back garden. I notice as we enter the front doorway that two jazz musicians are playing quietly in the corner, and I immediately think of Nick and the occasional 'mood music' gigs he used to suffer through—patiently strumming jazz standards to the sound of clinking forks and murmurs about stock prices. *I close my eyes and make a face like I'm getting a blowjob,* Nick used to say. *Makes me look like I'm into it.*

It's a very nice restaurant, whatever Nick might say about it; it's exactly kind of place I never go. Ollie glances at my little black dress and smiles.

"Another devastating dress, I see," he says as we follow the hostess to a table in the corner.

"I had to go cave diving for this. It was shoved into the back of my closet."

"Pining for fresh air."

"I took pity on it. This is a mercy outing."

"No mercy for me, clearly."

He says it with enough amusement that I can't tease him for such a slick line. How am I supposed to respond to charm?

A server comes over as soon as we are seated. "Wine list?"

"No, I think we'll have some bottled water to start," Ollie says without looking up.

I'm grateful that he remembered, assuming he said that for my benefit.

As he glances down at the menu, I feel like I don't know him at all. It hits me in a wave, and I tuck my hands into my sides as I stare at the list of overpriced duck and sea bass entrees.

My white trash origins always sneak up on me at moments like this. I can picture twenty-year-old Laura in a place like this, her eyes lined in black smudge, wearing a bustier instead of a shirt, telling Ollie she'd like to give him a blowjob in the bathroom. When things get too quiet, she tends to crawl from the depths of my subconscious and try to get me to say something wildly inappropriate. I can practically smell her hairspray and knock-off Calvin Klein perfume as I look over the menu. I say nothing. I've inherited my mother's tendency to like to blow things up, but I don't have to act on it.

"So where did you grow up?" Ollie asks quietly. I guess we're doing small talk, now.

"Nowhere as interesting as Australia," I say. "How did you end up here?"

He shrugs. "Not my decision. My father is a businessman. Major player in Melbourne, but he always wanted to come to New York. I think he loved the movie *Wall Street*. Probably took the wrong message from it." He frowns slightly. "So when my older brother got accepted to NYU, my father moved the whole family here. I think he didn't want my brother to conquer the city before he did."

"And did your dad conquer the city?"

Ollie shrugs. "He does okay. Not as well as he wanted to. That's why he wanted me and my brother to become lawyers. He thought that was the missing piece in his success. I followed the path my dad wanted for us. Undergrad at Fordham, NYU law. But my older brother rebelled, did a whole bunch of other things. Worked on a fishing boat, drove around the country selling antiques. He eventually became an auctioneer."

"An auctioneer? Like, 'Going once, going twice...!'"

He grins ruefully. "He's at Christie's now, doing quite well. You can make millions of dollars at that if you're good at it. He's a real charmer. The kind of guy who can work a room." Ollie frowns; his charming brother definitely charmed his wife, and I wish Ollie knew that I knew, so we could talk about it. "He's more like my father than I am, in a lot of ways. I was the shy one growing up."

"But you're so loud and abrasive now."

He chuckles. "My father was appalled when I chose tax law. He thinks it's boring. But it was one of the few parts of law where nobody's angry, sad, or injured."

"Unlike criminal or divorce law?"

"Exactly." Even divorce law seems like a loaded topic. Is there any non-loaded topic with Ollie?

"And the dancing?" I ask gently.

"That was Eliana, my ex. I started dating her when I was in law school and she was a senior in college, studying dance at Marymount. She was the driving force behind West Coast Swing. She wanted to learn it and then she wanted to compete. And I went along with it because it made her happy." He shrugs. "It was probably a little act of rebellion. My father is convinced that only gay men can dance well. And I used to do small things that annoyed him, just to prove him wrong."

"But it must have been tricky when you were in law school, putting in time to compete."

"It wasn't that bad in law school." He frowns, remembering. "But once I got out, it was harder. I ended up quitting my job at a big law firm. That's why I landed as a legal consultant to an accounting firm. It was impossible for me to be on the partner track at Big Law, putting in billable hours all weekend, and still dance. What I like about my job at Murano is that they genuinely expect us to be there from nine to five and then go home."

"So you can have a life." I smile.

"Well, that was the theory. I'm not sure how much of a life I have at the moment."

I nod. That is one thing we have in common. "So why did you stop competing?"

"I never officially stopped, but Eliana and I never did especially well. We weren't winning any big competitions, which I didn't care about, but it bothered her. She wanted to become better known, get teaching jobs. And there was this guy, Connor Yung. Amazing dancer based in L.A. We used to love watching him. And one time, he and Ellie were picked to do a Jack & Jill together."

"That's the improvised dance where you get a random song and a random partner?"

He nods. "Right. They'd never danced together before, but they won the whole thing. And I guess Connor decided they had chemistry, because he asked her if she'd move to California to train as his partner and teach at his studio. He has his own dance school out there, working with movie stars as a private trainer, teaching classes. I guess he wanted to move on from his old partner Sarah. So Eliana went out there to do that."

"And that's when you broke up?"

"No, we tried doing the long-distance thing. But she was always talking about Connor or texting him when I came for the weekend. It was clear that she was falling for him. I confronted her and she said that nothing had happened, but she wasn't in love with me anymore."

The very calmness of his demeanor makes me sense that it was brutal. There are few things worse than realizing that the person you love is slowly pulling away.

"Are they a couple now?" I ask.

"They're still partners. They dated for a while, but I'm not sure what they are now." He shrugs, his rueful smile creeping back.

I do the math in my head. "You must have been with her a long time."

"Eight years. We talked about marriage, but she kept saying she wanted time, and then..." He shakes his head. "I'm not angry with her. She was twenty-one when we started dating, and I was her first serious boyfriend, and I think it was hard for her to commit to me without knowing what else was out there. And the one thing I couldn't be for her was *what else is out there*. We're still friends. We chat sometimes. She's a good person."

I consider this. It's usually a good sign when men are friends with their exes, but it makes me nervous. Why is he so emphatic about her being a good person?

"It must have been frustrating for you, though," I say. "You gave up so much to help her with her dream, and then she moved on when things started to take off for her."

"I try not to think about it that way. I really like my job. I'm glad I didn't end up on the partner track at some huge law firm. I landed in the right place for me. But it hurt. Not just losing her but feeling like she traded up."

"Sounds like the music scene. I always worried that would happen with Nick. Like if he ever did succeed as a musician, he would dump me for someone younger and hotter." I pause. "Not that that's what happened to you."

Ollie smiles. "Connor is only two years younger than I am, but he probably is hotter."

The whole conversation seems full of landmines, and I'm not sure whether I'm planting them or setting them off. "And after that you met your wife?" Another landmine.

"I already knew her. She had dated my brother for a while. Then he dumped her when he dropped out of college and went on the road. I reconnected with her again in the swing dance scene. She seemed fun, low drama. The irony is that I thought... I thought if she'd already dated my brother, then she had that out of her system. Eliana had needed to explore the world, but I figured Phoebe had already done that. She had dated a bit, had some wild experiences, and was ready to settle down."

"And then?"

"And then it didn't work out." He shrugs, his eyes sliding from mine. "At first, I thought it was great that Phoebe could also swing dance. But now it means she could appear anywhere I go dancing."

"The whole dance scene seems a little incestuous."

He shrugs. "Not completely. It's a great place to meet new people. The problem is that if you have a history with someone, you'll keep seeing them. If I were ever in a Jack & Jill competition with Eliana, and our names were picked out of a hat, I would have to dance with her, and I'm not sure I want to go through that. Not that it's her fault. She feels really guilty about what happened between us. But I only do competitions if I'm sure she's not going to be there."

I nod. "But you love it. Dancing."

"It's a nice break from tax law." Then he grins at me. "So where did you grow up? Don't think I didn't notice you dodged that question."

How do you talk about your poverty-stricken, broken childhood on a first date? You make it sound boring.

"My story is way less exciting. We grew up in Troy. Near Albany. Working class city." I shrug.

"And you liked to dance, you said?"

"I wanted to be Ginger Rogers as a kid. My mom watched a lot of old movies. And in college I liked to drink and dance. It took me a while to learn to separate the two. My childhood was not always fun. I was helping raise my sister. So when I went away to college, I wanted the carefree childhood I'd never had. Turns out that trying to make up for lost time can be dangerous if you inherited addictive tendencies."

"I bet your sister appreciated that you helped raise her, though."

"I think so. But she moved to Newfoundland recently

because she fell in love with someone up there, so I'm dealing with that, right now. Abby once said it was like we were married. We raised Hannah together, you know? But she needed to move on, and I'm happy for her, but..." My voice sounds emotional, and I pull myself back together. "Anyway, all that stuff is why I became an accountant. I wanted to give Hannah the opposite of my childhood."

"Because your mother wasn't an accountant?" His eyes are sharp. He has missed nothing about the little omissions in my story.

"My father left early and then we moved a lot because my mom kept switching jobs and boyfriends. She was a drinker, too. So I wanted to do better for Hannah. Steady income. Two parents. And then of course I picked a husband who was completely unreliable."

"It's hard to know who to trust," Ollie says quietly.

"Or we keep repeating our parents' mistakes."

He grimaces. "Or that. My parents have one of those marriages where they overlook casual infidelities, which is a different kind of toxic. Because they never actually overlook anything, they just needle each other. My brother became like my dad, and I became like my mom. My brother cheats, and I pick women who cheat on me. That was a fun day in therapy when I worked that out."

"So is your brother still in New York?" I ask.

"They have a house up in Dobbs Ferry."

I don't ask who 'they' is. I watch something close up behind his eyes, and he looks away from me again. He has the chance to tell me the whole story, and he doesn't. The jazz band keeps playing, but there is no room to dance.

. . .

After dinner, he offers to walk me home as we're only about fifteen minutes from my apartment. It's a warm night, the sky still violet-green from the summer sunset.

"I feel like…" he begins as we wander down the street past shops and restaurants.

"Yes?"

He looks into the distance. "I feel like I'm about to walk you home, and maybe I'll give you a kiss goodnight. And someone will ask you how your date went, and you'll say, 'It was fine.'"

I smile and shake my head. "I'll say, 'It was nice.'"

"Nice. Okay." He looks away, a distant smile on his face.

"Nice is good. Believe me. Nice is much better than I've been experiencing on dates recently."

"That sounds like a low bar."

I catch his eyes, thinking of that casual remark I made about us having no chemistry. Now I think about his stories, his worry about being cheated on. "Would you like me to tell you you're sexy, Oliver?"

He laughs. "See, now you're being patronizing."

I consider this for a moment. "You know what it is? It's that I don't know how to do this. Last time I was dating, I was still drinking. And there isn't much I miss about drinking, but I miss how easy it was to get to know people. Like, if you and I were in a bar, and we were a few beers in, we would be telling the real story of our divorces. I would go on a whole rant about Nick, and you would tell me about your ex-wife, and we would get out all the messy stuff. But when I'm sober, the messy stuff stays in. And most of the time that's good, it's really good, but when I want to get to know someone, I want to hear about their messy stuff, and I don't know how to get there anymore."

"You want to hear my messy stuff?" His hazel-green eyes are lit up in the fading light.

I feel vulnerable. "I want to know you."

I wonder if he's going to dodge the question. He takes a breath. "Alright," he says. "We can try it."

"Try what?"

He takes off his suit jacket and points to a large public library a few steps ahead of us. He gestures to the stone wall wrapped around the building at knee-height and spreads the jacket on the wall. "Sit down, and pretend this is a bar, and give me your drunken rant about your ex."

I am startled into a laugh. "It doesn't work that way. I'd have to be drunk. Or at least sit in a bar for an hour, drinking ginger ale and working up to it."

"We don't have time to get you to a real bar if you need to get home by eight-thirty. Just sit on my jacket so you don't ruin your dress." He doesn't mention that this might ruin his jacket, which warms me inside. I was always too cynical for old-school chivalry, but now I'm realizing it feels amazing when it's sincere. Ollie didn't practice that line; he just means it. My insides feel fizzy and soft, like I'm filled with champagne.

We sit down together, and I consider what he's asking me to do. What would I say about Nick if I was really being honest? If I were four drinks deep, midway through a night on the town?

"Okay," I agree. "But you have to promise me your drunken rant, too. This can't be one-sided."

I watch his jaw clench for a second, but then he nods. "Okay."

"Okay." I take a breath. "Nick," I say, imagining what would pour out of me if I was wasted. "I *loved* him."

I watch Ollie's jaw tighten again, but he just nods.

"I mean, I thought we were on this romantic, once-in-a-life-time journey, because he was loyal, and supported my sobriety, and was really sweet when we were together. But he never put me first. It was always his music. And it's not like he was obsessed with money or fame. It was more like, he was good at guitar. He got gigs and made money. But never *great* gigs, and never for *that much* money. And it's not even self-sabotage! That would almost be better, if he was ruining things by fighting with the lead singers or something. It's more like, he was good enough to be a replacement guitarist, but not great enough for a band to take him on tour. And that broke his heart, that he'd spent his whole life working on something and wasn't exceptional. But it meant that whenever he got an opportunity, he felt like he had to take it."

Ollie nods. "Because the next opportunity was going to be the one where he made it big."

"Exactly. And I didn't even mind that he stayed with music. That's the thing. People would tell me he was immature or irresponsible for staying in music, but I didn't expect him to get a desk job. He would have been miserable. What bothered me was that Hannah and I always ended up coming in second. It was like he was in love with another woman—the music industry —and she kept breaking his heart, and he couldn't give her up because he wanted to believe *this time* would be different. So he couldn't say no, even if a gig came up on my birthday. Or...this past year, he promised Hannah he'd come for Christmas."

Ollie winces a little. "And he got a gig."

"It was a good gig, but she was so *sad*, because he promised her. I let him promise her he'd be there Christmas morning, and then I had to deal with the fallout when she realized he wouldn't be. And a few weeks ago, he was supposed to come for Hannah's spring break, and he missed half of that for another job. And I just stopped being in love with him. It took years, but you can't be madly in love with someone who's in love with something else. It burns you out. I think Nick thinks that once he makes it big, he can turn around and make it all up to us, but

I'm done waiting, because he stopped being a man worth waiting for."

Ollie nods. Our shoulders are almost touching. "But last summer? You went back to him?"

"That was him trying to prove that he'd changed. He had a steady gig at a jazz club in Atlanta, and he promised that if I came down, he wouldn't take any more gigs away from home. He'd be with us."

"Right." Ollie's eyes are sympathetic.

"And that lasted four weeks, five? And then…"

"Something good came up," Ollie finished.

"Really good." I nod. Tears come into my eyes. "And it made me feel so stupid."

"No, you weren't." Ollie leans forward and speaks gently. "It's okay to trust people."

"You told me that you don't trust anybody," I remind him.

"I'm working on it," he says with a rueful smile.

"We have a kid, so I felt like I owed it to Hannah to try. But the reality is that I owed it to her not to try."

He is gazing at me, watching the expression on my face carefully.

"Your turn," I say, pretending there aren't tears in my eyes, willing the tears away like they will dry on their own if I ignore them even though that has never worked, not once.

His smile turns ironic. "Okay. Let me think about what I would say if I was totally drunk. You want messy? My wife left me for my brother, who got her pregnant. You may remember I was expecting a baby the first time we spoke a couple of years ago."

It is my turn to nod. I don't want to admit I've heard any of this.

"Well, that was the day I found out that the baby wasn't mine. She had slept with him at least once, and she figured out the timing and realized it could be his child, so she took a test, and she had texted him the results. But I picked up her phone that day by mistake, so I saw his response."

"Oh no."

"I always wonder if I subconsciously knew, and that's why I grabbed her phone. Or what would have happened between us if I hadn't. But...I told you she dated my brother before me. So they had a history. And if...if it had just been some random guy, I might have forgiven her. But I realized she had only ever loved him. I was the backup plan."

"I'm sure that wasn't it."

There's a skeptical look in his eyes. "Anyway, I broke it off. And then two months later, she and Sean were married. And I still don't know if my brother really loves her or if he just wanted to take her away from me."

"That's horrible."

He smiles bitterly. "And I can't talk to my family about it because my parents have forgiven him, and now I'm the problem because I'm unwilling to do the same."

"They can't possibly expect you to forgive him."

"You haven't met him. He can spin a really good yarn, and he was working on my parents, selling his side of the story, for the years I was away. I'm sure he told them I had stolen his one true love, never mind that they broke up several years earlier."

"How can they not be furious at him?"

"They were. But on some level, I think the whole thing pleased my father. When I was in college, I used to act superior to my dad, like...*I'll never treat a woman the way you do.* I think he likes seeing my me and my brother rolling around in the mud like this. It means that we're on his level. Cheating is what real men do, you know? And my mother just wants a grandkid. She wants her family to stick together, and right now I'm the problem for not agreeing to it."

My jaw drops open. "Your mother said that?"

"She says that I have to forgive Phoebe, because I don't realize how guilty she feels, and you can't help who you love. Which I know is true, of course, but…"

I roll my eyes. "Oh come on. You're not upset at her for her feelings. You're upset at her for her choices. Including her choice to lie to you about her feelings."

He blinks once, startled. "Can I bring you with me next time I see my mother?"

"Oh, I would have words."

Ollie looks away for a moment. "I was always trying to measure up to my brother, you know? As a kid, I was trying to be as cool as Sean. And when I couldn't do that, I tried to be more successful. And I didn't manage that, but at least I had a stable relationship, while he hopped from woman to woman, and now he has the marriage and the kid and the wife."

"You're amazing."

He shrugs. "You haven't met him yet. That's what I'd confess to you if I was really drunk. That I think if any woman I'm dating meets my brother, she's going to fall for him instead."

I can see that he means it. It is shocking how much he means it. "I'm going to fall for the asshole who slept with his brother's wife?"

Ollie shrugs.

"Does he dance?" I ask.

"He's probably taking swing lessons, for all I know. Phoebe still dances. But that's why, when she left, she took everything good with her."

"No, she didn't." I stare ahead at the traffic nearby as it piles in front of a stoplight and then speeds away. "You know what I know about that story, and you don't?"

He shakes his head, gazing at me. His eyes are close enough

that I can really see their colors, the dark rings of green and brown.

"There is no way in hell your brother would have done that if he wasn't intimidated by you."

Ollie shakes his head. "Nice thought, but he just likes to win."

"He didn't win. He lost his brother. I mean, my sister, no matter how screwed up I was, I always tried to be there for her. Because if I lost her, I lost everything. And you're telling me he doesn't care that he lost you?"

Ollie looks into the distance. "He still thinks I'll come around. Sometimes he calls my office phone at work and leaves messages telling me to call him. And I don't. But sometimes I think about it."

He looks so sad that I don't think; I just put my hands on his shoulders to meet his eyes. "Listen. You should do what you want. Just because you're the better man doesn't mean you have to be the bigger man. If he's counting on that, if he's using your own decency against you, then he can go fuck himself. Because you have a right to be angry. Don't let him take away your anger, because you earned it and you get to keep it for as long as you want to."

Ollie opens his lips to say something and then places a hand on my cheek and kisses me fiercely instead. It's startling for half a second until he slows down, giving me space to move away. Another kiss comes more gently, then another, and our arms are around each other, and his hands are slipping around the back of my dress. It's messy and uneven and not polite at all, and I feel the blood racing up to my cheeks. He slows down a little, taking a breath. When he finally pulls away, he meets my eyes. I kiss him once, gently, like an answer to a question.

For a long moment, I can't speak. He looks a little dazed too.

"You're so beautiful," he whispers. "You're so staggeringly beautiful it's unreal."

I feel myself blushing harder, unsure what to say in the face of a direct compliment

"It feels like a trick that you're single," he adds. "It feels like I can't trust it. I can't..." He trails off. "Can I kiss you again?"

"I think you should, because that kiss needed some work," I tease. It was probably the best kiss in my life.

"Oh really?" He looks, a little wary.

"You need more practice. A lot more before you get it right, I think."

He kisses me again, hard and confident, just long enough to melt my insides, then pulls back and puts his head down on my shoulder for a second, making a sound of frustration.

"I have to get you home," he groans into me. We don't move for a long moment. I kiss his neck, once.

"That's not helping to motivate me," he says.

He stands up and offers me a hand and sweeps me into his arms in a dance position. I am about to joke that there's no music, except I realize there is, vibrating through the windows of a car that's pulled up to a stoplight. A Justin Timberlake song. Ollie grins and runs me through a couple of moves on the sidewalk. He is still grinning when he pulls me back into his arms to dip me. I hear the cars near us moving away, and I wait for the car with the music to leave, but it doesn't. The driver rolls down the window, the booming music getting louder.

"Awesome!" the man calls. He's a young guy in a white tracksuit with an earring. "You guys are awesome!"

"Thanks!" Ollie says. "She's a famous dancer!"

"Shut up," I whisper into Ollie's neck.

"I believe it!" the man calls. "She's great."

To be clear: I am not great, but Ollie can make anyone appear that way.

He spins me around again as the driver calls, "Have a good night!" I hear the car engine speeding away, taking the music with it.

"I love this city," Ollie murmurs.

My heart feels open as I finally meet his eyes. My brain is trying to absorb everything: the way his lips felt and the warmth of the city and the music I can still hear in my head. The faint, enticing woodsy scent of him. I put one hand gently on his shoulder.

The thought flashes through my head that for the first time since Nick, I want to drag a man somewhere that we can be alone, exploring each other for hours. But we don't have hours. We have no time at all.

He gently lowers his hand down my side and then threads his fingers through mine. We turn together to continue our walk. My whole body is vibrating like the subways rumbling below us and the buses idling on the corner. We say nothing at all for the last few blocks as he walks me home, holding hands like we're teenagers. When we arrive at my door, he kisses my hand and slowly lets it go. Another chivalrous act that shouldn't work—that wouldn't work if I thought it was anything but sincere—but I sense that he means it, and it makes me swoon inside.

I walk up to the door of my building and look back to see that he is still there, still handsome, still watching me intensely. The moon is out tonight, giving his hair a faint blue halo against the greasy glow of bodegas and the hazy green of my building's lobby lights. In his suit, his hair disheveled and his eyes dark, he looks like a romantic hero.

I walk back to him and kiss him one more time.

He grins at me. "So how was your date?" he asks softly.

I smile. "It was nice."

I can still hear his low laughter as I turn and enter the door.

6

THE WHIP

THE FIRST MEETING of the Interoffice Relationship Policy Revision Team meets on the Monday after Ollie and I have our dinner date. There are six of us in the group: two senior managers (Ollie and Destiny), two accountants (me and Brant), and two client service workers (Lana and Niamh) whose job it is to answer questions on our customer hotline. Lana and Niamh are both in their early twenties and seem like good friends; when I enter the conference room, they are grilling each other about their weekend.

"No, but seriously, you must still be hungover," Lana is saying.

"I had a juice cleanse on Sunday so I'm fine."

"Was there vodka in that juice?"

"We are at work, Lana. Don't come at me like that."

"Don't come at me with 2 a.m. texts that you met Chris Hemsworth only it's some bartender in Hoboken."

I take a seat at the table opposite Ollie, who looks silently amused by this discussion.

Destiny arrives and calls things to order quickly. "Okay, folks," she begins. "We are here because of a serious sexual harassment complaint, so let's take our work seriously. Our job is to review the company policy, get some input from employees about the current guidelines, and then write a recommendation for our proposed policy revision. I have been told that one of the key expectations is that we will write up a better self-disclosure policy, meaning that people who start dating will be required to disclose it to H.R."

Ollie and I carefully look anywhere but at each other.

"With that in mind, I wanted to mention that one reason you were all selected for this group is because nobody here is believed to be in any kind of serious relationship with another employee, so you can be fairly neutral and not push for policies that benefit your interests. Hopefully that is accurate."

Ollie and I glance at each other. Do we need to self-disclose? Are we 'serious and monogamous' or not? He says nothing and neither do I.

Destiny outlines a plan for the committee: we will have a couple of initial meetings, send out a questionnaire to employees, then have an all-day meeting (probably as an off-site) where we lock ourselves in a room to work out the details of our write-up, and then revise the initial report and talk about how and when to present our plan.

The word 'off-site' is a red flag for me as a single mom. It could mean renting a nice conference room two blocks away where we can isolate ourselves and work, but it could also mean an all-day trip to somewhere like a sculpture garden in New Jersey or a horse farm in Connecticut, where everyone else will be enjoying the scenery and I will be fretting about how much I have to pay a babysitter because I won't be getting back to the city until 9 p.m.

"I love off-sites!" Lana looks delighted.

"Remember that time we did a ski weekend last year?" Niamh asks.

"I remember the Baileys and hot cocoa," Lana says. "The skiing not so much."

"We should make them pay for a spa day!" Niamh directs this to Destiny, who already looks a little tired of their enthusiasm.

"I think off-sites could be challenging for some people," Ollie offers, glancing my way, "if they have kids or commitments in the city." He briefly meets my eyes, and I am filled with gratitude.

"I have kids, and I like off-sites," Brant replies dryly. "Gets me out of the house." I want to roll my eyes, because he has complained to me multiple times that his wife has custody of his daughters ninety percent of the time.

"Alright, let's do a quick vote," says Destiny. "Who wants to have our off-site outside the city?"

The vote lands in favor of leaving the city by four to two. Ollie glances at me and looks away again, and I think about how ridiculously attractive he is. Somewhere deep inside me, Rebel Laura pops up her head again, telling me to rub my foot against his leg under the table. *No, I'm not going to do that.* Because I'm an adult. And because Destiny doesn't look like she wants to deal with any nonsense. And because I don't want to look completely desperate.

I wish Vivi were here, so I could at least confess to my sexual frustration on a yellow notepad. When the meeting wraps up, we walk out into the hallway and I lean against the wall, pretending to check my phone while giving Ollie space to catch up with me if he wants to.

"Thanks, Laura," Destiny says as she walks past. "Your input was helpful."

"I'm really looking forward to this," I say with forced cheer.

Ollie pauses across from me in the hallway, glancing at his

cell phone as well. Brant steps between us and glances at Ollie and then at me.

"Well," he says, "want to chat on the way back?"

There's no way to dodge the request without being obvious. "Of course," I say. I follow Brant toward the elevator bank.

"Ten percent," he says to me as we step on the elevator. "They're talking about a ten percent downsize next year. So you're putting in some face time with the VPs at exactly the right time. I'm sure that's why Lana and Niamh are there; some of the managers want to replace half our customer support team with artificial intelligence."

"Well, shit," I say quietly.

"My thoughts exactly."

When I get back to my desk, Ollie has texted me: *We should talk.*

I feel a brief flash of nerves as I text a reply. *I have to get Hannah by six, but I could duck out a few minutes early to chat somewhere nearby?*

His reply follows quickly: *Sure.*

And then he adds: *By the way, I was lied to. Someone told me that if you put enough accountants in a room, there'll be an orgy.*

I type back: *If you don't put it on the meeting agenda, it's not going to be in the meeting.*

WE END up sitting in the back of an Irish pub a few blocks from work, well before the evening rush, hidden in a scuffed wooden booth tucked behind a column.

"So," he begins, "I noticed that neither you nor I jumped in to announce that we were in a serious, monogamous relationship."

I smile. "I didn't want to spring that on you and have you look surprised, like, 'That makes one of us.'"

"Me neither." He gives me a meaningful glance. "But are we, I mean...it's probably too early to have this discussion."

"I was hoping you weren't juggling six other women, but I was going to wait another date or two before I put the ankle monitor on you."

"Right." He smiles, too. "But just to be clear, I'm not seeing anyone else."

"I'm not either. To be honest, I can't imagine wanting to." At his look, I hurried on. "I just mean it's been a long time since anyone could compete with a nice cup of tea and a home renovation show."

"Good, yeah. That's how I feel, too. Less so about home renovation shows. Those are too high stakes for me. I get worried as soon as they start fighting about wallpaper. But what is our move, here? We don't seem to be keeping to the spirit of Destiny's request. I mean, legally, I don't think they can actually require us to be single; that might have some discriminatory overtones. But they wouldn't like it. And I don't mind resigning from the committee, but that would force you to resign too, potentially, unless I didn't say who I was dating. I didn't know if you'd rather avoid the committee entirely, or if this is helpful for you professionally."

"Well, the problem is, I had to beg for my job back last summer, so I need opportunities to prove to them that I'm a loyal soldier. Brant volunteered me for the committee because he thought it would help. And he keeps mentioning layoffs, so..."

"Right. Similar with me. I only just got back from requesting a transfer. So it sounds like we'd both like to stick it out." He seems to be picking his words carefully. "Do you want to postpone things between us until after the committee is done?"

"Do you?"

"Personally? No, I really don't." He smiles ruefully.

"Me neither," I agree. "I mean, I suppose we could just say that we're friends. And then make it public that we're dating later on."

"Has your friend Vivian told anyone we're dating?"

I frown. "I mentioned we had a date, yeah. Have you told your friend Katy?"

There is silence for a moment. "Shoot."

"Yeah," I agree. "We're not a secret now."

"I don't want to ask you to lie..." he begins.

"You can ask me to lie," I say quickly.

He grins. "This feels like a very shaky start to a relationship."

"Can we tell everyone that we decided we're better off as friends because you're still hung up on your ex-wife?"

He raises his eyebrows sky high. "Why is it me who has to be hung up on my ex? What about you and your musician?"

"I was picking the more believable scenario," I reply.

"You mean I'm more damaged?" His eyes sparkle with ironic amusement.

"I meant you're so charming that it would be hard to believe I didn't want you."

"Nice save." He considers. "Alright, let me think. We could tell our friends that we went on a date, but decided we're too busy, and we're just friends for now, but we'll try again in a few months. But we'd have to stick to that story with everyone. I don't feel safe telling Katy that I'm lying. It's not that she would sabotage me on purpose, but..."

"And I would have to tell Vivi we're just friends for a while."

"Yeah."

"And during the meetings I'll have to refrain from crawling across the table to make out with you."

"Great. Now that's all I'm going to be thinking about during every meeting."

I reach over and hold his hand under the table, and he flushes a little.

"So that's a plan." His voice is not entirely steady, and I suspect he is feeling what I'm feeling right now. Never have I wanted him more than at this moment, when I can't even kiss him. It's like the very forbidden quality is amplifying the feeling. He runs his thumb lightly across my wrist. "So in the meantime," he says softly, his eyes so warm they seem to be lit by a fire burning somewhere within him, "can I ask you on another date?"

"Yes." My heart flutters like I've been asked to the prom. "We'll just need to be extremely well-behaved in public."

"Only in public?" There's that mischievous look again.

"Only in public," I repeat, and his gaze grows so intense that I can still feel it on me as I slip out of the booth to leave. I can still feel it on me for the entire subway ride home.

"Let me get this straight," Vivi says at lunch as we watch Ollie getting into line at his favorite lunch cart across the street. "Neither of you thinks you're ready for a relationship?"

I always knew that Vivi was going to be the hardest person to convince, but I feel obligated to stick to our story. The goal is not to tell Destiny and the committee one thing and our friends another—not when everyone circulates around the same water coolers. That's a recipe for getting fired.

"So he must be the problem, right?" she asks. "Because you are definitely ready for dating."

"He told me he doesn't trust women." I figure I should stick as close to the truth as possible.

"Oh. Huh."

"Yep."

She ponders this. "Hey! Ollie!" She calls loudly above the sound of traffic. I glance over at Ollie, who is gathering his lunch to head back to the office. "Ollie!" she shouts a second time.

"Vivi, stop it!"

"Come eat with us!" she calls to him. He nods and approaches with his lunch.

"Hi," Vivi says, gleeful in the way she always is in the face of conflict. "So Laura told me you're not ready for a relationship?"

Ollie glances at me and smiles. "I think we agreed to take a few months off while we're working on a committee together, so that the whole relationship doesn't blow up in the middle of it."

"Sit down. I want to talk to you about this," Vivi replies.

Ollie sits down, a grave, polite smile on his face. "Okay."

"So Laura is great, right?" she asks.

Ollie nods, his eyes flickering to me. "Laura is amazing."

"So what's the problem?"

Ollie laughs. "The problem is that I need to take a couple of months to deal with some personal stuff and I thought the timing meant we should delay the start of this."

"Bullshit," Vivi says. "Bullshit, bullshit, bullshit. What's the real problem?"

"Vivi, please?" I beg.

Ollie sighs. "I had a panic attack on our first date when I saw my ex-wife. And realized I need more therapy."

"Oh." Vivi looks skeptical for a moment.

"Laura has been very kind about not mentioning it. There may have been some tears involved." Ollie is absolutely committed to the bit, I'll give him that much. "So I figured, I don't want to waste Laura's time until I get that worked out."

"We should let Ollie go back to his lunch, Viv," I add.

"No, no, no. I want to talk to him. So. Oliver. Some questions. Let's get to know you."

Ollie shoots me a look, but fortunately, he still seems entertained. He settles in with his lunch as she considers him.

"So where did you grow up then?" she asks.

"A suburb of Melbourne called Toorak."

"In Australia? What's that like?"

"It's like...Beverly Hills, maybe? The closest I've seen around New York is probably Upper Montclair, New Jersey."

"So fancy as hell," Vivi replies.

"Yeah." He hesitates for a moment. "My dad is a successful businessman, and he wanted everyone to know exactly how successful he was."

"Melbourne is in the southern part of Australia, right?"

"Yeah. There are palm trees there. A lot of swimming pools."

"Do you miss it?"

He shakes his head. "I fell in love with New York when we moved here."

Vivi considers him for a moment. "So your parents are still there, or..."

"They live on Long Island now. In Great Neck."

"How Gatsby of them."

"I think that was exactly the idea."

"So what would your parents say if you brought home a divorced single mom?"

"Vivi—" I feel a little appalled at her bluntness, and faintly worried she'll scare him off. I remind myself that in Vivi's mind, he has already been scared off.

"Well," Ollie begins, "I'm thirty-seven years old, and I don't really talk to my parents, so I don't have much interest in what they would say."

Vivi looks impressed. "Okay. Once you're done with your spiritual journey, you can date Laura." Vivi stands up. "I'm getting an iced coffee. Talk amongst yourselves."

"She's a lot," I begin as Vivi walks away.

"She's looking out for you," he says.

"So did you tell Katy that we're not dating anymore?"

"Yes. It was a little simpler than that." He chuckles ruefully. "She knew about all the stuff with Phoebe and pretty much assumed I was too screwed up to date anyway, so convincing her wasn't hard."

I take a breath. "I wanted to tell you...Hannah will be away a bit this summer. She's spending three weeks with my sister Abby in Newfoundland. So if you can wait until then, I'll have a few weeks where I'm pretty free, and we can figure out something to do."

"You're already taking West Coast Swing."

"I mean something like, I don't know, a weekend away or something. To show you I can actually be a fun person."

He has a strange look in his eyes as he shakes his head. "Why do you keep..."

"What?"

"You don't owe me anything."

"I know." I feel puzzled at the wary look in his eyes. Is it so hard for him to believe I like him enough to do something nice with him?

He sighs. "It feels like you feel guilty for what you said about me at the party, and you're trying to compensate for—"

"I don't feel guilty, Ollie. It just wasn't true."

Vivi returns then, and we drop the conversation. "Okay, one last request," she adds. "Oliver? Don't waste her time."

Ollie nods solemnly.

"Hey," I say, "even if we do start dating again, no one is wasting anyone's time in the first four months of a relationship."

"Lies," Vivi says. "If you want my brutal opinion, I think most people are pretty sure how they feel by the second date."

7

FOOTWORK

IT TURNS out that the most convenient time for Ollie and me to have our next date will be on a Saturday afternoon when Hannah is at a four-hour-long ninth birthday party for her friend Nina. Nina's parents are the kind of Brooklyn monsters who joyfully turn their kid's birthday parties into gala affairs involving rented bouncy castles and a private frozen yogurt truck, leaving the rest of us parents looking like peasants when we buy our kids sheet cakes to serve in the playground. The timing will keep Hannah from feeling jealous of my date, though...plus my Saturday plan with Ollie means that I won't be busy Friday night, which—as Jody points out to me via text message—means that I have no good excuse *not* to turn up at the weekly 'open social' session being held at our dance school on Friday evenings.

I don't know what I'm expecting when I get to Manhattan Swing on Friday night: a classroom environment, a workshop, a club... What it feels like instead is a junior high dance: a few single people clustered around the sides of the room nervously and lots of couples in the center of the room trying out moves that they don't fully understand yet. The event is held in the largest classroom at the studio, in a huge room with mirrors on one wall and disco balls spinning overhead. No one is dressed up, really; there are lots of jeans and t-shirts, and a few fancier outfits from folks who are presumably beginning their evening with awkward footwork practice before continuing on to the rest of their Friday plans. After my gaze swings across the two dozen couples on the dance floor, I am relieved to spot Helen and Jody against a wall, chatting. If I didn't have Jody here, I might not find anyone to dance with.

Our regular teacher, Maria, is helping to run the evening, and she gives everyone a quick five-minute lesson at the start of the night: a discussion of 'the whip,' one of the more common West Coast moves, and then three different variations on the whip—only one of which I am likely to remember. Class works that way for me a lot of the time; a lesson starts out slow, and I feel pretty confident about how I'm doing, but by the end, the instructors are giving us 'next level' challenges that only about five percent of the class (that five percent being Jody) manages to keep up with.

As the music starts and the lights are dimmed further, I spot our young blond friend Ben walking in, looking a little awkward without his fiancée. I wave him over.

"Paige is doing her bachelorette weekend," he explains. "Even though we're still a few weeks out from the wedding, her sister has a baby due soon, so we scheduled it around that."

"Vegas or Atlantic City?" Jody asks.

"Nashville."

"Of course," Jody drawls. "Please tell me there's an Elvis stripper on the agenda."

"I didn't ask. I just hope it calms her down," Ben mutters. "It's still five weeks to the wedding and she's so *stressed* all the time."

"Nothing calms someone down like a good hangover," I reply. "Come on. Do you want to dance with me?"

Ben nods a little bashfully and then puts out his hand. He has mercifully moved past his stepping-on-toes phase but is still visibly counting off steps. It's always relaxing to dance with him because there's no pressure to look smooth. I get just as confused as he does during his attempt to lead me through a turn and we both debate the different hand positions for 'inside turns' and 'outside turns' before consulting with Jody, who explains to us that we are both doing it wrong and teaches us the right way.

Then I take a turn dancing with Jody, whose confidence continues to make her the strongest leader I've danced with aside from our instructors. While we try out the various moves from class, she mentions that she has her eye on a different follower, Téa, whom she met in an East Coast Swing class and who is now also learning West Coast. She points her out to me: a young woman with lavender hair who has the sweet, dreamy look of someone who talks about vibes and crystals. As soon as we've stopped dancing, I command Jody to cross the room and make her move, and Jody rolls her eyes but reluctantly agrees.

I spot Helen dancing with one of the young men from our intro class while his wife watches from the sidelines; they are one of the married couples, and they seem much more relaxed than the engaged couples whenever they have to split up. The husband, Tim, joked with me about it during our lesson. ("When you're engaged, you're worried someone will steal your fiancée, and when you're married, you're hoping they give you a break.") Ben dances with a pretty young woman with light brown skin and long braids who appears to be a few months ahead of him in experience level but cheerfully smiles through his attempts to lead her through various entry-level moves. The leader/follower relationship always seems particularly ironic when it's only the follower who knows what they're doing.

I take a few moments to watch the really experienced couples, seeing if I can pick up any tricks, and that is when I catch sight of a woman who is exactly what I hope to be someday: confident, creative, adding her own little spin to steps. She is very pretty and very blonde, with a familiar face that makes me wonder if I've seen her in a movie. I keep an eye on her during the next couple of dances as she takes turns with various leaders. I wonder if she's a teacher or just stopping by to get some practice in.

"I want to be like her when I grow up," I joke to Helen when she and Jody return to our corner.

"Everyone wants to be like her," Helen replies. "She's a champion-level dancer."

"Do you know her? Who is she?"

Jody opens her mouth to speak, but before she can say anything, our instructor, Maria, stops the music.

"Folks, we have a special treat!" Maria calls out. "Eliana Macri is back in New York, and she is going to give us a special guest demonstration on follower footwork at the end of the evening, so be sure you stick around because that is taking place at exactly nine p.m."

My breathing becomes a little more shallow. No wonder the blonde woman has a familiar face. She is Ollie's old partner, and I've seen her in videos with him, back when her hair was shorter and three shades closer to mousy brown.

"She's ranked like, fourth in the country," Jody murmurs to us.

I find my voice. "She used to dance with Ollie, right?" My voice sounds more high-pitched than usual, and Jody gives me a sharp glance.

"She may be again," Helen says blithely. "Now that she's back in town."

There are a million reasons why I should stick around for Eliana's 'follower footwork' lesson, but I use my babysitter as an excuse and head home, trying not to panic as I ponder the return of the woman who broke his heart.

I'll be seeing Ollie tomorrow for our picnic at the bandshell in Central Park, where we are supposed to hang out and try some dancing to a big band show. If he is planning on being a dance partner with Eliana again, he'll probably tell me, won't he? My heart lurches a little at the thought.

After I get home and tuck Hannah into bed, I spend the evening torturing myself by watching old YouTube videos of Eliana and Ollie. She is incredible, perfectly matching his elegant moves step for step, but I'm not really watching her. I'm watching his face. In the videos, he looks at her like he is madly in love.

Then I watch some videos of Eliana in various competitions over the last few years dancing with Connor Yung. They have good chemistry, too. There is even a video of them placing third at a huge swing dancing competition in Barcelona only six weeks ago.

What happened there?

I WAKE up in the morning to a text from Nina's mother, the host of the elaborate birthday party that Hannah was supposed to go to today.

Hey everyone so nina woke up with a fever so we're going to have to postpone the party so sorry

I write her back an appropriately sympathetic response; it has sometimes been my turn to have my kid pick up something in the petri dish of New York City public schools. Then I start to text Ollie and sigh. I guess he really is learning the realities of dating a single mom. I explain the situation in as few words as possible, trying to make myself sound wryly amused instead of deeply frustrated. I send the message and wait, giving him a chance to formulate a polite reply.

While I am waiting, I get another text, this one from the NYC transit system. Apparently, the subway line leading from our Brooklyn neighborhood into Manhattan is temporarily down, so we probably wouldn't have been able to make it to Central Park today anyway.

No subway either, so I guess this is fate, I text Ollie.

My phone buzzes a few seconds later. *Can I call you right now?*

"So here's what I'm thinking," he says when I pick up. "It's an outdoor picnic environment. There are playgrounds nearby. Is there a reason we can't take Hannah with us?"

I sigh. "It wouldn't be a date," I say, "which is fine by me, but you need to be aware that as soon as my kid is there, the whole day will be about keeping her entertained."

"I'm okay with that. I like your kid." I try not to let myself react to that. "And we won't say we're dating, obviously," he goes on. "We can say we're work friends."

"We don't have an easy way to get there," I reply.

"I could pick you up in my car."

A car? He's a lawyer, so I shouldn't be totally shocked, but I forgot that people had those in New York. "You can't just drive to Brooklyn and pick us up in your car to go to Manhattan. Where would we even park?"

"In the worst-case scenario, my lot isn't that far away from Central Park. I have a monthly spot near my building."

A reserved parking space near Central Park? Why not offer to fly us on his Concorde jet?

"Alright," I say, glancing outside. The weather is really perfect. "I'll let Hannah know."

"Thank you, Laura."

I don't know what he's thanking me for. I don't know why that makes me happy.

When I explain the plan to Hannah, she is reluctant to go into the city to sit and listen to music, but I promise her there will be dancing, and playgrounds, and that she can bring a bag full of snacks and coloring books…and I promise that she gets to use her Nintendo Switch on the car ride, which seals the deal. Apparently, I am one of those terrible parents who buys good behavior with screen time, but I have decided to live with it. If anyone wants to come after me for it, they can find me on Single Parent Lane, with the rest of the residents who don't give a damn.

Ollie calls my phone when he is downstairs, and Hannah and I come down to find him waiting in front of our building next to a tan Mercedes that's at least ten years old. It feels like a reverse image of the dates in my early twenties when the guy was smoking a cigarette and leaning against his shabby red sports car. Ollie is wearing a button-down short-sleeved shirt, and he looks put-together and nicely groomed, but emphatically not cool.

"It's my mom's old car," he says as he gestures behind him. "It's not exciting but it only has thirty thousand miles on it, so I feel like I have no excuse to get rid of it."

I glance around at the lovely, soft seats as I sit down. The car smells faintly of leather and Ollie's warm cedar scent. "I usually refuse to travel in a mere Mercedes," I announce, "but I will make do."

"I'll bring the Bugatti next time."

"Please do." I introduce him to Hannah, who doesn't remember him from 'Take Your Child to Work' Day and seems largely uninterested in chatting, as she immediately settles into playing her Nintendo.

"I bribed her with screen time."

He shakes his head. "Shameful. Next, you're going to tell me you sometimes buy her ice cream from a truck."

"Ice cream?" Hannah immediately perks up. "Are we getting ice cream?"

Ollie glances at me. "Sorry."

"Oh, you're buying it for all of us now."

We don't end up needing to go to his parking lot because Ollie finds street parking only two blocks from the park—a miracle that I don't think I've ever managed once. We walk through the park and track down an empty bench to one side of the large open performance space. A small crowd of people, mostly over fifty, are seated in chairs as the big band warms up on the outdoor stage. Ollie unpacks the picnic basket he's put together, and I pull out the cold drinks and coloring books that I brought with us in a cooler.

"Do you want to dance when the music starts?" Ollie asks me.

"What kind of dance?" Hannah narrows her eyes, looking between us.

"You know Ollie teaches dance," I tell her.

"Ballet?" She examines him.

"Not ballet."

"My friend Fiona does Irish step dancing," Hannah says.

"I do not know Irish step dancing."

Hannah frowns. "Tap dance?"

"No, but I can tap dance," he says. He catches my delighted look and shakes his head. "No."

"I will give you one of these very nice grapefruit seltzers if you demonstrate some tap dancing for us."

"Oh, is that how things are going to be?"

"Please?" Hannah says. "I want to see you tap dance."

He sighs and looks around. "I feel like a smudge-nosed 1920s shoeshine boy." He does a quick little tap dance for us, about thirty seconds long.

"I couldn't hear the tapping," Hannah sighs. "But good otherwise."

"Oh, thank you."

"He teaches swing dance," I say. "West Coast Swing."

Hannah demands an explanation, and Ollie takes my hand to demonstrate just as the band starts up. Hannah watches us for a few moments, then jumps out of her seat.

"Teach me," she says. "Mommy's not good."

Ollie laughs and gives me a glance to get permission, then begins to teach Hannah some steps. It reminds me of two years ago in the conference room at work: Hannah is an absolute sponge for his attention, and I can see right away that Ollie is not going to get a chance to sit down anytime soon.

He runs her through three separate twists, and then she tells him to spin her as many times in a row as he possibly can. He counts them off for her. "Ready? One, two, three, four…"

She gets dizzy and stops after seven times.

"It's harder on concrete," he says. "You need a slippery floor to get up to ten."

"I can't work in these conditions," Hannah says wearily, sitting back down. I think of Abby; that's a phrase that probably originated with my sister.

"Laura?" Ollie smiles at me. "I know you're not as good as Hannah, but do you want a turn?"

I smile and concede to dance with him for a minute or two before I step back. Hannah is looking at us suspiciously.

"Can we go to the playground now?"

"Let's eat first," I reply. Hannah wolfs down her sandwich and announces that she is ready to go.

"Hannah," I say, "why don't you read or color for a minute while the rest of us finish eating?"

For some reason, I want to prove to Ollie that my daughter actually does read books; she isn't a feral creature who insists on having her way all the time. But she's not letting me have that small victory. She flatly refuses to read any of the books I've brought and then starts begging for more time on her Nintendo, arguing that there's no real difference between letting her use it in the car and letting her use it in the park, which makes more sense than I can admit to.

"There are squirrels here," I say. "See if you can find their hiding places in the trees."

"That's boring," she wails.

When she sees that I'm not going to budge, she flops down on the bench and watches us eat, sighing wearily.

I feel exposed. I've never been around Hannah in the context of a date. Even though she's not being particularly terrible, I can supply the monologue in Ollie's head: *This is how she raises her daughter? When I have children, they will sit quietly landscape painting and reading* Watership Down *while their parents finish their conversations.* I thought like that myself once. I figured that being the opposite of my mom would be sufficient for doing a good job: I would not drink heavily, I would set boundaries, and I would take my children to enrichment classes and cultural events. My children would be creative, academic, confident but polite, definitely not addicted to video games.

All of those plans relied on having another parent to help me out, it turned out. The best I can say is that Hannah has never had to drape a blanket on me while I sleep off a bottle of wine. It's something, but it's never felt like I'm getting it right.

Ollie watches me closely as we pack up the picnic. When

we get up to walk toward the playground, we fall behind Hannah by a few feet.

"Thanks for putting up with her," I say.

"There is no putting up involved," he says firmly.

"She's being deliberately difficult."

"I can't imagine where she picked that up from."

I laugh, and he squeezes my hand once. I think about how we're supposed to act like we're not dating in public, not just because of Hannah but because of our jobs. The very prohibition is making me feel rebellious.

And because I can't leave well enough alone, I say, "So is your dance partner Eliana back in town? I think she came to one of our practice sessions at Manhattan Swing this week."

He nods, his eyes fixed on Hannah running ahead of us. "Yeah, she's back in New York for a bit."

"Oh yeah?" I sound really casual. Definitely cool and not jealous at all.

"Yeah. She texted me. She is looking for a new partner."

"Ah." Is she asking *you?* Does she want you back? Do *you* want *her?*

"I have to talk to her about it. We're going to get a coffee," he says.

"Okay."

He stops walking and looks directly at me. "Hey. Don't worry, okay?"

"Even if I was the type to get jealous, I would have no excuse after two dates."

He nods. "I appreciate that, but I'm still asking you not to."

"So I should cancel the private detective I hired to track your every move?"

"Completely up to you. I don't want to cut into a small businessman's freelance income."

"As long as he's filling out his 1099-MISC forms," I say lightly.

"And doing proper withholding of his social security taxes."

Hannah decides to introduce Ollie to the giant playground in the middle of Central Park, with its mountainous rock to climb, and then immediately takes off to play with another child. She seems to have her Aunt Abby's tendency to want to befriend strangers in New York City.

"So where was your favorite place to play as a child?" Ollie asks as we lean against a wall near the giant climbing rock, watching Hannah from a few yards away.

"Where was yours?" I say.

"Ha," he says. "I'm not falling for that twice. No changing the topic. You go first."

"Well, the place where I lived the longest had a really fun abandoned garage that we would play in." I catch Ollie's appalled glance. "It wasn't unsafe. It was actually magical. The house behind us was abandoned, and the garage was right by my yard. We collected garter snakes, and we made a little gang with the other neighborhood kids where we pretended to solve crimes, and that lasted until we moved again."

"That sounds fun," he says warily.

I point to a tattoo on my wrist of two flowers. "That was the house where my mom grew these."

"Japanese peonies," Ollie says, surprising me with his accurate identification.

"They were the only plant my mother succeeded in keeping alive. I got these flowers when I was twenty-one because I thought they represented Abby and me. The one good thing that survived my mother."

Ollie's eyes are filled with sympathy.

"We weren't abused or anything." My voice sounds defensive. My childhood wasn't *all* bad.

"You were neglected," he says gently.

I shrug. "It's why I was determined never to do that with Hannah. I was going to stay in one place. Not date casually. The kid comes first." He nods, looking serious. I add, saying it for the first time, "I think I thought if I got back together with Nick, it would prove that I wasn't like my mother. That I wasn't going to keep bouncing from man to man."

He frowns a little. "I'm sorry you had to go through that."

I nod. "You mean as a kid? It had its upsides. I learned to cook. By the time I started college, I knew how to make a mean spaghetti carbonara."

"And now," he adds, "you don't rely on anybody but yourself."

It is so staggeringly accurate that it forces me to laugh. "Well, men don't have the best record of showing up. I trust Abby."

"And then she moved away."

The fact that he gets it feels unexpectedly huge. I feel tearful, which feels ridiculous in the middle of a playground. "Your turn. Tell me about your playgrounds growing up."

"Well," he says, "this giant rock reminds me of this beach I used to go to as a teenager. I was a lifeguard. And the beach had this huge rock we'd climb on." He smiles. "I lost my virginity behind that rock."

"So this rock brings back dirty memories?"

"Not the playground part, but yeah." He grins, but then the smile fades. "She was the first girl my brother stole from me, actually."

"So he makes it habit of this."

"I went to therapy for a while," Ollie says as we watch Hannah debating some finer point of her makeshift tag game with another child. "I told you that. And I realized my father was the one who pitted us against each other. I think he thought it would give us a competitive edge. Sean and I dealt with that differently, though. Sean ignored everything my father wanted: he left Australia to get away from my dad, then dropped out of college, didn't go to law school. And I emotionally checked out. I stopped reacting. It hurt Sean's feelings, I think. Like I stopped caring about him when I stopped trying to one-up him."

"And Sean restarted the game by stealing your wife?"

Ollie lets out a breath. "God, I hope not. I hope Phoebe means more to him than that. But it definitely means that he won, if there was a game to win."

Hannah appears beside us, wiping sweat from her brow. "Ice cream?" she says pointedly to Ollie.

We introduce Ollie to Mister Melty-Face, our nickname for the SpongeBob popsicle that you can buy from the ice cream pushcart vendors in the park. It has two large, dark eyes that tend to roll slowly out of its head, and Hannah and I have a tradition of eating it while making horrified screams.

"Noooooo!" Hannah demonstrates. "Not my face...!"

"Not my eyes!" I cry.

Ollie pretends to melt down onto a park bench. "Noooooooooooooo... I'm melting! I'm melting! What a world, what a world..."

Hannah considers him. "You're not a good actor."

"That's why you have to do the acting, not me."

"I'm very good at acting."

"I remember," he agrees.

Hannah's energy starts to flag after a couple of hours, and Ollie drives us home. When I glance at her in the backseat, she is playing Nintendo with her eyes drooping and her head leaning on the window. Eventually, even the cheerful beeping and golden coins can't keep her awake.

"Thank you for today," I say quietly as Hannah snores behind us. "I know it wasn't..."

He looks surprised. "It was a good day," he says.

I try to force a smile instead of getting emotional; there's no point in being desperately grateful that he stuck around for an afternoon if he's not planning to do it again. "Well, for the record, I thought your Wicked Witch of the West was brilliant."

"I believe that's known in theater circles as getting mixed reviews."

I look out the window. If he is deciding between getting back together with a cute blonde dancer or an overworked single mother, I can't blame him for choosing the simpler option.

He glances at me. "You can rely on people, you know," he says gently.

"Thank you." My voice is so quiet that I am not sure he hears me.

Ollie's god-tier parking skills are still in effect when he arrives on my street and finds an available space thirty feet from our front door.

Hannah is still asleep—or feigning it, more likely—so I pick her up while Ollie grabs our cooler. Hannah blinks herself awake on my shoulder, then squeezes her eyes shut, ready to hitch a ride by pretending she's still out cold. Ollie offers to take her, but I shake my head. I get a vision in my head of some future where I could just hand her off to him and think it was the most natural thing in the world, and the thought feels dangerous. Don't get addicted to that idea, I tell myself firmly. You're an addict; don't get drunk on a fantasy of happiness. You know where that leads.

As we approach the building, I notice a motorcycle parked right outside my building in the usual no-parking zone. I stop walking entirely when I see who is leaning against it, looking at his cell phone. Hannah senses my tension and sits up.

"What's wrong?" Ollie asks, but Hannah is already sliding herself out of my arms.

"Daddy!" she calls, running forward.

Nick glances up and then throws his arms out to Hannah. "Baby!" he calls. He is wearing another one of his 'bad boy rebel' outfits: signature cowboy boots, tight black t-shirt stretched across his chest, dark jeans. He looks stupidly handsome; that's one reason he's gotten away with so much over the years.

Ollie lingers behind as I step forward.

"Hey, Nick." My arms fold across my chest out of habit.

"Laur," he says, his eyes flickering to Ollie and then back again, "sorry to drop in like this. I was staying with a friend in Philly when I got the news that I booked the tour with The Big Lie. I borrowed his bike to drive up and tell you."

I know the band—it is the same one that hired him as a replacement guitarist during Hannah's April break. They are a successful rock band, their sound a pop/alt-rock hybrid somewhere between the All-American Rejects and The Strokes, and much more mainstream than anything Nick has booked before. Their lead guitarist made the tabloids a couple of months ago when he went to rehab, and Nick filled in for a couple of shows.

"That's great news," I say kindly, because it is, and I'm not going to deny Nick this victory. I can sense Ollie's tension as he stands nearby.

"I'm officially part of the band, too," Nick goes on. "Not second guitar, not filling in... I'm lead guitar player for the next few months while they see what's happening with Theo."

"Congratulations. That's fantastic, Nick."

Hannah eyes him curiously. "Will you be in New York?" Hannah knows how to cut to the chase.

"Well," he shrugs, "we have a couple of dates here, yeah. I won't be around much this summer, but I can take you on tour with me for a while if your mom is okay with it." He looks at me. "We can get a nanny for her or something, if you have work."

A nanny? That means Nick will be making real money. Nick glances again at Ollie, who finally steps forward.

"Nick Marceau," Nick says, putting out his hand. Of course he's going to mention his last name, because it is still my last name.

"Oliver MacCormack."

Nick shakes his hand, his eyes drifting to me again, an unspoken question there.

"I'll just say good-bye to Ollie," I say, letting Hannah continue to pepper her father with questions.

Ollie and I step a few feet away and he politely hands me the cooler. Part of me thinks I can read Ollie's mind perfectly: the irony, the awareness that Nick is handsome, the fact that Nick has finally 'hit it big' and decided to show up immediately.

"Is this where I tell *you* not to worry?" I ask, trying to sound teasing.

He smiles flatly and leans forward slightly. "You don't owe me anything," he says quietly.

That's the exact wrong thing for him to be thinking, but I can't come up with a way to convince him of that in front of my ex-husband. "Thank you for today. It was nice."

"Nice." He nods. We can't even hug good-bye without rousing Hannah's suspicions. I squeeze his arm once, then watch him walk to his car. When I glance at Nick, his head is tilted slightly to one side as he shifts his gaze between me and Ollie's old Mercedes.

I walk back toward him; Hannah has wrapped herself around his leg like a boa constrictor.

"I'm not staying," Nick says. "I gotta get my friend's bike back. But we could grab some dinner?"

I nod. What else is there to say in front of Hannah?

·   ·   ·

WE HAVE dinner at a Mexican place around the corner that I know from past experience is willing to cook Hannah some chicken nuggets, another one of those parental compromises that I swore I'd never make until I was making it. My plan was to expose my daughter to all sorts of interesting world cuisines, but it served only to reinforce her unwavering love for bland Middle-American fare. The great nugget compromise feels emblematic of my parenting.

Nick doesn't ask me about Ollie during the meal. He asks Hannah about her day, though, and gets all the important details: Hannah got to play on her Nintendo Switch but only in Ollie's car. She hasn't met Ollie before, but he teaches dance. She wants to learn dance. Taekwondo is going pretty well. Mom is learning to dance. Every one of these comments is punctuated by Nick looking at me and then very deliberately looking away while I sip my iced tea and look out the window. Nick talks a bit about the tour, which is covering almost the entire country, followed by a possible two-month leg in Europe. He is radiating quiet excitement about it all, and I am happy to see him so happy. In spite of everything, I can't begrudge him the joy that fills his whole being. He has worked hard for this; that much I know.

When we leave the restaurant at sunset with half of Hannah's nuggets in a take-out container, Nick walks us back to our building and gives Hannah a huge hug, then sends her inside so he can speak to Mommy alone for a moment.

"It won't last," Nick says quietly, "that guy."

"It's really none of your business. And it's not serious."

"You let him meet our kid and it's not serious?"

I look away for a moment. "Hannah had a birthday party

that got cancelled. I brought her along. And I don't have to defend myself to you."

"Fair enough. But I know you, Laura. And he's not the one. He's going to bore you."

"Because he shows up on time?"

"Is that the best thing he has going for him?"

I sigh. We both seem to decide not to fight. "Congrats on your tour," I say.

"Thanks." Nick gives me a gentle smile. "I'll call you soon, okay?" He runs one hand down my arm, then waves at Hannah, gets on his borrowed motorcycle and drives away. Hannah watches him through the window of our lobby with a dreamy expression, like his exhaust fumes are made of rainbows.

8

WEDDING SEASON

THE DAY after the Central Park date with Ollie is my Sunday afternoon West Coast Swing class while Hannah takes Taekwondo. It is starting to be a favorite part of my week. Ben, Helen, Jody and I have formed a little team of singles: we look after each other, trade tips, and step up whenever a quick pairing is required, since we form an equal number of leaders and followers. We have all decided to continue dancing through June as well—though Ben acknowledges he'll quit after his mid-June wedding.

"How is the planning going?" I ask him when we take a brief break in the middle of class.

His eyes take on the thousand-yard-stare weariness of someone in the middle of a Himalayan trek. "It's been pretty rough."

"Do you want to tell me about it?"

He breathes a long sigh. "Paige's family has more money than mine, and they're footing the bill for the wedding, so my parents offered to pay for the rehearsal dinner. But now the place my parents picked is not fancy enough to satisfy Paige's mother, so her parents want to pay for the rehearsal dinner, too, but my mom got insulted."

"You should have the rehearsal dinner at a biker bar," Jody says from next to us. "There are a ton of those on Long Island."

"If only," Ben agrees. "And apparently, the song Paige wanted to dance to, *Disturbia*—" (As if any of us could forget that particular choice.) "—got nixed by her parents, and they gave us a list of approved songs. All by Tony Bennett or Frank Sinatra. So we have to choreograph our first dance all over again."

We offer sympathy with varying degrees of sincerity. I suspect Jody finds Ben's plight amusing, though she is nice enough to tell him that she has a friend who manages a fancy restaurant out in the Hamptons, if he needs a connection for the rehearsal dinner.

"He's a bit of cokehead," Jody says, "but he'll hook you up."

"Thanks." Ben looks sincerely grateful. He's a good guy in his quiet way. I wonder if this makes him an easy target for manipulation by his wealthy fiancée's parents.

"Well, whatever song you pick, you are going to knock Paige's socks off with how good you're getting at dancing," I remind him.

He looks down. "I just don't want to step on her feet. She's under a lot of pressure, and I want to make her happy. This is one of the few things I can control."

Helen looks thoughtful. "It must be hard when her parents are paying for everything, mustn't it? Because if you put your foot down, they can threaten not to pay. But if this is the pattern for the whole marriage, they will use money to control you."

"I know that. I think they think I'm not good enough for her or I could pay for the whole thing myself."

"What do you do for work, Ben?" Jody asks.

"I'm an investment banker."

"Are you kidding?" My jaw drops. "What the hell would be good enough for them?"

"An investment banker with inherited wealth," Jody replies, then softens and pats him on the arm. "Come on. We've got you. We're going to make sure you literally sweep your bride off her feet."

Eliana Macri's return to New York is the talk of Manhattan Swing. I hear someone chatting about it in the hallway when I'm refilling my water bottle, and then again after class when our instructors are talking about scheduling. Apparently, Connor Yung, Eliana's partner for the last few years, has moved on to yet another new partner—some Finnish woman named Jaana who is a rising star on the European circuit—leaving Eliana with no one to dance with, only a few weeks before a big swing competition and a couple of months before the nationals.

"Connor thinks being national champion will help his dance studio," the pink-haired young woman at the front desk is saying to Maria as I walk past after class. "And he doesn't think he can get there with Eliana."

"Ouch," I hear Maria reply.

The young woman sounds thoughtful. "Do you think Ollie has forgiven her?"

I'M at my desk on Monday answering painfully dull emails when my phone rings.

"I'd like to take you swing dancing this weekend." It is Ollie. We have seen each other at work a couple of times, once in a meeting to prep for our 'off-site' next week, and twice in crowded elevators, but we haven't spoken. It's gotten both easier and harder to see him around the building: easier because I finally know he's attracted to me, and harder because there's more that we need to hide.

I take a breath. "As long as you are aware that I have had a grand total of about six hours of experience and I'm not going to be very good."

"Oh." There is a pause. "Never mind, then."

He hangs up on me. Funny.

I wait a long moment before the phone rings again.

"Yes?" I say, torn between amusement and annoyance.

"I've thought it over and I think you'll be acceptable."

"I'm going to murder you," I reply.

There's a pause, and I feel like I can see his smile over the phone. "Is Saturday evening an acceptable night for murdering me?"

I pretend to consider my answer. "I can probably wait that long."

When I hang up, I turn to see Brant behind me, his eyes narrowed. "You're murdering who, now?"

"A friend," I say.

He nods, slowly. "First step to getting back out there?"

"I guess I'll find out."

He nods. "Fair enough. One of us should test the waters. See if it's actually as bad as we remember."

I calculate when the last time was that I told Brant he needed therapy. Three weeks ago? Four? Is it safe to do again? "Brant? Have you thought about therapy?"

"Nah. People like us don't need therapy. We've pulled back the curtain. Seen the Great and Terrible Oz. Marriage is the disease, not the cure."

I grimace, hoping it resembles a polite smile.

"By the way," he adds, "I made sure with Destiny that the off-site would end early enough to get you back here by five. I know you've got to get home to your daughter."

"Thanks, Brant."

He nods, a strange smile on his lips. "Anytime."

. . .

THE LOCATION of our off-site is a beachfront hotel near South Norwalk, Connecticut. The plan is to work on the committee report in a big conference room overlooking the water all day, then take a one-hour boat tour on the Long Island Sound as a team bonding event at the end of the afternoon. As Brant promised, the boat trip will end at 3:45 p.m. and we will go straight back to the city; even with traffic, this means I should be able to pick up Hannah by 6 p.m., when her afterschool care program closes.

Lana and Niamh arrive for the day in what I can only describe as yachting outfits, matching navy and white sundresses with little scarves around their necks. They clearly went shopping together, and part of me feels envious. It's been a long time since shopping was a fun activity I did with friends instead of a lone, late-night internet search for off-season deals on casualwear.

Brant turns up in a polo shirt and khakis, while Ollie is wearing a pale linen suit that looks as fashionable and buttoned-up as always. He takes a seat near me in the plush passenger van, and I fantasize about being able to hold hands. Maybe it's just as well we won't be tempted, since Lana and Niamh immediately surround us in nearby seats.

"We should do a warm-up exercise," Lana announces. "And we have a suggestion."

"Go ahead," Destiny says warily.

"What was the most illegal thing you've ever—"

"No," Destiny says firmly.

Niamh smirks. "What about the wildest place you've ever been naked?"

"Oh, I have such a good one for that," Lana says.

"Also no," Destiny says. "We are here to come up with policies to prevent sexual harassment, remember?"

"Trust me, my nudity was very unsexual," Lana says.

"How about favorite vacation spot?" Ollie offers.

"Ugh, boring," Niamh cries. Ollie looks out the window.

"Please," Destiny says, "no warm-up exercises." She has the tone of a weary kindergarten teacher.

"I've got a compromise suggestion," I offer. "What is the weirdest thing a client has ever claimed on their taxes as a write off?"

Niamh claps her hands together, delighted. "I have one. I had a guy write off his dog food expenses because he claimed his dog was private security for his home business, which was hand-rolling people's joints for them."

"People can't roll their own joints?" Brant frowns his disapproval.

"No, it gets better. So we do this whole thing, right? Writing up why he needs a security system, and dogs are more effective et cetera, in case he needs to prove the validity of the expense. And then at the end, I ask him what kind of dog he has. It was a cocker spaniel."

We laugh.

"If he ever gets audited, he's screwed, but I had no idea!" Niamh insists.

"I had a client who was an actor," Brant says, "and he said every movie, tv streaming service, or play he saw qualified as research for learning his craft. So his entire entertainment budget was a business expense."

"I had one like that," I reply. "Film producer. He wrote off an entire three-week trip to Europe as a location scout because he had a script that required filming in Switzerland, France, and Italy, so he said he needed to explore all three countries to properly do a budget for the film. So I say, okay. You can try this as a write-off, but it will help if you have an established screenwriter and financing for the movie in place, right? I say, 'Just tell me that it's not a script written by your wife or something as an excuse to take this trip.' And he goes, 'Oh, my wife knows nothing about this. I'm taking it with my girlfriend. She's the screenwriter.'"

Destiny laughs. "I win this one, y'all," Destiny says. "I had a client who was a dominatrix. Enough said."

"Hey, Ollie," Lana says. "Remember that question about sex toys?"

"Hard to forget," he agrees.

"Someone thought a sex toy was a write-off?" That's a new one even for me.

Ollie sighs. "Apparently the client had anxiety issues, and their therapist had recommended frequent physical pleasure as a tool for managing it, and they believed the vibrator was supporting equipment necessary for them to do their job. I explained to the client our usual policy about mental health equipment."

"Alright, that's enough," Destiny says, laughing. "We have officially bonded, and now we should be looking over the meeting agendas, okay?"

Lana and Niamh sigh but settle down, looking at either the meeting agenda or something more entertaining on their cell phones. The passenger van gets quiet, and Ollie leans closer to me.

"Your ex is still in New York?" he asks quietly.

"He never was," I reply. "He was visiting a friend in Philly when he got the news of the tour. He decided to drive up and surprise us."

"And he didn't text you he was coming?"

"He expected me to be home. Which I usually would be."

"How do you feel about him getting the tour?"

I shrug. I glance over at Brant, noticing that he's watching our conversation. "It's good for his career."

"It's a big deal, though, right?" Ollie asks quietly.

"Yeah." I sigh. "Hopefully it works out. Nick doesn't have the best luck with bands."

I watch Ollie visibly relax. Did he think that Nick was staying in my apartment?

"What's this about your ex? What band is he on tour with?" Brant asks me.

"Nick booked a gig with The Big Lie."

Niamh and Lana spin to stare at me. "Is he like, a roadie?" Lana demands.

"He's a guitar player," I reply, and as soon as the words are out of my mouth, I know I should have avoided the question.

"Wait a second," Niamh says, "you are telling me that your ex is the new guitar player for The Big Lie?"

I sigh, nodding. "Temporarily."

"To replace Theo Jones while he's in rehab?" Lana asks.

"Yes," I say. "What bands do you guys like?"

They have a lot of opinions on that question, and I make sure to ask them follow-up questions, a distraction tactic that works only long enough for them to circle back with even more enthusiasm. Lana explains to me that my ex-husband is "the coolest" and asks whether I can get them backstage passes.

"I'll see what I can do."

Ollie leans over to me a minute or two later. "I'm okay without a backstage pass."

BRANT PULLS me aside as we all get off the passenger van at the hotel.

"You and Ollie seem like good friends," he says quietly.

"Yeah. We went on a date once, but it didn't work out," I tell him. I figure that it's best when lying to stick as close to the truth as possible. "We're friends now."

"Okay." He raises his eyebrows and nods, slowly. "I think he might be interested in more than that."

"It's not that, I'm sure, Brant," I say. I feel uncomfortable. A vague, floating thought that Brant himself might be interested—and if so, might not easily forgive me for the lie—floats through my head.

Brant's eyes are full of wary cynicism, but then again, they always are.

THE MEETING at the hotel feels productive, though, and after a while I stop feeling frustrated that I can't be alone with Ollie and start appreciating how he behaves in meetings: how he lets everyone speak, how he takes notes, how he never makes the meeting about him. He makes relevant comments and then listens. He lets Destiny do her job and lead the group. He smiles when someone makes a joke but never prolongs the joke enough to waste time. It feels ridiculous to stare at a man who is quietly typing on a laptop and think, *I love the way he types*, yet there I am. Being attracted to him while he was dancing was comprehensible. This feels like something else entirely.

Eventually, Lana pulls out a document summarizing how employees feel about the current policy for office relationships.

"So I got the responses to our questionnaire."

"Global or New York office?" Brant asks.

"This was all U.S., not global," Lana says. "And to the question of 'Are our current policies clear?' we got eighty percent yes."

"So twenty percent don't understand the policy?" Destiny asks.

"Well, when we poll folks about whether any policy is

clear," Niamh says, "twenty percent of people almost always say no, so that may just be the idiocy factor."

"We'll use that exact language in the report," Destiny jokes.

"Anyway, when people ask if there should be more reporting of relationships, eighty percent said no," Lana goes on.

Ollie and I glance at each other and then away.

"A lot of the comments talk about how it's intrusive," Lana adds. "I specifically got two complaints: one is that it is hard to label relationships when they are in the casual phase and announcing them to the office after a date or two feels like an intrusion. The other was that casual relationships can create blowback that people aren't willing to deal with."

"Did anyone give an example," Destiny asks, "of the kind of blowback they expect?"

"One person mentioned that he suspects his manager might have a crush on him and she might get jealous if she knew he was dating someone else in the office. But since he can't prove the crush exists, he has no clear protection against potential retaliation every time he has to mention dating another employee."

"What did people say when asked if they wanted all employee relationships forbidden?" Brant asked.

"Ninety-four percent said no," Lana replies.

Niamh smiles. "That six percent is probably the manager who has a crush on her employee and doesn't want anyone else getting to him."

I shudder. The implications of that feel a little close to home.

"My take," Lana says, "and I'm not, like, a lawyer or whatever, but I feel like the more we demand disclosure, the more likely we could be liable for potential issues. Like if we force employees to discuss that they are dating someone else, they can argue that we forced them to experience retaliation and that the whole company is more liable."

I am impressed with Lana. She has always seemed unserious, but I realize now that I've mistaken youthful exuberance for lack of intelligence.

"The simplest solution," Brant says, "is just to forbid all relationships entirely."

Destiny nods. "That would be easiest, I agree. But that's quite tricky in practice sometimes. I know you're not an employment lawyer," she says to Ollie. "But any thoughts?"

"I think the company will be sucked into lawsuits regardless of guilt and any policy could be used in either direction," Ollie says. "All lawsuits tend to include all possible parties so as to avoid finger-pointing at whoever was not involved in the suit. But I do think we should take into consideration what employees are telling us."

"True," I agree, determined not to look at Brant. "You can't report someone for having a crush on you, which is often the more loaded situation. Can't we have a policy of leaving it to the employee to assess the impact on their work? Unless they're obviously in an employee/manager situation?"

Brant's eyes are still narrowed as he glances at me. What is going on, exactly?

I start to worry as we get ready for the boat tour. Will he notice if I wind up alone with Ollie? Should I avoid Ollie because it will be obvious that we like each other? But I already told Brant we were friends, and I don't want to look like I'm hiding something.

The boat turns out to be a fairly large one, holding perhaps fifty people, and it has several distinct groups on it: a handful of senior citizens who are clearly birders, laden with binoculars and lists of shore birds in their hands; a couple of smaller groups of tourists from France and Japan; and a large family group who are on some kind of reunion trip. It quickly becomes clear that the parents at the family reunion are occupied with their smaller children, and their teenagers have turned into a loud, cackling gang, busy impressing each other with loud remarks and phone memes.

As the boat leaves the dock, Ollie and I stand with Brant and Destiny for a few moments, watching Lana and Niamh take photos for some kind of Instagram 'I own a yacht' concept.

"Did they really suggest we talk about being naked as an ice breaker?" she asks us. "That really happened, right? I didn't hallucinate it?"

As I shrug, amused, she glances between Brant, Ollie and me. "I am so thankful for you three. You're my grown-ups."

I feel vaguely guilty that I'm going to try to sneak off on the field trip for a moment alone with my boyfriend.

As our boat negotiates its way among smaller Connecticut pleasure boats, Ollie and I deliberately walk in opposite directions on the deck without saying anything, as if to throw people off our trail. After a few minutes, we land in the same spot, a quiet place to stand on the deck together, looking out at the Connecticut shoreline as we slowly circle an island. It is hard to stay apart like this. It is beautiful and quiet, the wind in his hair and the sun on his face, and I can't kiss him.

"Brant is interested in you," Ollie says quietly.

My stomach sinks. If someone else has noticed Brant's behavior, that makes it real. "I hope not."

"Every time he talks about his cynicism about dating, his eyes go right to you."

I shrug. "I'm hoping if I ignore it, he will get bored and fixate on someone else. He's my direct supervisor so he can't ask me out."

"I wonder if that's why he put you on the committee with him. To figure out your feelings about it," Ollie says quietly.

I shrug. "I'm worried he won't forgive me for insisting I'm single and then starting to date you, whenever we do tell people."

"We'll have to keep well away from each other in the meantime," Ollie says. "Especially around work. I was thinking we could start having lunch together, but..."

"Yeah, no. Bad idea."

"He can't retaliate against you, you know that, right? That's illegal," Ollie says quietly.

"There's what's legal and what you can get away with. He could come up with some other reason that I'm doing a bad job. He's talked about layoffs a lot."

"Alright. So," Ollie says, looking around, "I guess I'll give you space. But tell me if he escalates anything. I know good lawyers." Ollie smiles, but it doesn't reach his eyes.

"Just one more minute out here," I say. "It's nice to be here with you."

"One more minute." We look out at the distant water, and I tell myself not to ruin things. Try to have fun. Keep things light, I remind myself.

"So do you want kids?" I ask. Keeping things light.

He keeps his eyes on the horizon. "Sure. But I'm not dying to have them."

"You like them, though."

"Selectively," he says with a shrug. "Your kid is good. Those ones, on the other hand..."

He tilts his head toward the group of teenagers who are now leaning precariously off the side of the boat, just pushing the limit of where Ollie or I would feel the need to yell at them.

"I'm forty-one," I say quietly. "So I'm not sure I can have any more."

"I'll have to ask out Lana instead, then," Ollie replies, still not looking at me. "I'll wait until she's done posting selfies."

"I'm being serious."

He looks at me and then glances around to make sure no one is nearby us. "If things work out for us, I would be getting a kid."

"But not your kid."

"My father was impressed with the high quality of his DNA. He wanted to have children to carry on his bloodline. Mind you that our bloodline goes straight back to thieves and murderers. But it's safe to say that continuing my DNA is not something I'm obsessed with."

I find it hard to believe him. I find it hard to believe someone would give up all of that just to be with me.

"You'd never get to experience the toddler years."

Ollie smiles. "From what I hear, the teenage years are the toddler years all over again."

"Speaking of," I say, glancing over, "I have to go talk to that kid."

I walk over to one of the more daring teens just as he leans so far off the side of the boat that both feet are off the ground.

"Hey," I begin. "Can you come down, please?" My voice sounds irritating even to me.

The boy I'm addressing has straight black hair and a chipped front tooth and looks like he's about fifteen. It's clear that he doesn't want to back down in front of his cousins.

"It's fine!" he drawls. "I do this all the time."

"It would make me less nervous if you had both feet on the ground," I say, just as the boat lurches slightly higher as we hit a wave.

He groans at me and puts his feet back on the ground pointedly, glaring at me. I turn to walk back to Ollie, who is watching me with amusement. The boat lurches again, sending me sideways to grip the railing, just as I hear a gasp and a cry behind me.

I turn to see that the boy is gone. His cousins are shouting as they point to him in the water, and I rush forward to see his dark head spinning in the wake of the boat. There are "man overboard" shouts. I stare at the waves, hoping the little idiot has learned his lesson, but then he goes under again, and I watch the foam from the boat's wake drifting where his head used to be. He doesn't emerge from the water. He has vanished.

Without thinking, without giving myself time to think, I glance around, grab the round life preserver that sits on the front deck as a decoration, and jump off the edge of the ship after him.

I know it is a stupid decision as soon as I'm falling toward the murky water of the Long Island Sound. My stomach drops, waves splash up my nose, and I sink deep into the yellow-green water, which is bracingly cold in mid-June. I kick off my shoes so I can force myself up to the surface, then bob for a moment in the salty waves from the boat wake, coughing. The boat is still moving away from me, sending a set of strong waves bobbing me up and down.

I scramble around to grab hold of the life preserver and turn and start to swim after the boy. The one thing I remember about drowning people flashes through my head: I will need to push him the life preserver but not let him get a grip on me and pull me under. Panicked people sometimes drown their rescuers, and Hannah needs me alive. I can vaguely hear shouting in the distance behind me, but I can tell that the boat is still getting farther away.

I'm not a fast swimmer, but I can still make it... unless he's too deep in the water already.

"Hey, you want to give me that?" Ollie's head appears next to me. Also swimming.

"What?" I'm confused for a moment.

"The life preserver? Give it to me?"

Bewildered, I push him the life preserver and he shoves me a large orange mass that proves to be two brightly colored life-jackets tangled together.

"Put one on," I hear him say, and then he swims forward with the circular life preserver around one arm, easily going twice as fast as I was. It's almost comical how quickly he leaves me behind as he swims.

Strong, tall man, I realize. *Childhood on the coast of Australia.*

I pause where I am bobbing, badly out of breath, clinging to the tangled pair of orange life jackets that Ollie left me with. The water is shockingly cold now on my feet, and I can feel my body starting to shake. I glance back to see that the boat is finally slowing and that we have a crowd of observers. I watch Ollie reach a point in the foamy wake of the boat and then dive under the water, and I feel a flash of fear, my breath coming and going in uneven puffs.

The boy could die. Ollie could die. I should have stayed on the boat. Ollie has rendered my efforts pointless. My white shirt and work pants are soaking wet and slopping around me. What was I thinking? Is Ollie okay? Is the boy going to drown him?

After a moment, Ollie and the boy emerge at the surface and my breath comes out in a rush of relief. The boy is gasping and choking as he clings to Ollie, the life preserver floating abandoned nearby, and I realize that I should have swum behind Ollie with the two other life jackets. I begin to kick forward as fast as I can. Everything feels impossibly slow as I try to reach them.

"Put one of those on!" Ollie shouts almost angrily when he spots me. He is shoving the round life preserver toward the boy.

I awkwardly link one of the life preservers around me and clip it on, pretty sure I'm getting it under my arm somehow.

"Give me the other!" he calls.

I give a big push through the water to toss the other one to Ollie, getting a wave full of saltwater down my throat as I do. I start choking a bit, pushing briny water from my eyes as I try to understand what's going on.

I expect Ollie to put the other life jacket on, but instead he pushes it to the coughing boy. "I need you to put this on, okay?" he calls loudly.

The boy shakes his head. "My phone," he groans. "It fell."

"It's dead," I shout, wondering if he disappeared underwater in pursuit of his phone, not because of imminent drowning. If so, it's possible I will kill him before the boat has a chance to turn around.

"I need you to put this on!" Ollie says to the boy again, more firmly.

The boy just keeps shaking his head. "My phone..."

"Now."

The boy groans and awkwardly holds on to the second life preserver, still coughing. He slings it under one arm as Ollie treads water.

"Good news," Ollie calls to me. "I think they're coming back for us."

A rush of relief brings tears that blend with the water. Ollie gives the boy a glance and, deciding that he's not going under again, swims the few feet toward me.

"You are amazing, Laura," Ollie says as I cough near him, the salt stinging my eyes. "You didn't hesitate. You went right in."

"Because I'm impulsive," I say.

"No, you're brave."

My head begins to clear, the salt water mostly out of my eyes, and that is when I let out a long, highly visual set of swearwords that leaves both Ollie and the coughing boy staring at me.

"You okay?" Ollie asks.

"Hannah," I say. "I was barely going to get to her in time, and now I won't, and if I'm late they'll kick her out of her after-care, and I don't have any back-up."

"It's going to be okay," Ollie says. The wrong thing to say right then.

"No, it's not going to be okay. Because there is no one else to get her, do you understand? My ex-husband is eight hours away and my sister is in Newfoundland, and I have nobody. And my phone was in my pocket, so I can't even fucking call anybody!"

"Hey," he says. "Hey. Come here."

I don't move, so he swims closer to me.

"Come here. Listen."

"Don't tell me it's going to be okay!" I yell at him. "Don't tell me it's going to be okay. You don't understand my life!"

"You're not alone," he says.

But that is exactly what I always am. Have always been. Ever since I was a child. It's why I don't depend on anyone.

Except that Ollie jumped into the water after me.

"Hey," he says gently, "rescuing someone from the Long Island Sound probably falls into the category of a forgivable sin with your childcare, okay?"

"You rescued him," I say petulantly. "I just ruined my shoes."

He starts laughing. For a second I am angry. Furious.

"I hate this!" the boy cries from nearby, and then I start laughing too.

Ollie's eyes are full of warmth. "You know how we were talking about the teen years being like the toddler years?" he says. "Based on today, I think I can skip the toddler years, no problem."

We glance at the boy who floats near us, staring listlessly at the boat as it makes its awkward reversal. "Fuuuuucckk!" the boy cries in outrage at the sky. We both chuckle again.

"You getting cold?" Ollie asks me, coming closer.

"He probably is. You can help him."

"Screw him, he needs the life lesson."

I cough out water again as I laugh. I am shivering harder now. "I've been colder at an outdoor music festival, it's fine."

"The things you've done for My Chemical Romance."

He reaches out and puts his hand over mine where I'm clinging to my life jacket. His hand warms mine, then he rubs my shoulder to warm me more. We are coughing up seawater in Long Island Sound, and I realize I don't even feel that upset. He's here. He came after me.

"I love you." The words rush out of me.

There is a flash of something like panic in Ollie eyes.

"Sorry, I just meant..." I begin.

"It's okay," he says, but he won't look at me. "It's probably the stress talking."

"Right. Yeah."

We don't say anything else. We just watch as the boat slowly finishes its U-turn. I am really starting to shake, now. Ollie tries to rub my arms again.

"Stop," I mutter. "They'll see us."

He nods solemnly and goes back to check on the boy.

In another few minutes, we are being offered a ladder from the side of the deck. Without speaking, we mutually agree to let the world's worst teenager climb up first. His cousins applaud his return like he has just performed a cool trick.

Then it is my turn and my arms won't work. Ollie watches me, wide-eyed. "You okay?"

"My arms won't work," I say, my voice a little panicked.

"They will warm as soon as you get them out of the water," he says. "Just put one on the ladder and give yourself a minute."

I place a hand on the ladder, but the waves are bobbing, and I can't keep my grip.

"I can carry you," he offers, and that's it. He is not carrying me in front of everyone, not after I've said I love him, and he didn't say it back.

I swing one arm up and then slowly, awkwardly haul myself up a rung of the ladder, water sluicing away from my sodden work clothes, and then another, and then another, hauling myself up. I can do this. My clothes stick to my body like cling-wrap.

I finally get pulled up by strong arms, and then I am standing on the deck, water rushing down me in a torrent, the shivering making it hard to stand up. Ollie is beside me after a moment, equally soaking but not shaking as much. I glance over and see that the boy's parents are eying Ollie and me suspiciously, like we followed him into the water in a foiled attempt to kidnap him.

"What happened?" his father is asking his soaking son as the teen sits wrapped in a coarse wool blanket. "What the hell happened?"

The boy shrugs. "There was a huge wave, and I slipped."

Ollie and I accept blankets from the crew.

"Did those two go in the water to try to help you?" I hear a woman ask the boy.

"No, they slipped, too," he replies, the little traitor.

Destiny, Brant, Lana and Niamh are all surrounding us now and I blink salt out of my eyes and shiver hard, trying not to look at Ollie.

"Are you guys alright?"

"Is everything okay?"

"What happened?"

Brant sounds outraged, like either I decided to go for a swim or someone pushed me overboard. His eyes shoot to Ollie.

Ollie speaks first. "Laura jumped in to save that kid from

drowning, and I went in after her because she didn't put on a life jacket first."

"And then Ollie saved him from drowning," I add. "And I did nothing."

"But you guys are okay, right? Do you need a hospital? Medical attention?" Destiny asks. I can tell from her expression that she thinks we are idiots, which is a perfectly reasonable surmise.

"I don't think so," I say, teeth chattering. "Sorry about that. Should be okay once I get dry."

"They were ready to call the Coast Guard," Niamh adds. "But you guys looked like you had a handle on things."

I nod, pretending it's true. Lana appears with two coffees for us from somewhere on the boat.

"So I know this may be totally inappropriate, but since you guys are fine," Lana says, "how was the water? Was it swimmable?"

WHEN WE GET BACK to the hotel, Ollie and I both pass on a hot shower and medical attention in favor of dry clothes and cheap flip-flops from the hotel gift shop so that we can get back to the city faster. We are both wearing SoNo Inn sweatshirts by the time we climb back onto the bus, wrapped in two gifted hotel towels and still wearing our damp pants. I sit shaking by the window, trying to tap out the name of my kid's aftercare program on Lana's cell phone, as Ollie lobbies on my behalf to take the passenger van straight back to my kids' school in Brooklyn, even though we are supposed to be going directly to Manhattan. My heart feels almost entirely grateful, except for the part of it that is appalled.

Did I just tell a man who I've barely started dating that I *loved* him? Surely not. Did he just *decline to say it back?*

"You jumped in to save someone," Lana says, sitting next to Ollie and putting a hand on his shoulder. The salt water has turned his hair into an irritatingly attractive, messy tangle. "That's so heroic."

"Well," Ollie says with a shrug, "I was told that was the expectation when I joined the committee." Lana and Niamh laugh.

Everyone loves him, I think with irritation. Of course I do, too.

IN THE END, I am only twenty minutes late to pick up my daughter. I climb out of the van and race to the building to find a grumpy young afterschool teacher sitting on the steps outside her school's aftercare office, watching Hannah eat a slice of pizza.

"She was hungry," the young woman says in the same tone that you would give a death threat. Then she takes in my appearance.

"I jumped into the Long Island Sound to rescue someone who went overboard," I say.

"Oh." Her expression is flat.

I take out a twenty-dollar bill, which is damp like the rest of my things from being in my presence for the last ninety minutes. "This is all I have. For the pizza. I can get you more tomorrow, I..."

"It's fine. You'll be charged a late fee. Just don't let it happen again."

She gives a warm, sweet good-bye to Hannah and an assassin's glare to me before she walks away.

Hannah is staring at me, a little pizza grease still on her chin. "You went swimming?" she asks, accusing.

"I fell in the water," I say, and leave it at that.

Back at home, I get an email from Ollie, and my heart is in my throat. This is it. He will break up with me because I told him I loved him.

Hi Laura, I am still so impressed with your bravery today. You really are amazing. I'm sending you an email since your phone has probably not recovered. I hope you are drying off and that everything went okay with picking up Hannah. If you need anything from me, like help getting a new phone, please let me know what I can do. I will understand if you are not up for dancing on Saturday, but I would still like to take you. Ollie.

I stare at the sign-off for a long time. He didn't write, 'Love, Ollie.' He didn't write anything at all. So I guess we are going to pretend my *I love you* never happened.

Dancing sounds great, I reply.

His response comes a few moments later. *Perfect. Looking forward. Take care and stay dry. —Ol*

THE NEW YORK CITY PARKS DEPARTMENT organizes an outdoor West Coast Swing event once a month on a pier looking out over the Hudson River, with a DJ to play songs that fit within the slow-but-not-too-slow range that makes them easy for West Coast Swing. I've learned that every dance style tends to have its own music requirements, even within the more popular music styles. There are songs by Wham that are perfect for the jitterbug, and Ed Sheeran songs that you can waltz to. West Coast Swing requires a bluesy quality that's hard to put into words. Certain songs just click with it, and sometimes it's a surprise when you discover a new one that works.

It's a little after seven in the evening when I arrive, and I can hear a Sam Smith song crooning out across the sunset-orange water of the Hudson as I walk along the river path toward the pier. It is early June, the season of long days and warm breezes before the city slinks into the sweaty heat of summer. I glance at my new cell phone and see a message from Ollie identifying his exact location. *To the left of entrance, dressed like a spy.*

I spot Ollie waiting in a black button-down shirt and charcoal linen pants, glancing around with the body language of someone who isn't sure where to look. West Coast Swing tends to be informal, so after much deliberation, I went with a form-fitting red shirt with a sweetheart neckline and black jeans.

"First time swing dancing?" I say as I walk up to him.

He lights up as he sees me, and the smile makes him look especially handsome. "I watched some videos online and thought I would give it a try," he replies with a grin.

I nod and lean forward, saying in a conspiratorial voice, "I've been doing it for years, but I convinced this guy I was learning it for him. Boy is he in for a surprise when he sees how good I am."

He puts out a hand. "Can I dance with you until he shows up?"

"You're going to be dazzled."

"I already am."

It really is annoying that he is so good at this: looking good, dressing well, saying exactly the right thing. *I don't trust women.* He said that, and now he's being charming and sexy. I need to be careful, and I keep failing at my goal. I could get in trouble at work just for being seen with him, yet here I am.

Ollie leads me straight onto the dance floor, and I think: this is it. This is the moment I've been thinking about since I first saw him dance. What will it be like to dance with him, out on a dance floor with other people, having him lead me through steps and spins? Will I be so terrible that I won't enjoy it? Will it be sexy? Will it be like dancing on clouds?

What it is, initially, is hilarious. I miss easily one out of every three moves that he's trying to guide me through. Every time I miss something and start to panic, I see his green-gold eyes light up with amusement.

"I'm glad you're having fun laughing at me," I say as we pull away from each other and then back again.

"I'm just having fun," he calls back. "I wish I could kiss you, but I don't know if we'll be spotted by the Murano accounting paparazzi."

"What could they prove? We're just friends having a fun dance."

"Sure."

He pulls me in close and then releases me again.

"The last time I danced this much outside of class was probably a twenty-four-hour rave," I say to him the next time he pulls me closer.

"Your teen years were way more fun than mine."

"Who said anything about teen years? That was way into my twenties. You're looking at someone who once gave the finger to a police helicopter topless."

He blinks at me, momentarily rendered silent. I feel panicked.

"Did I just ruin your opinion of me?"

He pulls me close and says into my ear, "You are the most interesting accountant I've ever met."

After another few mistakes, I am starting to get the hang of it. Social dancing is not so much about nailing amazing moves as listening to the music and paying attention. Once or twice, he looks impressed that I did a spin correctly. Once or twice, I might even be enjoying myself.

When a cheerful pop song comes to a close, he gives me a hug.

"Hey," he says, looking down at me, his eyes warm.

"Hey."

"You're doing so well."

"Don't patronize me, MacCormack."

He looks at my lips, and I remind myself not to move closer. Just in case someone from work sees us. Just in case we're being watched. He leans over and says quietly, "I'm honestly really touched. No one has ever done something like learning to dance for me before."

"Does it make you less impressed if I tell you I'm enjoying it?"

He looks at my lips again, and I wonder if we are going to risk it. *Please risk it*, I think. He glances around, then he freezes, spotting something behind us.

"What is it?"

"Nothing." The warmth has left his expression.

"Is it someone from work?"

He shakes his head.

"Eliana?"

He shakes his head, his expression grim. "It's my ex-wife. I haven't seen her since the divorce."

I think of that made-up story we told to Vivi about Ollie having a panic attack after seeing his ex-wife. Suddenly I wonder if maybe there was some truth to it. I glance around, looking at the crowd.

"Has she seen you yet?"

"I don't think so. Maybe."

"Come on," I say, taking his arm and pulling him toward the side of the pier. "We're not leaving. We're just going to talk."

When we are positioned looking out at the milky-pink surface of the river, our arms resting against each other on the handrail, I risk a closer look at him. His eyes are haunted as he stares at the horizon.

"Is your brother here, too?"

He shakes his head, taking a moment to find his voice. "I

don't think so. It looked like she was with some people from Dancing Up a Storm, where she used to take classes. I recognized a few of them." He glances at me and then away. "You deserve better than this. I'm sorry. I feel like I'm letting you down."

"It's fine. It's not like you ran up to her and begged her to come back. Unless that's the plan for later."

He huffs out a laugh. "No. Definitely not. I'm just not sure what to say if she wants to talk. I haven't had to deal with this before."

I consider for a moment. "So okay. This woman—I'm not going to say skank..." The corner of his mouth twitches. "She did something really hurtful. And instead of telling her to avoid you, you quit the field, right? You left New York. And when you came back, you stopped doing any social dancing. So can you explain that to me? Why are you the one who thinks you have to avoid her, when she's the one who did something wrong?"

He shakes his head. There's an answer, but he doesn't want to say it.

I glance back at the crowd to see if anyone is watching us, but I can't spot anyone. "If she sees you, I know what she's going to be thinking. She's thinking, 'What does he think of me? Does he still hate me?' And if you want the upper hand, all you have to do is not give her that. Just be polite, and tell her nothing, and let her fixate on it. That's your revenge."

He shakes his head. "I don't want revenge."

"Then what do you want?"

"I just keep thinking..." He hesitates again. "I guess I'm scared."

"Of...?"

"I don't want to hear her say that she picked the better guy." The words burst out of him. "That she's happier now because she's with him." His eyes are on his fists, his shoulders tense.

"She didn't pick him at all!" I step closer to him until he looks at me. "They both screwed up and their whole marriage is an attempt to make it look like this was something they wanted the whole time."

He is shaking his head. "Maybe they did want it the whole time."

"No. Look at me." Ollie glances up. "Right now, she is married to a man who is capable of sleeping with his brother's wife. Don't you think she's wondering whether she trusts him? Don't you think she is aware that you are the one decent person in the whole situation? I mean, there is no one in New York City I would pick over you."

He looks at me for a moment, then leans over and kisses me until I feel a little limp. I can't even speak for a moment.

"Sorry," he says, his voice husky. "We're not supposed to do that in public. I know that."

"Well," I glance around, "if there are any spies from work around, we'll just have to assassinate them."

He takes a slow breath. "Let's go back and dance. I know what to say if she talks to us."

"You're ready?"

"I'm ready."

He takes my hand. Sure enough, as we walk back to the dance floor, a petite woman with golden skin and dark, straight hair walks toward us. She has the perky look of a 1960s flight attendant, and she's dressed in a flowing sundress and ballet flats. She looks much more put-together than I did when I had a young toddler at home.

"Ollie," she says. "Hey." Her expression is earnest, wide-eyed, faintly apologetic.

"Hi, Phoebe." The weight of the unspoken hovers between them like a raincloud.

"Good to see you." She glances at me nervously and then back again.

Ollie takes a breath. "Phoebe," he says, "I'd really like to forgive you at some point, but I haven't yet. I'm sorry. So if you'll excuse me, I'm going to go dance."

Her face falls. "Okay. Sure. Of course."

Ollie leads me onto the dance floor just as a Tracy Chapman song starts playing. He takes my hand and leads me into the throng. I can tell that his mind is elsewhere, but he is still wonderful to watch. He has an indefinable quality that I love in dancers, the ability to let each movement flow outward, carrying it all the way, letting each gesture hang for a moment with an intuitive sense of suspense. I wonder if his ex-wife is watching us. I wonder if she's noticing that I'm not nearly as good as he is.

After a moment, his eyes refocus. He's back with me. His face lights up in a little smile. I smile, too.

After another song, he leans over to me. "She left, I think." He glances around. "I feel a little guilty. I should have been calm enough to introduce you, but I can't quite yet."

"Don't you dare feel guilty," I say. "You just told her how you felt."

He looks like he wants to kiss me again, but then another song starts up, this one a little faster. We dance to a Rihanna song, and I think about the bride-to-be from my intro class, learning to dance to a Sinatra tune approved by her mother. We dance to a Lorde song and a song by Coldplay. We dance to Billie Eilish and Salt n Pepa, to Hozier and Sam Cooke.

My first impression of Ollie's dancing comes back in full force. Ollie is sexy. I can't help but notice every time he pulls me into his arms and then sends me away again. I am making mistakes, but I can't even worry about them. All I keep thinking is that I want him alone. Maybe he doesn't love me, maybe he is obsessed with his ex, but I still want to go to bed with him. I want him like I'm a teenager who's never gotten my heart broken.

He catches my gaze. "What time do you need to get back?" he asks in my ear.

"I still have three hours."

He nods. "Can I take you to my place?" He winces a little at the words. "I know how that sounds, but I want to be where I don't need to worry about being seen with you."

"Let's go."

"Now?"

"Now." He looks amused as how fast I answered.

"Right now?" he asks, teasing now.

I roll my eyes, and he laughs, then squeezes and releases my hand. We walk away together, carefully not touching, carefully not looking like we're all over each other. As soon as we're inside a taxi, I meet his eyes and am caught again in his gaze. I could kiss him right now. No one would see. He smiles and leans a little closer. I lean a little closer, too. He puts one hand to my chin and rubs a thumb along my jawline. A careful delay, a hesitation. His eyes look vulnerable and then his gaze shifts out the window.

He is going to break my heart.

When we arrive on his street, I discover that his apartment is in a four-story brownstone in the West 80s near Riverside Drive. It is the first time I've really registered the fact that he must have a lot more money than I do. This neighborhood is all understated elegance and ten-foot ceilings.

"I'm on the third floor of a walk-up," he says apologetically as he gives me a hand out of the cab.

"I can't make it," I say. "Too tired. You're going to have to carry me."

He looks me over, shrugs, and then picks me up to carry me

up the front steps. I laugh as he slides me down to get his keys out. Once we're inside the building, he slides me down against him, our bodies close.

"Need a lift again?" he asks gently.

I shake my head, my eyes on his lips, my heart pounding.

As we climb the stairs, I can feel his eyes on the back of my neck. The flights of stairs seem to take an eternity. When we reach his apartment, he unlocks the door and then takes my hand to lead me inside. As soon as the door closes, we both spin at the same time, pressing toward each other as he kisses me, pushing me up against the door.

It is an explosion of a kiss, his hands sliding behind my back, my hands slipping around his waist to pull him closer. I hear him whisper my name, and then we are wrapped around each other, all over each other like teenagers, his lips on my cheek, on my neck, on my shoulder.

"Do you need anything?" he says after a moment, breathing hard, his mouth against my collarbone. "Anything to drink, water?"

I shake my head, dazed and hot.

"A shower?" he asks. "After the dancing?"

"We're both sticky," I murmur. "I don't mind if you don't."

He shakes his head against my shoulder as he keeps pressing me against the wall, then licks the salt from my neck. My knees almost melt beneath me. His hands glide around my waist and pull me even closer and everywhere that we're touching lights up.

Another pause for breath. I can't remember the last time I was this turned on.

He pauses and heaves a long sigh, not looking up. I wonder if he's thinking about his ex again. "What is it?" I say, afraid for a moment.

"I just feel..."

"What?" I try not to sound worried.

"Relieved," he says. "I'm so relieved that I saw her, and I got through it, and I didn't lose you. You didn't give up on me."

I run a hand through his hair, meeting his eyes. "I'm not going to give up on you."

He gives me that same unreadable look for a moment, then kisses me again.

"Let me get you some water," he says.

His apartment is high-ceilinged but narrow, a railroad-style one-bedroom with limited furniture: I suspect that his wife must have taken a lot of furnishings in the divorce, and he never bothered to buy more. The living room has only a television, a classic leather sofa and an old-fashioned rolltop desk. There are two barrister bookcases filled with various paperbacks and law school tomes. It all seems very Ollie, special but a little buttoned-up; even his books are behind glass. He walks around his clean, minimalist kitchen, pouring two glasses of water.

"What you said the other day, when we were in the water," he begins quietly, handing me a glass of water. So I guess we're going to talk about it now. My casual little 'I love you.'

"I was probably drunk on seawater," I try to joke.

He shakes his head. "It's not that I don't..." He takes a breath. "It's not that I don't think things are going that way."

"It's okay. I didn't say it so you would say it back."

"I just...I don't want you to think I'm trying to play it cool. It's not that at all. It's just that I'm superstitious about that particular word."

I nod once. "Okay."

"But I'm serious about you."

"Okay." I give a little smile. He takes a step forward and puts one hand on my waist to kiss me gently, and I can't tell whether he's trying to tell me that he loves me or apologizing that he doesn't. His eyes are warm, the rings of green and brown so beautiful this close that it's hard to look at them for long. When he leads me to the bedroom I feel a brief sense of panic. I haven't slept with anyone but Nick in years.

He pauses as he notices my hesitation. "We don't have to—I'm just afraid my back will stick to my leather sofa if we sit down there."

"That old line," I whisper.

"You're so stunning," he says quietly, his expression entranced. "I don't know what you're doing with me."

"You're sexy. And handsome. It's just been a really long time since I did this with anyone," I say.

"Me, too. Two years."

I wonder if it's true. He could have anyone, I think.

His bedroom is high-ceilinged and clean, with pale sheets and wide, old-fashioned windows covered by light grey curtains. I sit on the bed, and a moment later he is kissing me. I lean back, and his arm cradles my head as it lands. This could actually happen.

He rests on his elbows above me, his hand trailing up my side. I have a sense of clarity about how much I really want this. It has been so long since I truly wanted to do this with somebody, but I want to know everything: what he looks like with his shirt off. How he will undress me. Whether he will be bold, or shy, or intense.

He leans down and kisses me through my shirt, and I think: he is not being shy. He's being assertive and tender, and I need more of him, and of this, and I am lighting up like an old-fashioned carnival ride, all flashing bulbs and whirling motors...and then my cell phone rings, with the inevitability of single parenthood. I reach into my pocket and pull it out, glancing at it.

"Not the babysitter," I say, tossing it aside.

Ollie murmurs a laugh and then kisses me softly as I start to undo his shirt buttons...first the top one, then the next. This is actually going to happen.

He begins to undo his own buttons even more quickly as I slide one hand underneath his shirt, feeling how warm his skin feels beneath my fingertips. He pauses to peel away my shirt and tosses it, then takes in the sight of me in my black bra and jeans. He runs one finger along the bra strap and slides it aside to kiss the skin underneath it.

This is actually going to happen.

He finishes pulling his own shirt off and tosses it. I look at the shape of him, his shoulders strong and dotted with freckles, his chest lean and strong. I run one of my hands through the light layer of hair that runs up his chest. He slides one hand behind me and unlatches my bra.

He shivers a little, then leans forward to pull my bra away, to tease me with his mouth.

"I like you so much," I whisper. *I love you.*

He kisses me tenderly, and it is almost enough. This is actually going to happen.

My cell phone buzzes. Someone has left a message. I glance at it.

I slide a hand along his thigh, touching him as his head bows against me.

My cell phone buzzes again.

"Just one second," I say breathily.

I run my hand along his back and then look at the phone again.

"Just one..." My back is arching as I glance at the voice message that is being constructed visually by my cell phone. "This is Dr. Yukovitz calling from Rochester Memorial Hospital. Please contact the..."

I sit up quickly. "Hold on."

"What's wrong?"

"It's a hospital, I should…"

Ollie's face is pure concern as I listen to the full message. I grab my discarded shirt as I listen.

"It's Nick," I say at last. "He's gotten in a car accident. I guess I'm his emergency contact."

Ollie nods, once. His mouth forms into a frown.

"This doesn't mean…" I trail off.

"I know," Ollie agrees. His voice is kind, but his eyes look distant.

"I should probably…"

"Yeah. Of course," he says quietly. "Can I help, or call a cab, or…"

"A cab sounds great."

I get dressed and then lean over and press my face into his neck. I kiss him once softly on the shoulder, then once on the lips.

"I'm so sorry," I whisper.

He nods. "It's okay. It's not your fault."

He almost sounds like he means it.

9

ACCIDENTS

I CALL the hospital staff on the taxi ride home from Ollie's place; the hospital is a few hours north in Rochester, New York, where Nick is on tour. I still feel hot from Ollie's touch, my body lit up even as my nerves are making my phone shake in my hands. After being put on hold for fifteen minutes, a nurse finally picks up to tell me that Nick is conscious and that he will call me when he can. I sink backwards in the taxi seat in relief, then text Nick to check in.

As soon as I send the message, I get a text from Ollie. *Let me know if you need anything.*

Thank you, I write back. *Nick is conscious. Still sorting out the rest.*

Good to hear, he writes back.

When I get home, our babysitter, a young woman named Allison, informs me that Hannah is in bed but has not actually fallen asleep yet.

"I tried, you know? She just wouldn't go down."

"It's okay," I say. "I'll go sit with her."

I pay the sitter and then tiptoe into Hannah's room, where she is still tossing and turning in the darkness. This is not unusual for her, especially since we came back from Atlanta. She seems to have too much on her mind to drift off to sleep. I was like that as I kid, but I always chalked it up to being nervous about what my mother was getting up to; now I wonder if it's genetics. I find my usual spot on her small armchair in the darkness, keeping my cell phone on my lap.

"Where were you?" Hannah asks when she notices me there, and I immediately get a vision of kissing Ollie on his bed.

"Practicing dancing," I say.

"I don't need to practice Taekwondo," Hannah says. "I'm just good at it." I can tell that she's upset at me.

"I know," I say gently. My mind is on Nick, and what I may have to tell Hannah, but she doesn't speak again.

My phone buzzes from a phone call about ten minutes later, and I pick it up and walk to my bedroom, hoping Hannah isn't still awake enough to notice I've gone.

"I'm sorry," Nick begins. I feel a wave of relief at hearing his voice and knowing he is alive and unhurt. "I know I should have taken you off the list of emergency contacts, but I didn't know who else to put on there." I think about his retired parents in Florida and his brother, a long-distance trucker along the Northwest coastline. He is probably right that I was the sensible choice.

"It's okay, Nick. Just tell me what happened."

"A drunk driver hit us."

"Who is 'us?'"

"Me and Elliot." He means the lead singer of the band, a handsome young man in his late twenties implausibly named Elliot Steel. "Our show got cancelled today because of a bomb threat, so he was out partying and got totally wasted all afternoon at this dive bar. I stayed with him so someone would be there to drive him home. I'm like the dad on this tour, I swear. I'm the most responsible one of the whole group."

I don't mention that he could be a real dad to Hannah if he weren't on the tour.

"Okay, and then?" I prompt.

"We were on the road, a little after eight—not even late—and this guy just ploughed into us. Crossed the median line. Elliot thinks I saved his life, so that's the good part. I was sober. I mean, I had a drink or two but basically nothing, so I managed to dodge the worst of it and Elliot got through without a scratch. The band is giving me a couple of weeks to recover and then I'll come back on tour."

"Recover from what? What happened?"

"Sprained wrist. It's in a temporary cast for the next week or two. The problem is that right now I can't drive," Nick said. "I can't play guitar. I can't even do my own buttons."

He sounds rueful, but I can sense the inherent question in his words. I can decide to help him...or not. One option is to let Nick sit alone in a hotel in Rochester for the next couple of weeks, struggling to change his clothes by himself. I could help him get home to Atlanta or tell him to hire a nurse. And there's the other option, the one that will delight my daughter, where I offer him my sofa and look after him.

"I know I have rotten luck, Laur," he says, interrupting my silence, "but I swear this is different. The tour has been going really well. The guys really like me."

"I'm not mad at you. It was an accident, and I'm glad you're not too badly hurt."

"I just need to do some exercises, and I'll get better. It's a small delay." His voice is quiet, gruff. I used to love that voice so much.

"I think you should hire a nurse or a home health aide if you can't take care of yourself. Someone who can help you get changed and stuff. It makes the most sense." I know that's easier said than done, but I don't want to admit that.

Hannah bursts in the door and climbs on my bed. "Daddy? Is Daddy hurt? Can I talk to him?"

Of course she is awake. Of course she heard all of that. Hannah reaches around my head as I attempt to dodge her grip and finally pulls the phone from my hands.

"Daddy, are you hurt?"

I close my eyes in frustration. Hannah is near enough that I can hear Nick's response. "Just a little, baby. Not badly. It's my wrist."

"You can stay with us, and I'll take care of you."

I freeze. "He's very busy, Hannah," I say.

"Please? Just for a little while?" Hannah is wheedling now. "I'll take care of him. Please? Why can't he stay with us?"

I recognize Hannah's tactic for exactly what it is, but that doesn't make it easier to say no.

"Your dad is very busy with his tour," I say.

"Daddy," Hannah says into the phone, "are you too busy with your tour?"

"I am busy with the tour," Nick says flatly.

"Playing guitar?"

"Healing my wrist for a bit. I can't play guitar right now."

"You can't play guitar?" Hannah looks horrified. "Then come visit! I miss you."

"It's...whatever your mother says," Nick replies, which is both the best answer and the worst. He didn't promise anything, but now if he doesn't come and spend time with her, it will be my fault.

"Please?" Hannah says to me. "Please, please, please. I want him to stay with us so I can take care of him."

There is a long moment of silence as I take back the phone. I sigh.

"I'll be okay in Rochester," Nick offers. "But if you think it would be good for me to spend time with her..."

"All right," I say at last. "You can stay for a week or two on the sofa until you can use your wrist again."

Hannah practically jumps up and down from enthusiasm.

"Thank you," Nick says. "I'll take the bus down. I'm having the tour hold onto my instruments, so I just have to wait this out until the cast comes off. I know this is a huge favor."

"It's okay," I say, but I can't feel it. I feel numb.

THE NEXT MORNING, Ollie texts me: *Everything still ok?*

I text back right away: *nick is ok, injured wrist, has to take time off the tour*

Ollie replies: *glad it's not more serious*

I think about hiding the fact that Nick will be staying with me, but I can't bring myself to do it. Ollie might as well know the worst of it.

I write, *Hannah insisted Nick come stay with us since he can't use his wrist. He'll be here for a week or two on the sofa to spend time with her. It doesn't mean...* I take a breath, picking my words. *...anything*, I finally write.

It is a while before Ollie responds, probably a full five minutes.

Then my phone buzzes. *Sounds like you'll be busy the next week or two.*

Unfortunately, I write back.

There's another long pause. *Let me know when he's gone.*

Then another pause, and then Ollie adds: *And if you need anything in the meantime.*

I understand what Ollie is saying: he's not going to go out again until he finds out whether I'm getting back together with my ex. I would probably be the exact same way, but it still makes me want to scream. It makes me want to confess my love all over again. It makes me want to act like a teenager and gush that Ollie can't give up on me because he's the best thing that ever happened to me.

I don't write any of that, because I won't be able to handle it if he doesn't believe me.

Thank you, I write. Sometimes I hate grown-up Laura.

NICK ARRIVES that night on a bus and takes a taxi from Port Authority to our place in Brooklyn. He looks like an utter wreck when he arrives, his shirt torn, his arm in a sling. I wonder if it's a bit of a put-on, how wounded he looks, because it's hard to be mad at him when he is crawling over my doorstep like an injured cat, a tired smile on his unshaven face.

Hannah is almost frantic in her excitement, showing him the sofa-bed and then making him sit with her in her room for almost two hours before she finally goes to sleep. I hear her peppering him with questions about his injury while he gently reassures her.

"Let's let your dad gets some rest," I finally have to tell her.

When I've gotten her into bed, I find him in the living room looking more tired than ever.

I make him a mug of tea and a plate of snacks. He smiles and drinks the tea quietly, sitting at my table, his eyes occasionally glancing over to take me in. We talk about the tour a little, and it sounds like he has been playing the role of adult among a group of reckless and unruly kids who don't quite know how to deal with their sudden, overwhelming fame. I would be proud of him if we were still together. In spite of everything, I still feel proud.

"Okay," I say finally. "I have work in the morning, so I need to get to bed."

He rises with me.

"Can you uh...?" he asks. He lifts one arm. "Just help with the shirt."

He gives a grin like he knows he's being a little ridiculous, but that's okay, right? Because it's us, the two of us, like it always is.

I help him get his shirt off, ignoring what this involves. He is inches away, his skin warm, and I pull my attention elsewhere.

"I'll buy you something stretchy to wear tomorrow," I say. "Do you need any painkillers?"

"I have some. Prescription strength. I should be okay."

"Good. There's everything you need in the bathroom. Sleep well."

"Thank you," he says quietly. He is watching me.

"You want me to get the light?" I ask.

"Nah, I've got it."

The atmosphere between us feels heated.

"You still seeing that guy who dresses like a golfer?"

"More or less," I reply.

"The sex is great, or...?"

"Do you really want an answer to that?"

"No," says Nick. "I'm sorry. Thank you for letting me stay. I wanted to see Hannah."

"She wanted to see you."

I look at him once and then leave him. Back in my room, I have a mental conversation with my mother.

"Unlike you, Mom, I did not sleep with Nick. You would have slept with him, but I did not."

I can almost hear my mother speaking to me. "You didn't manage to sleep with Ollie, either, did you?"

AT LUNCH ON MONDAY, I explain to Vivi that Nick is now back on my sofa.

"Just as well you aren't involved with Ollie if you're busy giving sponge baths to your ex-husband."

"I am not giving him sponge baths. I helped him get his shirt off once."

Vivi rolls her eyes at me. "And you don't think Nick is pretending to be less capable than he is to get back in?"

"He would choose a rock tour over me any day."

"You should kick Nick off your sofa and tell him to get a hotel. You know that, right?"

"Which I would love to do, but he spends so little time with Hannah, I can't justify it to my kid. Oh, and speaking of Ollie, his ex-girlfriend is back in town and wants to dance with him again. And she's gorgeous."

"But he's not dating, right? While he goes through his whole personal growth thing?"

I shrug. "Dancing with her wouldn't be the same as dating, I guess."

"So you're screwed."

I nod slowly.

"I don't know. I still think Ollie is into you. What's this I hear about Ollie jumping into the ocean to rescue you?"

"He jumped in to rescue a teenager."

"Well, all the women on Katy's floor are enraged. They think you jumped in on purpose so he would rescue you. You're on some kind of hitlist up there. Watch your back, the female lawyers probably own dart guns."

Did Ollie really jump into the ocean for me? I cling to the thought like it's a life preserver.

Brant walks up to me shortly before the end of the day. "So Ollie's heroics on the boat tour are the talk of the office."

I frown. Brant has become especially hard to read since we've been serving on the committee together, and I keep suspecting that he knows more about me and Ollie than he's saying.

"It was nice of him to save that boy."

Brant leans against my desk. "I don't think he went into the Long Island Sound for a random teenager."

"I told you that we're friends." The further I get into this lie, the harder it will be to back out of it, I realize.

He sighs. "Laura, as someone who knows men, I think his intentions are a little different than friendship."

"I appreciate the warning, but nothing is going on."

He shrugs. "I'm just saying, I don't want you to be blindsided."

"My ex-husband is currently staying on my sofa for a couple of weeks, so that is plenty for me to deal with right now." That part is true, at least.

Brant's frown grows deeper. "I thought you said things were over with him."

"They are. He's just recovering from an injury."

Brant doesn't seem appeased. "You're not moving to Atlanta on me again, are you?"

"No. Definitely not. I promise. My plans here are permanent and long-term."

He nods slowly. "Just remember there's a reason you split up with him in the first place."

"I am aware, Brant. Thank you."

On Tuesday, I get a call from Jody on my walk home from the subway.

"Have you heard from Ben?"

It takes me a moment to process whom she means: our

young blond friend from class. "No, I don't have his phone number. Why? His wedding is coming up soon, right?"

"Yeah, but...oh right, you weren't in class on Sunday," she goes on. "Apparently the wedding is on thin ice."

"What? Why?"

"The fiancée's parents are trying to get her to ditch him."

"Our sweet little investment banker? Why would anyone ditch him?"

"The usual rich person insanity. Speaking of ditching people, why weren't you in class on Sunday?"

"Family drama." I barely remembered I even had swing class, to be honest.

"I was hoping it wasn't because of Ollie," Jody says, and I can feel her eyeroll over the phone.

"No, it wasn't because of Ollie."

"Good. I was worried you were upset about him being partners with Eliana again."

It hits harder than it should. "He is? When did you hear that?"

"It's what the instructors were talking about on Sunday. Anyway, I know you started dancing because of him. I was worried you were one of those people who starts something because of a man and then quits as soon as he's not available anymore."

It takes me a moment to answer. If Jody hadn't called, I might not have come back to class at all. And now Ollie is back with his old dance partner?

Jody absorbs my long silence. "Is that a yes?"

"No, sorry, it's just... My ex-husband got injured and he's on my sofa for the next two weeks and I have a lot to deal with."

"Okay." I can hear Jody considering this. "So what I'm hearing is that you have free babysitting for the next couple of weeks and can come to as many swing dancing practices as you want?"

I laugh in spite of myself. "You're right." And she is. I don't want to be someone who quits dance because a guy hurt my feelings. "I'll be there for the Friday evening social for practice and for class. And let me know if you hear from Ben. I hope he comes back to us," I say.

"Yeah, me, too."

THAT EVENING, I tell Nick that if I'm going to buy him clothes that are easy for him to wear, bring him soup, and help him order taxis to get to a physical therapist, then he can watch Hannah for me for a few hours while I go dancing.

"Dancing?" he asks. "Is this like, electronica, or..."

"It's swing dancing."

"Swing dancing." He is smirking.

"What?"

He shrugs. "Do people wear newsboy caps to these events?"

"Am I hearing this correctly? Is a forty-three-year-old man taunting me for not being cool?"

Nick rolls his eyes. "Sorry. I just wondered if this was because of him. The dance teacher."

Now is my opportunity to lie, but I don't want to. "His name is Oliver MacCormack if you want to look him up. He had a dance to a Bruno Mars song that went viral a few years ago."

"A Bruno Mars song?"

"Yeah. It's West Coast Swing. A lot of it is to rock music. Anyway, Hannah is really happy to have you here, Nick. So you guys can have fun together while I go practice."

I leave the room because I don't want to know if Nick looks up Ollie. I should be above making Nick jealous, but not if he's going to tell me that Ollie dresses like a golfer.

. . .

THE NEXT DAY, I receive an email from Destiny: *Can you and Ollie have a meeting to go over the language in my draft report? You're the best writers on the team. Use track changes.*

I write back at once, then email Ollie and offer to book us a conference room. He replies: *I think my office should work.* Of course he has his own office. I have twelve square feet in a cubicle sea, and he probably has custom window shades and a view of the Hudson.

"Hey," he says to me as I enter. His tone is friendly but polite. He is wearing a blue pinstripe suit that looks tailored and vaguely British; the jacket is hung neatly on a coat hanger behind the door. His office is unreasonably large and lined with bookcases and a framed photograph of startling orange and grey cliffs above a cool blue ocean. I gaze at the photo for a moment as he steps beside me.

"Australia?"

"My brother took it," he replies quietly. "He was always a good photographer. That's around Wilsons Promontory. We went there a few times growing up."

"And you put it up even though you're upset with him?"

Ollie smiles. "Well, sometimes I imagine shoving him off the cliffs, so there's that."

I turn to face him. "Listen, Nick and I—"

"It's okay."

"I don't want you to think there's anything going on. Hannah is so desperate for time with her dad, she insisted he stay."

"Laura, it's fine. Just tell me when he's gone."

"Okay." I wonder if he's going to bring up Eliana; I wonder if I have the courage to ask. "So anything new with you?"

He looks at me, then looks away, shrugs. "Not really."

Cool. Nothing to see here, right? Not like he is dancing again with his ex-girlfriend. "So," I begin, "shall we talk through this document together?"

He catches something odd in my tone and looks at me for a long moment. "Yeah, of course." He turns to his own computer and clicks on a file. "Let's start with page one."

For the next forty-five minutes we are completely professional. My inner rebel Laura keeps making wildly inappropriate remarks in my head, and I keep batting her away successfully. The topic we're discussing doesn't help.

"So I guess we're saying that office relationships are complicated, and we recommend but don't require disclosure?" I ask.

"Right. Right." He gives me a sharp look and then looks down and coughs. "I can finish this. I'll just summarize it for Destiny and send it back to her."

"Great."

I stand up. He walks to the door with me.

"Wait," he says. "Wait a second."

I turn to him. His hazel-green eyes look unusually dark. I wait for him to speak and he doesn't.

"Well," I say brightly, "at least I know that if you break my heart, we'll both be professional about it."

His eyes flash with something, and I see something that looks surprisingly like longing in his expression.

Then he pushes me gently against the wall and looks at me for a moment before he gives me a long, lingering kiss, his whole body against mine, hot and close. One of his hands drifts up to caress my neck. My knees seem to melt, but the warning light is flashing again; I wonder if this is the kiss you give someone if you're never expecting to kiss them again.

When he pulls away, he does not meet my gaze.

"Sorry." The word sinks quietly into my shoulder. "I know we're at work."

"I'm not," I say. I run one hand along his shoulder, and he takes it in his own, gently, and then places it at my side.

Ollie cuts me off. "Tell me when your ex is gone."

He stands up straight and turns and opens the door for me.

I give him a last look and then go.

JODY MADE a good point about Nick being around to watch Hannah, so I decide to make the most of it: to go to an open West Coast Swing night at a different dance school on Wednesday night, my Friday night practice at Manhattan Swing, and my lesson on Sunday. If I get nothing else out of Nick's stay, I'm going to learn to dance better.

I'm not going to quit because Ollie is dancing again with Eliana.

I finally have a babysitter, though it bothers me that I'm mentally calling this babysitting. Nick is watching his own child. He is putting in his time as a father, like he is supposed to do all the time, not when he's too injured to do something more important to him.

I put on a flowy sundress and leave Nick and Hannah on my sofa watching *Moana*.

"She practices dancing *so much*," I hear Hannah say as the door closes behind me.

The event I'm attending is called Hot and West, and it is held at a smaller dance studio in Williamsburg, a little north of my place in Brooklyn. When I arrive, I discover that the studio is located over a Greek restaurant and has more of a dance club vibe than Manhattan Swing Workshop. Their dance space is a function room dimly lit with colored lights, the kind of place you might hire for a small wedding. The thirty people on the floor all seem like they know more styles of dance than I do: I see elements of the hustle, of blues dancing and salsa. I feel like the Jennifer Grey character in the movie *Dirty Dancing*—stumbling upon people engaged in something intimate and a little illicit. Officially, this is a West Coast Swing event, but people are clearly making their own rules.

Part of me is wondering if I'll see Ollie's ex-wife again, but I don't: running into her really was a fluke. That whole night when we went back to his place feels like a fluke now, an almost-was, the start of something that may never happen. Ollie hasn't broken things off, but it feels like we are in a holding pattern, waiting to see which of us gets our heart broken first.

Standing against a wall, I briefly worry that no one will ask me to dance, but then a man approaches me after a few moments. He is a blond-haired man in the kind of tight red shirt that Warren Beatty would have worn to a 1970s movie premiere. I explain how new I am to the whole dance scene, but that doesn't stop him from leading me through steps forcefully. He's very skilled and confident, but a little intimidating. He doesn't say much, just whips me around and occasionally gives a little frown when I entirely miss a step. He dips me low enough that I get nervous he'll drop me. After our dance, he nods, smiles briefly, and then crosses the room to approach another partner.

I watch them dance. She is much better than I am, and he guides her through an elaborate series of dips and spins that would definitely have cracked my head open.

"That's not safe," mutters a woman beside me, watching my most recent partner.

"Are there unsafe dancers?" The thought hadn't occurred to me.

"Oh, definitely. There are moves you should not try unless you have a very experienced partner and you've practiced a lot. No one is getting hurt right now, but I don't trust that guy."

This is new information to me, and it is reassuring to know that my intuition was correct. Some leaders can be dangerous, which makes dancing not that far away from dating. I watch for another few moments, wishing I'd brought Jody with me, and then decide to ask a different man to dance rather than waiting for the red-shirted guy to circle back. The man I approach is much older, much more relaxed, and much more fun to dance with. He explains that he's recently retired from driving a subway train and does this to stay in shape. I tell him about my widowed friend who is doing a different dance every month.

"Very impressive," he says. "This is my only dance right now, although I guess I know the Electric Slide. You should bring her here," he says.

"Maybe I will." I grin, and he gently guides me through a brand-new step that I've never tried before, but that I somehow manage to keep up with.

At the end of our song, my partner sees a friend of his and I let him excuse himself to chat with her. I scan the room and conclude that the only other single person I could dance with is Mister Dangerous, and I decide to head home.

When I get back to my apartment, Hannah is in bed and Nick has muted the tv and is doing wrist exercises.

"How was the movie?" I ask.

He looks me over. "Fine. Can you uh...help with the shirt?"

I walk over and help him get his shirt off, then turn to go.

"I should shower," I say. "I'm sticky."

"I'll bet."

I spin around. "The guy I'm seeing wasn't there, Nick. I do have the decency not to ask my ex-husband to watch my kid while I go to bed with someone."

Nick leans back on my sofa. He looks good shirtless, and he certainly knows that. "Sorry, I was being an asshole."

"I don't want to fight with you."

"You're learning dance for him, though, aren't you?"

I shrug. "Well, I got my motorcycle license for you."

"That's my point." He frowns. "You're serious about him."

I can sense how embarrassing all this will be if Ollie dumps me. "If there's ever anything to tell you, I will."

"I watched some of his dances." Nick smiles dryly. "You knew I would. You told me his name to make me jealous."

I shrug, feeling called out. "Well, I didn't like you insulting him. Because if you insult him, you're insulting my judgment."

"It's the fact that you picked a guy who is the complete opposite of me."

"It would be weirder if I picked someone exactly like you."

"Not necessarily. Depends on who he was." Nick gives me a charged smile. "I mean, don't get me wrong. He can dance. He's very...competent. He isn't what you need, though."

Competent. Of course Nick would pick that word. We look at each other for a long moment. This is what I used to call sexual chemistry, this tension between us. Now I wonder if the feeling in my chest isn't just Nick very successfully stringing me along, never letting me get comfortable with anyone else, convincing me that what we have is an eternal, irreplaceable passion. I wonder how much of the sexual tension between us was always calculated, created on purpose from the first moment when we locked eyes. My father figures growing up all abandoned me, and maybe Nick intuited that he could keep me hooked by always being on the verge of leaving.

I wonder why I never saw it before. And once I see that, I have another realization. It isn't just that Nick is hooking me in and then constantly leaving. It is that he is hooking me in, now, at this particular moment, *because* he is leaving. Because he knows he's about to go, and this will keep me waiting for him. He has always been at his most passionate, his sexiest, his most loving, right before he goes away.

"Goodnight, Nick."

His eyes flicker with an expression I can't read. "Goodnight, Laura."

ON FRIDAY NIGHT, I go to our usual swing club practice at Manhattan Swing Workshop. Ollie's cute, blonde ex-girlfriend—and apparent current dance partner—Eliana is not there this time, which improves my mood a bit. Instead, one of the other instructors does a quick run-through of five different variations on the tuck-turn. A tuck-turn is a move in which a leader pulls the follower in and then spins them away again, and it feels like a reasonably good metaphor for my love life right now. I practice the move with Jody as my partner, and I manage to keep up with the instructor for the first time ever, all the way through to the end of the lesson.

"Did I just follow that entire lesson without getting lost?"

"You're getting better," Jody agrees. "It's really noticeable."

Jody is not big on compliments, so this one, although made with her typical blunt candor, warms me inside.

"I hope Ben is okay," I tell her. "The wedding is supposed to be tomorrow, right? I'm sure he's fine, but..."

"Yeah. I have his cell phone because I was trying to connect him up with my friend who manages a restaurant, but I'm scared to text him. His crazy fiancée probably checks his messages, and I don't want her saying, 'Who is Jody from swing class? Why didn't you tell me you're taking swing class? Are you having an affair?' She'll probably think I'm a man named Jody and he's hiding that he's gay."

"There has to be a way to phrase it. Give me your phone."

I compose a text to Ben. *Hey Ben, it's Jody and Laura who gave you that help with wedding planning, just wondering if everything is going well or if you two have decided to elope instead. Hope everything is coming together for your big day.*

Jody considers the message. "Oh, that's perfect."

"You should see my passive-aggressive work emails. When I'm really mad, I sign them, Cordially yours, Laura."

Hank, the co-teacher for our class, is helping to run the evening, and he surprises me by asking me to dance. Dancing with him feels like a pleasant mix of learning things and trying out my steps. I should enjoy myself, but instead I find myself asking the one question I don't want the answer to.

"So, do you know if Ollie is back with his old partner Eliana?"

"Ollie MacCormack?" Hank considers. "I think they're dancing together for the Garden State Swing Festival. You should sign up for that, by the way. It's in Jersey City, and it's a great experience for new dancers. It's one of the best swing dancing festivals on the East Coast."

"When is it?"

"July 12th weekend. You could even compete if you want. All the big names will be there, getting ready for the national competition in the fall. And Ollie and Eliana, if you want to see them. They're really great together."

"I'm sure," I say with a forced smile.

"There's a Newcomers category, for brand new dancers, and one step up is Novice, which you could also try if you want. It's very low-key at that level. Lots of people dipping their feet into competition. On the last day, there's a fun event where the top Novice competitors get to do a Jack & Jill with the Champion followers and leaders."

"That sounds terrifying."

"It's fun. I did it years ago and I got to lead Paula Michaels, who is the national champion with Dion Reyes. She's really nice. I learned a lot just from dancing with her."

A plan starts to form in my head, right out of a teen movie.

I am going to become an amazing dancer in the next three

weeks. I am going to win the Novice competition and then dance with Ollie in the Novice/Champion Jack & Jill competition, even though the names will be picked out of a hat and by definition, as with any Jack & Jill event, I won't get to pick my partner. And I am going to prove to Ollie that his (top ten in the country) ex-girlfriend doesn't have nearly as much chemistry with him as I do.

My wild scheme might even be possible. Hannah is going to Newfoundland for a visit with Abby and will be there through the first two weeks in July. I will have the time to prepare. Aside from my job, I could do nothing but dance until the festival weekend.

It feels like a Rebel Laura move. When I was young, I did a lot of things that pushed my limits. I worked as a bartender, followed a band across the country, drove a motorcycle, jumped off cliffs into swimming holes. When I had Hannah, I became the grown-up, the one who set limits. I forgot what it was like to want something just for me. And I want Ollie. As stupid as it sounds in my own head, I want him to choose me.

I am out of breath by the time I return to our usual corner of the dance floor. Helen has arrived, and we watch Jody dancing with Téa. The two of them have been circling each other for a while and tonight may be the night when one of them finally asks the other to meet outside class. But at the end of the dance, Jody gives Téa one of her friendly, brisk nods and returns to us.

"What happened?" I ask.

"We danced. It was fine." Jody is still hard for me to read; I can't tell if she feels nothing about Téa or feels a lot and is determined not to talk about it.

"I like her lavender hair," Helen offers.

"She wanted to talk to me about gifts," Jody says, a bit wearily. "'*What do you think your gift is in life? Mine is being able to pick out people's outfits.*' I told her mine was sarcasm and she said she wasn't sure that counted." Jody sighed. "I don't know if we really click, but we're going on a date."

"That's great!"

"Maybe." Jody glances down. "Anyway, I just got more interesting news. Ben texted me back, and the wedding isn't happening. They broke up."

"What?" Helen and I look at each other, aghast.

"And he's quitting dance," Jody says. "Of course."

"Can you text Ben and tell him to come with us to practice?" I say. "Or maybe to the Garden State Swing Festival in a couple of weeks?"

"You do it." Jody gives me her phone, and I send the message.

"Nobody else should stop someone from dancing," Helen says. Jody gives me a meaningful look.

When I get home, Nick has put Hannah to bed and is sitting in the living room, watching an action movie at a barely audible level.

He takes me in. "Black tank top, black jeans. There's a look I haven't seen in a while."

"Wearing a cream blazer while dancing to Nelly Furtado is frowned upon."

"You look good."

"Thanks."

He takes me in. "You're different, Laur."

"I hope so." I walk back toward my room to take a shower.

10

TRAINING MONTAGE

WHEN I OFFERED to let Nick stay with us, I was worried it would lead to Hannah trying to get us back together, like some low-rent Brooklyn version of *The Parent Trap*.

That's not what happens, though. After a few days together, Hannah begins squabbling with her father over TV shows and bedtime. She gets annoyed at his unwillingness to leave the house every time she wants to visit a playground or go out for ice cream, and I have to remind her that he is letting his hand heal so he can get back to work.

It reminds me of what it was like to live together in Atlanta; Nick and Hannah had a lot of friction then, too. As an only child, Hannah can be pushy when she doesn't get her way, like one of those high-strung movie stars who is charming as long as you are bringing her matcha lattes and highly unpleasant when you are not. And Nick can get grouchy when he is hungry or it's early in the morning, which Hannah likes to turn into an epic crisis.

Within a few days, Hannah is talking about how much she's looking forward to staying with her Aunt Tabby in Canada once school is over, not how pleased she is to have her dad around. I can sense that she's been happy to have Nick visit but is equally happy to let him leave again. It feels like an unexpected gift, this reminder that we don't quite work as a family. Maybe if Nick had been here all along, we would have found our way to an equilibrium, with both parents setting the ground rules. As it is, Hannah and I are the family unit, and Nick is our charming but troublesome houseguest. I wonder if Nick feels it, too.

The night before Nick is going to switch out his wrist brace for something more flexible, I hear him swearing in the bathroom. I knock softly and he grumbles for me to enter. He stands there with his t-shirt caught over his head, half twisted up in his arm. He was clearly in the process of getting undressed when something got twisted the wrong way.

"Would you like me to take your shirt off again?" I offer, amused.

"If you have a moment." His voice is dry, and I pull off the shirt and hand it to him, feeling a rush of affection. He's much more appealing when he's not trying to be appealing, much sexier when he isn't giving me long, slow glances.

There's a brief moment between us that I manage to shake off; it's only because we're standing so close. He doesn't tempt me the way he used to. It's like when I stopped drinking alcohol: after a while, you can miss something but not crave it, because you know your life is better off without it.

When I turn to leave him, I almost miss him saying my name. "Hey, Laura?"

I turn around. "What's up?"

He gives me a tired smile. "Thanks for helping me."

I smile gently, feeling my heart wrench. "No problem."

He nods. "When you left Atlanta, I thought things were still open for us to try again."

"They were. Then," I reply. I don't know when the window closed. Maybe Christmas. Maybe Hannah's April break.

"But not now?"

I look away.

"Laura."

I sigh and shake my head. I watch as an awareness dawns in his eyes.

"You really like that guy."

My heart lurches a little. "I'm barely dating him. Don't get worked up."

"So can he make money at that? As a dance teacher?" Nick gives me a dry smile, trying to get me to admit the apparent irony that I've picked another unreliable artist who can't support me, just at the moment that Nick is finally doing well.

"He teaches in the evenings. He works as a tax attorney at Murano."

"Fuck." Nick grimaces. "Now I want to date him."

I laugh, feeling a well of affection for Nick, some hopeful vision of what it would be like if we were actually friends instead of whatever we are now: tortured soulmates turned disappointed co-parents. Maybe we can get to the kind of friendship where we can laugh together. Maybe. Maybe all it takes is not expecting anything and he will stop letting me down.

His laughter attenuates into something painful. I loved him so much, for so long, and I can feel it in the air: this is the last time I will ever have a chance to kiss him. He is still handsome, and he is right there, and I don't want to kiss him. Not even a little.

As Hannah and I wait outside our building with Nick for his ride to the airport, I can sense that he is happy to get on the road again, to be somewhere that he gets to play 'Dad' to a bunch of cool young rock musicians instead of being 'Daddy' to an eight-year-old who already suspects that he's a screw-up. It must be nice to be somewhere that your strengths are visible and your flaws won't be; it's why politicians seem happiest when shaking hands and kissing babies.

"Two minutes until my ride," Nick says, glancing at an app on his phone, and then turns to Hannah and gives her a huge hug that turns into a three-hundred-sixty-degree spin. Once she is wobbling back on her feet, he smiles, sets her right, and then leans over and gives me a kiss on the cheek.

"Thanks again." There's an unexpected amount of sadness in his eyes.

"What's wrong?" I ask.

He glances at Hannah, who is a few feet away now, watching for the taxi, and says quietly, "You're going to end up marrying that guy, aren't you?"

I ignore the pain at the words. "Almost definitely not."

A taxi pulls up, and he looks back at me. "I wish I'd done things better. I'm sorry." It's the most honest apology I ever remember getting from him.

I clear my throat. "You're going to be amazing on that tour. I'm really proud of you."

"Thanks." He smiles once, that old, crooked smile that once sent me reeling, and then kisses Hannah on her head and turns to get in the car.

When he is gone, Hannah looks up at me. "Do you still love Daddy?" Her insightful streak has its usual annoying timing.

"Of course. But he and I are not going to be a couple again. You know that, right?"

Hannah considers this. "You could marry him again if you want to. But you should only do what you want to do," she says. It's the eight-year-old's version of wisdom, but that doesn't make it wrong.

. . .

THE NEXT WEEKEND, I fly up with Hannah to St. John's, Newfoundland, to drop her off with my sister, and I spend the weekend with Abby and her fiancé Paul in Paul's adorable yellow townhouse in the middle of the downtown. Everything about St. John's feels foreign to me. It looks like some Irish or Scandinavian port city, remote and quietly adorable, but I let Abby try to convince me that it feels like Brooklyn. "We can walk to two different coffee shops!" she insists —and I pretend to agree. I know she's more in love with Paul than with anything else here, but it's nice to see her happy and reassuring to see that she and Hannah are immediately on solid ground. Within ten minutes of arriving, they are racing down the sidewalks singing Disney songs together. It makes me feel less guilty for leaving Hannah with Abby for three weeks.

When I return home by myself two days later, I get my courage together and finally text Ollie.

Hey, I write, *Nick is back on tour, and Hannah is in Canada with my sister for a couple of weeks. I am free if you want to meet up or talk.*

He calls me an hour later.

"Hi!" I try to sound cheerful.

"How is your ex doing?" Ollie asks, his voice sounding distant and polite. "He's recovered?"

"Yes, he's fine. You could drag a touring musician behind an 18-wheeler, and they'd still be on their feet to do the next show. He has to wear a brace on his wrist, but he's totally fine. I know that whole thing had terrible timing, but I want to tell you again that nothing is going on with him. It didn't, it hasn't, and it won't."

There is a long pause. "Laura." Another pause, so long and deep that it feels like I'm walking through a tunnel. "I don't think I can do this."

"Oh." I feel a gust of terror rising in my chest, ready to blow through me.

"It's not even...it's not that I think anything happened with him, but I just keep waiting for the other shoe to drop with you. You're too involved with him, and you have a kid together..."

"No." My voice sounds shaky. "This was Nick pulling his usual bullshit, but I can assure you it was a once-in-a-lifetime occurrence. And I would not have asked him if Hannah hadn't overheard me talking about how he was injured. She gets so little time with her father. I had trouble saying no to her, not to him."

"But that's my point. With Hannah involved, it's complicated. And if I were in a different place, and not going through my own stuff, I could handle it, but I was talking to a friend of mine, and I think that maybe I'm not ready for dating. I know we..." He pauses. His voice sounds unsteady, full of feeling. "I know we talked about that as a joke, but maybe we both were being more truthful than we realized."

"Okay." I'm trying not to react.

"After the way my marriage ended, I can't be in a situation where...it just feels like any second this will blow up."

I can't help but be angry; I don't want to be angry. "Ollie, you pushed me away. You told me not to call you until Nick was gone. And now you're acting like I'm the one who withdrew from you. I did what you asked me to. I could have called you every day, *every day*, and told you I wasn't in love with him, but you wouldn't talk to me."

"I know. It's my problem, not yours."

As soon as someone pulls out, 'It's not you, it's me,' the discussion is over. That's why it's the greatest hit in break-ups. You can't respond to it. It draws an uncrossable line in the sand.

"Maybe if I was capable of dating you casually, it would be different, but I'm not." So now he likes me *too much* to be with me. That's a good one, I think. Nick would be proud of that level of pretzel logic. "I'm better as your friend right now."

I realize this is timed conveniently with our committee work, too; it means that we weren't lying at all. I don't bother to ask him about Eliana. I don't ask if Eliana is the friend he confided in, the one who told him he wasn't ready to date me. I know I can't do that and not sound hysterical, jealous, screaming and begging him not to do this to us. I have some pride.

"I understand."

I don't understand, but I end the call as quickly as I can and then sit alone on my bed, my knees shaking. There's a hollow place in the middle of my chest as my eyes drift to the buildings outside: the burning brick red from the setting sun and the lemon glow from shops. I had this whole plan that I was going to become an amazing dancer and then win him back, but my plan is unwinnable. It was always going to be unwinnable, because I'm a single parent.

The rebel inside me wants to scream. To go to his house and yell outside his window. To get wasted. I am itching to get out of my skin, like I'll die if I sit in my grown-up apartment being grown-up about this, too. Nick is gone. Hannah is gone. Ollie doesn't love me. I can't even tell Vivi about this, because Vivi doesn't even know we were dating. I can't tell Abby, because she was angry that I let Nick stay with me in the first place and will blame the whole disaster on me.

I stand up and put on my sexiest club clothes. Black boots. Tight shimmering top. I want to go out and forget my rational brain for a while. Hannah isn't here. I can pretend I am twenty again.

A voice in my head is saying: *don't drink, don't drink, don't drink.*

I bat it away. *Of course I'm not going to drink,* I tell the voice. *I'm just going to go to a club and pick up a man and sleep with him and do every single thing that I used to do when I was drinking. Where's the risk in that?*

Where's the risk in letting Rebel Laura have a night out?

'Mercenary' is a new club in downtown Manhattan, tucked away in a space behind a popular steakhouse restaurant and below a yoga studio. When I make my way to the long entrance hallway, the music is booming and a bridge-and-tunnel crowd are lining up to get carded, dressed in New Jersey and Long Island haute couture. I'm not even feeling snobby about it; I grew up poor and spent enough time wearing faux leather pants that I can recognize my people. And they are definitely my people: dark-haired Italians or bottle blondes tottering in heels, exhorting each other with strong local accents about holding purses and where to find the strongest drinks.

As soon as I'm inside, I wade into the fray, dancing by myself, listening to the bass line vibrating up my spine. It's music I don't know, but it still feels familiar: the kind of assertive, mindless pulsing that always helps when there is something I need to forget.

I have apparently forgotten that even at my age, as a woman alone, I will become an immediate target. I wanted to feel attractive tonight, but instead I feel like prey. Within ninety seconds of thumping bass, there he is across from me: a young man who looks about twenty-five, dancing as close as he can, making his intentions clear with the subtlety of a subway train.

He grins at me and tosses out the universal club head nod. Then he comes closer, not quite grinding against me but suggesting that grinding is in the near future.

"Can I buy you a drink?" he calls into my ear. He's handsome enough to pull off his assertiveness, and he smells nice, but his hair is a little too slicked back, his diamond earring a little too large.

He's boring, I think, and feel unkind thinking it. He's so

unspecific, even though I know that if I talked to him, I'd hear the specifics: how he works as a trainer at his gym; how he's going on vacation with his brother to Miami soon; how he doesn't read a lot of books, but he likes girls who read. We would go to bed, and it would be a coin toss whether he could make me orgasm, but he'd try his best until either he succeeded or I faked it. Then in the morning, he would say something like, 'Laura, you're an amazing woman,' some line that he heard in a movie once when he was fifteen. He probably won't mention that I'm older than he is, or he might talk about how he 'likes older women.' Depends how smooth he is.

"Can I *buy you a drink?*" he shouts again, since I haven't responded.

"I'm going to go to the bathroom!" I shout back.

A moment later, I stand in front of a large mirror, my face glowing like a Renaissance portrait in chiaroscuro against the charcoal-painted walls. The bathrooms are still very nice, I notice. No graffiti, flattering lighting, dark wood decor. Women have vomited here, but not often enough yet for the smell to persist.

The only way this would be tolerable is if I were drinking. I look at my face and get a little teary, realizing how much this part of my life is officially over, even if Hannah wasn't in the picture, even if I weren't sober. It feels like going back to your childhood bedroom and realizing you can never stare up at your boy band poster with the same sense of yearning. I don't want this anymore. I will never want this again.

I want something real, and every time I reach for it, it slips through my fingers.

Ollie was supposed to be a mature adult, but maybe mature adults can't ignore that I'm a walking red flag, a series of problems. He did his best, but eventually there were too many issues for him to pretend them away. There was a neat line of red flags stretching out from me like a runway, directing him to get the hell away.

Maybe if I drank, I could lie to myself and act like I was young tonight. Maybe that's why people drink in the first place: to try to get back to the point where they aren't damaged yet. I wipe my face in the mirror, mascara smears leaving coal smudges in both directions, just as a young woman emerges from the toilet stall behind me.

She washes her hands as she glances over, taking in my expression as I listlessly wipe at my make-up with my thumbs.

"Man problems?" she asks.

"My boyfriend dumped me," I say blankly. That part is true.

She turns and puts her arms around me, this complete stranger. She must be very drunk. "He is not worth it," she intones. "No man is worth it." I nod into her shoulder. She smells like CK One.

EMERGING from the club a few minutes later, I decide to stop by an AA meeting on my way home. I track one down in the Village that's being held late enough that I can still drop in. A famous actor is there, which is the kind of thing I would love to tell my friends and won't. The glamor of big city life: twenty people sitting in a church basement, wary and exhausted, one of them fresh from shooting a movie with Sandra Bullock.

On the subway later, I think about West Coast Swing. It sometimes seems silly, all the formal positions like leader and follower, all the rules about frame and handholding, but I realize how nice it is when no one is likely to give you an unasked-for ass grind. In partner dancing, you never get surrounded by two men, one on either side, blocking your ability to exit.

I remember Jody asking me pointedly if I was going to quit dancing. I stand up in the subway, having a silent moment of decision as I stare at my face echoed in the dark window, tunnel support beams flickering behind my reflection like ghosts.

I am not quitting West Coast Swing because of Ollie.

I am not quitting at all.

I text Jody and Helen as soon as I get off the train, even though it's late at night. *Any time in the next 3 weeks that you want to go swing dancing, I'm in. I want to get as much practice as possible before Garden State Swing.*

Helen texts me back eight exclamation points in a row.

I HAVE eighteen days until the Swing Festival, and what follows is as close as I've ever lived to a training montage. I tell myself that I am Rocky running up endless stairs, the Karate Kid painting fences, Elle Woods studying for the LSAT. I am going to get good at this, and I am not going to quit because of Ollie. And while Hannah's away, I have all the time in the world to make good on that goal.

I sign up with Jody for the intermediate West Coast course that's starting on Saturday mornings in July.

I sign up for Thursday evening lessons at a smaller dance studio in lower Manhattan, and I bookmark another 'Hot and West' night near me in Brooklyn.

I sign up for four one-hour private lessons with Hank so I can learn how to do Jack & Jill improvs. I keep going to the Friday night open practice sessions at Manhattan Swing Workshop, too.

I even sit through an entire lesson taught by Eliana at one of our Manhattan Swing nights. She seems to have literally no idea who I am, but she has a lot of useful tips about pop-outs and footwork. Jody finds Eliana annoyingly perky, which I take as a sign of loyalty.

Jody tells me she has finally made a plan to see Téa.

"Meh," Jody says. "It probably won't work out anyway."

"No sparks?"

"I don't know if I believe in sparks."

Ben still hasn't returned to class, though Jody texts him again to check in.

I SEE Ollie now and then, and each time a crushing wave of feeling washes over me. We spot each other twice in the hallway at work, and he looks ridiculously handsome and not at all like he is going through a break-up, which I hate him for. The first time, I smile politely but do not wave, a flat, empty, polite smile that he doesn't return. The second time, he waves once but does not smile.

When I see him for a third time, this time in the hallway at Manhattan Swing Workshop, he walks straight toward me. Something in my chest turns into a gymnastics routine, all flips and spins and landing hard.

"Laura," he says. "I um..."

I feel it sharply then: the little mythical string that still connects his chest to mine, tugging. "Yes?"

"I am so sorry. I shouldn't have done that by phone."

Oh, *that's* what he wants to apologize for? The method of delivery?

"But you had to do it, right?" I feel anger rising inside me. I want to shove at him, to scream, but I keep my voice even. "It had to be done?"

He takes a shallow breath. "I was just waiting for you to..." The words trail off.

"Me to what? Break your heart? So you had to do it first?"

"No, I —" He looks appalled. "No."

I wait. He says nothing. He shakes his head; I can't believe he has the gall to look frustrated with me.

"I was trying to give you space—" he begins. The doors to the main classroom swing open and a throng of sweaty, cheerful dancers pour out.

"To give me space?" Am I hearing this correctly?

He looks pained.

"Well," I say, "mission accomplished."

He winces, and I turn and walk past him into the classroom.

———

A COUPLE of days after that, Brant approaches me at my desk and asks whether my ex-husband is still staying with me.

"No, he's back to drifting wherever the winds of pop music take him."

"Good," Brant replies with a frown. "I was a little worried about you."

I don't love that Brant feels comfortable saying that.

"You know, Laura," Brant adds, "one of these days I hope we're both ready to date again."

I nod. "One of these days." I pointedly return to my work. He stands there for a moment before he walks away.

At lunch, Vivi asks me whether Ollie feels ready to 'date' yet, and I try not to look like a want to set something on fire.

"Maybe at some point in the very distant future," I reply dryly.

"Oh," she says, taking in my look. "Do we hate him now?"

"A little."

"Well, good," she says. "I have no time for games. That whole thing about how he's still getting over his ex-wife? If a guy told me that, I'd assume he was seeing somebody else he liked better."

I think of Eliana. Vivi is more right than she knows.

———

Jody pulls me and Helen aside at the Friday social right after July Fourth, a week before our swing festival weekend. "We need to talk."

"What's wrong?" Helen looks between us.

"It's Ben. I'm worried about our little investment banker."

"I'm sure he is out drinking with his finance bro coworkers," I say, "and they are helping him forget the whole thing with the judicious use of lap dances and bottle service."

"That's what I thought, too," Jody says. She hands me her phone. There is a text thread with Ben.

If you're in the city just come hang out with us, Jody has written.

pretty much everything is pointless right now, reads Ben's response.

Not in a suicidal way, right? Jody has replied.

There is no answer to Jody's question, which was sent several hours ago.

I consider this.

Ben, suicidal? It seems unlikely. He has always seemed so even keeled. But it still reads as a cry for help, in the way that earnest, buttoned-up Midwestern guys will cry for help: the non-response.

"Give me the phone," I say.

Ben, I text, *it's Laura. Send me your address right now. We are coming to get you.*

I look at Helen. "Do you happen to own a car?"

She shakes her head. "I don't even have a license."

"I have a truck," Jody says. "I got it in the divorce."

"Hold on, you were divorced?" I stare at her.

Jody sighs. "I don't need to tell you *everything*, Laura."

. . .

BEN'S APARTMENT building is in one of the newer loft buildings in Long Island City that face Manhattan across a sweeping view of the East River.

"Of course he lives in one of these monstrosities," Jody mutters as we get into his sleek chrome elevator. Helen is sitting in Jody's truck outside to make sure it doesn't get towed; you don't find street parking in this neighborhood.

I push the button to the fourteenth floor as she continues her rant.

"I hate rich people. They ruin everything that is good in this city." Jody sighs. "Now let's go rescue that rich bastard."

Ben grimaces when he swings open the door to his apartment. There are weary smudges under his eyes, and his usual polished look has drifted into casual despair.

"I'm fine," he says, his voice gruff. "You don't have to do this. I'm not going to jump off the balcony."

"Can we just come in for a minute?" I say in my most maternal voice.

He leaves the door open for us to follow him inside, and sure enough, his place is a wreck...a grey and black, extremely expensive wreck, with pizza boxes littering the polished surfaces and piles of drinking glasses and Makers Mark bottles crowding the kitchen sink. Jody walks straight through the living room to take in the view.

"Holy shit, Ben," she says, taking in the Manhattan skyline. "This is so *American Psycho*."

He shrugs. "I'll have to get nicer business cards, I guess." He walks up and stands beside me. "I'm sorry if I sounded melodramatic in my texts," he says, his voice flat. "I'm just depressed."

"And you're going to a therapist about it?" I ask.

Ben groans and flops onto his sofa. "What would they even say? 'Your ex is horrible, and you were stupid for dating her in the first place, and then she waited to dump you until your entire family had flown in for your wedding.' 'Yeah, you're right, Mr. Therapist, thank you. I had no idea I was a loser.'"

I look around at the emptiness of his vast living room. "What do your friends say about it?"

"Which friends?" he asks. "The ones at work who call me the Mormon because I won't do cocaine with them? Or the ones back in Ohio who think I was dating outside my league and should give up and move home already?"

"Come on," I say firmly. "Stand up. We're taking you dancing."

He sighs. "I don't—I don't even—I don't even know what to wear."

Jody looks him up and down. "Put on your most offensive skinny jeans and your oldest band t-shirt. Helen is waiting downstairs in my truck."

"Where are we going?"

"A biker bar on Long Island."

"They'll probably beat me up," he replies dully.

"Good," Jody says. "Better to have a stranger do it for you than to do it to yourself. Come on, they have great live music, and I know the bartender."

He looks between us. "Can I shower first?"

"Make it fast," she says.

"And don't shave," I tell him. "The scruff beard thing is working."

"Yeah, you almost look interesting," Jody agrees.

He rolls his eyes but slowly walks toward a hallway that must lead to his bedroom.

When he emerges fifteen minutes later, he has scrubbed up into something almost handsome, which Jody and I seem to mutually register and decide not to mention.

No so with Helen, who shouts with delight when he gets

into the car downstairs. "My goodness, Benjamin! You look like that Chris Martin fellow from Oasis!"

"You mean Coldplay?" Ben asks flatly as he climbs into the back seat.

"Same thing. Who's he dating now? Not Gwyneth Paltrow, the other one. The one with that glazed look in her eyes like someone has stabbed her but she's trying not to react."

None of us can think of the person she means. Ben shrugs and looks out the window, but he's almost smiling a little.

An hour later, the four of us are at a Long Island biker bar that, as Jody promised, is having a 'blues rock' night, which is as close to West Coast Swing as we could find on short notice. Jody walks in and greets the bartender, a woman with long blond hair and sleeve tattoos who shouts over the music that our first two rounds are free.

"This isn't a true biker bar," Jody explains quietly as we take seats at a booth. "The line of Harley Davidsons outside belong to bankers and lawyers from the city."

"That can be your next step in life, Ben," I say. "Buy yourself a Harley and pretend you're tough."

"I'll need a raise first. Those things are expensive." Ben sips a drink. He looks surprisingly cheerful about having been dragged from his home by force. We are tucked into a booth near the bar, watching the band play: four men in sleek white shirts and black ties, looking like they stepped out of a Tarantino movie.

"I have my motorcycle license," I mention casually, to Ben's consternation. "It was a requirement for keeping up with my guitar player ex. I even owned one for about three months, before I got pregnant. After that it seemed stupid to keep it."

"That the ex who's living with you?" Jody asks.

"He was on my sofa, but he is back on tour. He just stayed around long enough that Ollie could decide that I was still emotionally involved with my ex and dump me. Which was probably Nick's whole strategy."

"Ollie dumped you?" Ben looks surprised.

"He is insecure?" Helen says. "I wouldn't have pegged him as the type."

"Well, he did announce he doesn't trust women before our first date."

Ben stares at me. "Oh, man."

"I know," I say. "I was stupid to go out with him. You can say it."

"No, it's not that," Ben says. "It's just that he gave himself an out. As soon as he messed up, he could say, 'Well, I warned you.'"

I pretend that the words don't hurt as much as they do. "Or he never liked me that much."

"No, he did," Ben says. "I saw how he looked at you during the first class. I thought you two were a couple already. But I think he must have walked into the relationship saying, 'What are fifteen ways I can screw this up?' And then he did them. I mean, with Paige, I went into the whole relationship thinking I wasn't good enough for her, and then, sure enough, her parents thought I didn't have the confidence to be good enough for her." Ben frowns. I wonder if he is realizing this for the first time.

"So what exactly happened with Paige?" Helen asks. "Can you tell us?"

He leans his head back against the plush booth and sighs up at the ceiling. "Do I have to?"

None of us say anything, waiting to see if he secretly wants to. Sure enough, after a moment, he launches in.

"So we were fighting a lot. And I thought it was the wedding pressure, I mean, her parents would make anyone crazy. So I figured we spend a couple of months of trying to please her parents, they pay for the big wedding Paige wants, and then we can start our life together. But nothing was ever good enough for them. And Paige kept getting angry about everything. The flowers, the bridesmaids, her bachelorette wasn't what she wanted. And finally, the night before the ceremony—after this ten-thousand-dollar rehearsal dinner..." (Helen whistles at the number) "...Paige is stomping around our hotel room saying that her sister's rehearsal dinner was better and I said, 'Are you sure you even want to do this?' And she told me 'I never wanted to do this. I'm not even sure I can be faithful to someone.'"

"So she was cheating?" Jody likes to cut to the chase.

Ben shakes his head. "I don't think so. Maybe at the bachelorette, I don't know. But I said, 'Well, fine. What if we didn't get married?' And she said, 'Then what are we together for?' And I said, 'To make each other happy?' And she started talking about how she hadn't experienced life yet, so I said, 'Paige, what do you want?' And she said, 'Why are you pressuring me?'"

"How old is she?" Jody asks.

"Twenty-six." Ben closes his eyes. "Here's the thing, though. The marriage wasn't even my idea. Her younger sister got married at twenty-four, and Paige kept telling me she didn't want her little sister being ahead of her with everything, like in terms of having kids and stuff. When we first started dating, she told me that I better not waste her time and not propose."

I nod. "So marriage was a box she had to check off to keep up with her sister?"

"Is that a woman thing?" he asks. "No offense."

Jody shakes her head. "That's a rich-girl-from-the-Hamptons thing."

Ben takes a deep breath. "Can my next girlfriend be poor? That sounds nice."

Helen smiles. "No, sweetie. My family was dirt poor, and I

was so desperate for a way out that I married the first man who bothered with me. What you need is a nice, normal, middle-class girl."

"In New York?" Jody snorts. "Good luck with that."

"Yeah, I should probably just move back to Ohio. And I hate Ohio," Ben says.

"You'd be hot shit in Ohio," Jody agrees. "Are you actually Mormon?"

He shakes his head. "Presbyterian. I'm not even that uptight about drugs. I've smoked weed like, four times." Jody tries not to laugh. "I'm not a loser. I'm just..." And he trails off, the way people do when they're trying to sum up all the good things that they are not.

"Hey." I put out a hand to Ben. "Come dance with me."

He meets my eyes and nods once. I lead him onto the floor where three other couples are swaying. There is a shocking amount of room around us compared to our usual swing prac-tices. Ben takes my hand and starts to lead me. He's too upset to be counting steps, which means that he's much better than usual. I can tell that his one beer is affecting him, too, making him a little more loose and impulsive, but then again, he prob-ably wasn't sober when we picked him up.

"You know I'd sleep with you if you were younger," he says to me over the music.

"Wow, thanks, Ben. That's the nicest thing anyone's ever—"

"No, I didn't mean it like that. I mean I'd probably sleep with anybody right now."

"That's even better. How are women not crawling all over you?" I laugh.

"No." He frowns. "I meant you're pretty. You're beautiful. I was trying to find a way to say that without sounding like I was hitting on you, because I don't want to hit on you. I just want to say Ollie is stupid." My cheeks warm from the sincere compliment that's hidden in there somewhere.

"I don't want to sleep with you either," I say. "But thank you. And Ollie's probably back with his ex-girlfriend, who is younger and hotter than me, so..."

"No way. I'm sure he's regretting screwing things up. You'd be a hard person to lose."

"Nice job digging yourself out of that hole."

Ben laughs. "Well, you know me. I've got a way with words."

Ben sends me through another move or two that we learned in class, still too caught up in his thoughts to be second-guessing himself.

"Am I boring?" Ben asks when we're close to each other again.

"No, you're handsome and fun and romantic."

"But...?" he asks. "You can say it."

"But I'm not sure that's obvious. On the surface, you seem straightlaced, but you're not."

"I think I bored Paige."

"Paige is going to want you back," I tell him. "So you have to decide what to do if she asks to come back. Because I'm pretty sure that she won't find anyone better."

He shakes his head. "Anyone is better."

"No. I'm one hundred percent serious. Have a plan for when she asks. Speaking as a woman, I think she will. And you have to decide if you still want her."

He nods, and a flash of vulnerability crosses his expression. "It's hard to imagine her crawling back to me."

"That doesn't make me wrong."

Another song starts, and Ben pulls me closer. It feels like something has shifted in Ben. He has decided to lead. This is the Ben who has soul, the one who knows how to make love. This feels like the real Ben.

I glance over and see that Jody and Helen are dancing near us.

"Look at you, Ben!" Jody teases. "When did you get sexy?"

Ben smiles weakly. "It just required getting my heart smashed into a million pieces."

"Worth it," Jody says.

When we are done with the song, Ben and I look at each other, and for a moment my heart races from panic. I am sure he wants to kiss me. I'm sure it would be a good kiss. But I give him a hug and let the moment pass.

When we drop him off at his place a little after 1 a.m., he gives me a warm smile, then thanks Jody for the night out, like a gentleman.

He's not boring at all.

"Swing festival," I call to him.

"I'll try to make it." He smiles at me as he closes the door.

"Were you flirting with our little banker?" Jody asks me.

"He needed the boost," I reply. "But I promise, literally nothing will ever happen."

"I mean honestly," Jody says, "that wouldn't be the world's worst one-night stand. He's probably a very patient lover. He had to be to put up with Paige as long as he did."

I end up crashing for the night on Jody's sofa because she doesn't feel like driving me all the way back to Cobble Hill. She introduces me to her roommate, a lean young grad student with dozens of books on anthropology who owns two chubby cats. Jody tosses me a blanket.

"Extra toothbrushes are in the basket by the sink," she says. "You can Venmo me for the cost." As sometimes happens with Jody, I'm not entirely sure whether she's kidding.

It's the first time I've crashed on anyone's sofa besides my sister's in a decade, and for some reason, it makes me happy. I like having friends with no kids. I am enjoying having a break from parenting. I would never change my life with Hannah—me and her, our little team against the world. But this night is a reminder of what it was like when my entire life didn't belong to someone else. It's a reminder that I'm still a person.

That may be the worst thing that Nick has taken from me, in the end. By making me into a single parent while he had adventures in L.A. and Georgia, he took away the moments that would remind me that I was still a little bit of the free spirit I used to be.

I think of how Ben talked about feeling boring, like no one wanted him, and I realize I have started to feel that way, too—like the real me is too hidden for anyone to see it. I wonder if Ollie felt that way after his wife left, and if Eliana is currently convincing him that he's exciting by begging for another chance. I wonder why I still care.

The Garden State Swing Festival is being held in an old theater complex in Jersey City near the PATH train station to New York City—the kind of place where the shabby gilt drama of a century ago still lingers in the gold paneling and rococo staircases. The festival isn't just for West Coast Swing: it's a mix of events for East and West Coast styles, along with dozens of lessons, demonstrations, and social dances. This glorious old decaying building will be hosting several hundred people from around the world over the next three days.

I arrive straight from work on Friday to get dinner with Helen before we pick up our badges and attend the opening night festivities and social dance; Jody has a work function at her nonprofit and won't be able to join us until later. Helen meets me at the train station dressed in her typical bright colors, with a long, flowing rainbow shirt and bright orange leggings, her silvery hair wrapped up with a matching headband.

"We're getting Thai food!" she announces emphatically. "I never eat the same cuisine twice in one week."

Over dinner, she makes me recap everything that's happened with Ollie so that she can fully appreciate why I am nervous about seeing him again.

"So if I'm getting this right," she says, "it sounds like he broke your heart, and this weekend he'll be dancing with his ex-girlfriend who is possibly his girlfriend again?"

"Pretty much. So I'm basically getting my heart stomped in a public forum."

Helen shakes her head. "You know it's way juicier than that, my dear."

"Why?"

Helen leans forward like she's about to share a fun secret. "Well, you know Eliana left Ollie a few years ago to dance with Connor Yung."

"Yes, that's what Ollie said."

"Well, last month, Connor Yung switched to dancing with Jaana Ahonen, and they're going to be here this weekend." Helen smiles conspiratorially. "And Jaana's former partner Hugo Persson will be here, too, dancing with Sarah Welsh, the woman Connor originally dumped for Eliana." Helen's eyes are gleeful.

"How do you even know this stuff?"

"There are dance blogs, and they are delicious." She points a chopstick at me. "So Connor is facing off against two ex-partners here. I know this is emotionally hard for you, but for the rest of us, the drama is exquisite."

I laughed. "I thought West Coast Swing was a nice, friendly community."

"Oh, it is. But Connor is the bad boy. And he'll probably win this year. Which I won't mind. He's gorgeous."

"I just don't want to look bad in front of Ollie while he's dancing with her."

"You won't," Helen says. "You've been working hard to improve because you're trying to win him back. I know Jody is very judgmental about him, but I think it's romantic."

"I don't expect to win him back."

Helen raises her eyebrows.

"I don't!" I insist. "The problem is, he doesn't think I'm worth fighting for. And I'm done with men who don't think I'm worth fighting for."

"Well, maybe I'm in no place to give advice, but I think if you want him, go get him."

"I know what I'm up against. I've watched Eliana dance."

Helen shakes her head. "Eliana is a sugar cookie. You're fire. I would dance with you over her, ten times out of ten."

"Oh, come on."

"She's very sweet and very bland. There's a reason she hasn't won a major competition."

"Can I have you announce me next time I step onto a dance floor? This is Laura Marceau. She's fire."

"That's the reason I've come, darling."

I take her hand and squeeze it.

Helen shrugs. "You and Ben and Jody are why I stuck with this for so long. I was supposed to be learning merengue this month."

When we arrive at registration, I ask if I can switch my sign up from the Newcomer to the Novice Jack & Jill competition, which is technically one step up. As a brand-new attendee, I'm allowed to attempt the Novice level, but I'm unlikely to win. The levels are based on a points system; anyone can try Newcomer or Novice, but after you earn a certain number of points in competition, you are generally required to go to the next step up, from Intermediate to Advanced all the way up to Champions. There are also a handful of competitions for age ranges like youth and seniors. Ollie and Eliana, with their competition history, are automatically competing at the top level.

While I wait for Helen to finish picking up her badge, I scan the lobby nervously for Ollie's auburn hair or Eliana's sunny ponytail. What I see instead is a sandy-haired, awkward figure hovering just inside the door.

"Ben!" I call, and Ben's smile widens when he sees us. "You came!"

"I came," he says. "And guess what? Paige called me last night."

"Are you serious? Did she want to get back together?"

Ben nods, slowly. "You were one hundred percent right, Laura."

"Tell us everything," Helen says.

"Is it okay if I don't?" He grimaces. "I basically told her off."

"I told you she would!" I say. "You're marvelous, and she's realizing what she lost. And if you wanted to try again with her, no one would judge you."

He shakes his head slowly. "Maybe the day after the wedding I would have, but now, no thank you. I realized that I always felt like I wasn't good enough for her, and it hit me that she was the one making me feel that way. She was playing hard to get, telling me I had to be serious enough to get married, telling me she expected to be treated well. It was a game, and I was tired of playing. I don't want to have to prove myself constantly anymore."

Helen pats his arm. "Good for you. I wish I'd avoided my first marriage."

"Wasn't that your only marriage?"

"Exactly," Helen says with a smile. "Now come join us. We'll find some lovely young woman and get you laid."

Ben looks amused in spite of himself as he heads to the social dance. I'm starting to hope this could be fun.

As soon as we enter the large ballroom space for the opening night dance, though, I start feeling less confident. The room is whirling with light and color and the faint scent of sweat. While the music is technically slow enough for West Coast swing, there are a bunch of styles to be seen, from the more bouncy, circular styles of East Coast to the sexier Blues dancers. I find myself scanning the room for Ollie, but he is not here. That feels like more of a relief than a disappointment, but only just.

Ben asks Helen to dance, which leaves me standing alone at the edge of the crowd. Almost everyone I'm watching is terrifyingly good, even compared to the events that I've been to in New York. After a while, I start to feel nervous that someone will approach me and ask me to dance and be disappointed by my lack of skill. I keep my eyes on Ben and Helen, reminding myself that there is joy in seeing how much better Ben has gotten and how much fun Helen's having. Then I notice a large man standing beside me with dark brown skin and startlingly attractive light-brown eyes. He is easily six feet tall and built like an athlete, but he has a warm, easygoing smile when he meets my eyes.

"Do you want to dance?" I ask him, just as a slower Leon Bridges song starts up. "I am completely new to this, and I only know West Coast, but I feel like if I don't get out there now, I never will. I'm a follower, if you know how to lead."

He tilts his head to one side like I've said something very funny, then puts out a hand to me. "I'd be happy to," he replies.

Within about three seconds, I realize my mistake. He is astonishingly good—better than Ollie, even. His dance moves are witty and polished, and he leaves me space to attempt my awkward but enthusiastic newcomer moves.

"You're doing great!" he says warmly.

It's a lie, but it helps me relax and start having fun. I manage to pull off three moves that I only just learned: a variation on a whip, a rock and go, and a new pop-out move that I picked up from my lesson with Eliana.

"How long have you been dancing?" the man asks, his hand warm in mine.

"About two months."

"You're wonderful for two months!" he calls back as he pulls me into a turn. He seems to be having fun even though he's guiding me through steps like you'd help a wobbly child on a bicycle.

At the end of the dance, I'm feeling a bit better about myself. "Thank you," I say with a grin. "You helped me get over my fear of getting out there."

"Dion," he says, holding out his hand.

"Laura."

"You're a natural, Laura."

We shake hands, and when I return back to the wall, I see Ben, Helen, and a newly arrived Jody watching me. None of them speak as I approach.

"What?"

Helen shakes her head as Jody opens her mouth and closes it before she finally gets the words out. "You know he's ranked number one in the country."

"What?" I turn and look after the man, who is now walking through the space greeting people.

Even Ben is amused. "So let me get this straight. For your first time social dancing at your first competition, you asked Dion Reyes to dance."

"Oh my God." I cover my face. "I didn't recognize him. I thought he was standing alone because he was new!"

Jody cackles. "He was standing alone because everyone is too intimidated to ask him to dance!"

"I asked him if he knew how to lead!" My face warms as everyone doubles over with laughter.

I lean back against the wall as Jody continues to shake her head at me. Then I see her notice someone, and I follow her gaze to Téa, standing across the room chatting with someone.

"Are you going to ask her to dance?" I nudge Jody.

Jody shrugs. "Maybe. I don't know. We had a date this week that went okay, but..." Jody sighs.

"You had a date? That's great."

"Okay, fine. You're right. Fine. I'll go." Jody pushes herself away from the wall wearily.

Helen and I smile at each other as we watch Jody cross the room. Right then I catch sight of Ollie. He is looking at me from across the dance floor, standing near Eliana, who has just arrived and is wearing a bright yellow outfit. He looks different, and I realize that he has shaved his beard entirely. He looks handsome without the beard, his chin sharply sculpted. I wonder if the loss of the beard is Eliana's doing and then wonder whether it is for competition reasons or to suit Eliana's personal preference. Not a useful thought at all.

He is staring at me like I'm the only person in the room, though, and for a moment, I can barely hear the music, barely notice anything but his look.

Helen leans over to me. "Ollie was watching you the whole time you were dancing with Dion."

I shrug. "Well, it doesn't really matter," I say, "because he's not going to do anything about it."

When I look back at him, though, he is walking straight toward me. I watch him cross the room, making as much of a beeline as he can without interfering with the whirling dancers. My heart does a small flip, which annoys me. I am angry at him. No flipping allowed.

When he finally nears me, he leans close. "Hey," he says in my ear over the music. "Can I talk to you outside for a second?"

"Sure."

My chest feels fluttery as we walk outside the ballroom into the lobby space, which is mostly empty aside from some dancers from the under-eighteen group twirling for each other to show off their brightly colored skirts. I feel a familiar rush just from standing near him again, the magnet-level attraction that I haven't felt since high school. I can see his lips better without the beard, the way the lower lip is slightly fuller, and that's not a helpful thought either. My brain isn't behaving.

"You looked really great out there," he says intensely. I can't tell what his emotion is. Guilt? Embarrassment? Not jealousy, as much as I wish it was.

"It's hard not to look great with such a great partner," I say honestly. I don't even mean it as a dig, but Ollie frowns.

"Listen," he says, "I'm competing here with my old partner Eliana. I uh...I should have told you about that. I don't want you to think I got back together with her. She just needed someone for this one weekend." He is looking at me very sincerely, like he earnestly wants me to believe him. But why would it matter, at this point?

"It's okay, Ollie." I take a breath, avoiding the intense eye contact and fixing my gaze on the group of teenagers nearby in their twirly 1950s dresses. "I heard about it at Manhattan Swing a few weeks ago." His jaw tenses a little.

"She asked me to do this as a favor," he continues. "She just got back to the city, and she didn't have anyone to dance with. Connor really hurt her when he announced he was switching partners, so she wanted to show up here with dignity, and I agreed to help."

"You don't need to justify yourself to me, because we're not dating." There it is, the little frown again. He looks down.

"I know, but it's only been a couple of weeks since we..." He takes a breath. "I didn't want you to think she had anything to do with my decision."

I take a breath. "Ollie, if I got my feelings hurt about you dancing with Eliana, that happened weeks ago, when we were still together. Now it's genuinely none of my business."

He says nothing for a moment, just takes a step closer. "Laura, can I ask you something?"

I nod once, still unable to meet his eyes.

"Are you back with Nick?"

My eyes shoot back to his. "What? No." I am almost too stunned to speak. "I told you I wasn't."

"I thought that maybe if I was out of the way for a couple of weeks—"

"So you broke up with me as a test? To see if I'd get back together with him?"

"No!" He looks shocked. "I wasn't testing you, I just thought that if you wanted to do it, maybe I was in the way."

"In the way of *what*?" My voice is getting louder, my will to act mature swept away by a wave of outrage.

"I thought maybe deep down, you still wanted him, and you felt guilty telling me—"

"I can assure you, I am not the one here who needs to feel guilty."

He takes another step forward, and I get the insane idea that he's about to grab me and kiss me, and I know that if he does then I'm going to shove him away as hard as I can.

"Laura." He raises one tentative hand.

The teenagers open the door to head back into the ballroom,

and music pours out the doors, along with Eliana, wearing her bright yellow tank-top and matching pants like she's made of sunshine and lemon drops.

"Hey! I figured out when the practice session is," she says brightly to Ollie, as if I'm not even there. She glances between us. "Oh, hi!" Her voice is full of sunny warmth, but I'm not buying it.

"Hi," I reply, my eyes returning to Ollie. Then I wait. Some stubborn part of me doesn't want to make this easy for either of them.

"Can I talk to you for a sec about the schedule, Ol?" she asks crisply.

He nods once. "Yeah, of course." He doesn't move.

Another long moment. Finally, I give him a smile and walk back inside the ballroom.

Just as the door closes behind me, I hear her say, "Wait, is that the woman you—"

The door shuts.

IN COMPETITION

ON THE TRAIN back to Brooklyn that evening, I think about everyone I danced with tonight: the national champion Dion, and affectionate, sarcastic Jody, and sweet, newly sexy Ben. It feels like I danced with everyone but Ollie.

Ollie, who apologized for not telling me about Eliana.

Ollie, who thought I would get back together with Nick?

I don't know whether to feel furious or depressed. Furious, I decide. Enraged. He said he wasn't testing me, but the fact that it was his first question suggests the exact opposite.

And his apology to me for dancing with Eliana? His assumption that I would care? I mean, of course I cared, but why bother? What exactly was he sorry for?

When I get back to my apartment, I vow to think about anything else but him, but I immediately break that vow to watch dance videos online, trying to figure out the identities of everyone from Helen's summary of 'the drama.' I watch the handsome champion Dion and his partner Paula. I watch some old videos of Ollie with Eliana, and then I watch more recent videos of Connor with Eliana, and Hugo Persson with Yukka

(Connor's new partner), and even an old low-res video of Connor from high school, dancing with his first partner Sarah.

They are all so good that it makes me not want to show up the next day.

I am not going to quit dancing.

My schedule for Saturday is full. An Intro to Lindy Hop Workshop. The Newcomers Jack & Jill competition, where I will be cheering on Ben and Helen. The Novice Jack & Jill competition, where Jody and I will compete. Then the champion-level West Coast pairs doing their pre-choreographed routines, when I will have to decide if I can stomach watching Eliana and Ollie dance.

And then another social night, if I'm up for it after my heart gets stomped into little pieces.

No problem, I tell myself. This'll be fun.

When I arrive at the festival, I am clutching a bag with a cushion to sit on during competition viewings and a back-up dancing outfit. I remember that if I do really well in the Novice competition, then on Sunday, I will get a chance to dance with one of the Champions. There's a chance I could dance with Ollie in the Novice/Champion Jack & Jill. I'm not sure if I still want that or not.

The Lindy Hop workshop is more fun than I expected. I first fell in love with West Coast Swing because it is slow and sexy, but classic Lindy Hop is bubblier and faster, like you're an excited teenager circling your partner on a trampoline. I decide I will definitely learn more swing styles, assuming I can survive this weekend.

One more victory achieved for my love of dance.

Next up is the Newcomers Jack & Jill competition where Ben and Helen will compete. The event takes place in a smaller theater across the street from the main venue, in a large, air-conditioned space that can hold about twenty pairs and forty observers. This event is a group contest where the dancers wear numbers, rather than each couple competing one at a time. I adjust Ben's number for him while we listen to the rules being explained. Dancers will get their partners' numbers picked out of a hat, and then they will dance to two different styles of song together—a slow one and then a fast one.

The atmosphere is light-hearted and supportive. Everyone is applauding, people are laughing, and nobody seems too worried about the outcome. Only Ben looks stressed.

"Why the hell did I let you talk me into this?"

"It'll be fun," I say. "Now go be sexy."

Ben's partner for the dance turns out to be a sweet, round-faced young woman who looks extremely nervous, and the first song that gets picked is a Frank Sinatra song. Jody is sitting next to me, and we give each other a quick look of alarm, hoping this was not one of the wedding tunes Ben had to suffer through in an attempt to please his future in-laws. But Ben just grins, puts out a hand to the woman, and begins.

He is not great. He is stiff and nervous, but somewhere in the middle of the song, he starts to gain a little confidence and move with the music. I see a little of the Ben from the biker bar emerging. By the end, he gives her a fun turn or two, and I recall Ollie's comment that everything can be taught except a complete lack of rhythm. Ben has rhythm. He even ends the song with a polished little mini dip. Meanwhile, Helen has been dancing with a very tall, enthusiastic leader, and seems to be having a great time.

Jody and I applaud enthusiastically as Ben flashes us a smile. At the end of the event, Ben and Helen don't rank in the top three, but neither of them seems too upset about it. No one at the Newcomers level is going to be competing again this weekend; the event is designed to give people their first competition experience.

"A Frank Sinatra song," I say to Ben quietly as we head out.

"Hey, I'm an expert," he replies. "I feel like I just did the first dance at my wedding, but I was being judged way less harshly." I wonder if this is the happiest, most relaxed that I've ever seen Ben.

I'm not feeling happy and relaxed.

My own competition is coming up, and I feel a brief flash of jealousy for Ben and Helen. At least their time in front of a crowd is over; now they can enjoy the weekend without a hovering threat of public embarrassment. But what am I so scared of? All I'm going to do is dance in front of a crowd of observers as part of a big group. How bad can it be?

What makes it better—and worse—is my discovery that Dion Reyes, my old pal and national champion, is acting as the host for the Novice competition. I glance at Jody as we wait for our partners. Then I look around nervously, wondering if Ollie will be there, but I don't see him.

Of course not. Why would he come watch me?

Before I know it, the pairs are on the floor. Jody is paired with a tall woman who looks like a good match for Jody's assertive but warm style. I am facing a handsome, dark-haired man who greets me with a grin. Our song turns out to be a Taylor Swift classic. I quickly realize that my partner is extremely good for someone calling himself a "Novice" dancer, and after a couple of moves, I start to relax. I miss one move he attempts, but it doesn't seem like a disaster. At least we are doing an interpretation of the song, picking up things in the music to express.

By the end, I feel euphoric as my partner gives me a thank you grin, and I scan the crowd to find Helen and Ben. Helen is audibly cheering me on. Ben gives me a thumbs up. I tell myself that it doesn't matter whether I make the top five. The whole point was to do this and survive.

As I have the thought, I notice Ollie standing at the back of the room. He looks away as soon as I see him, but why is here? What does that mean?

When the awards are given, it turns out that both Jody and I have placed high enough to compete tomorrow in the Novice/Champion event, which I credit entirely to my partner, but I'll take it as a victory. I try to tell myself that I don't even care who I dance with. I can't make myself believe it, though.

Then I pass him as we exit the event.

"Hey," he says gently when he sees me. "You looked great."

"Thanks." Bitterness has crept into my voice.

"Can I talk to you for a minute?" Ollie asks.

"Not right now," I say firmly. "My friends are waiting for me."

He nods. He looks like he wants to say more, but I walk away as quickly as I can.

"What just happened?" Ben asks as I catch up to the group. "Ollie looks like you just slapped him in the face."

"Ollie doesn't know what he wants," Jody comments. I wonder if that's true. Something in Ben's expression makes me turn around, though. Ollie is still watching me, his face perplexed. I turn and keep walking, feeling the tension pulling me back to him as I move further away, waiting for it to snap. The connection still hasn't broken, but I tell myself that it will with time. I never thought I'd be over Nick, either. A little internal bleeding is a normal part of the process.

AFTER LUNCH, Ben, Jody and I try another workshop while Helen rests her feet, then we prepare to watch the advanced pairs compete in the afternoon. It's not going to be easy watching Ollie and Eliana, but I want to see the other competitors, the best dancers in the world. Or at least that's what I tell myself. The truth is, I need to see them together. I need to know how they are together.

On our way into the ballroom, I am surprised to see Eliana wave me over. She is dressed in a sleek, sexy black outfit to perform, but she still has her hair in a youthful ponytail.

"Hey!" she says with a cheery smile, like we are already besties. "I saw you did well at the Novice competition. I remember you learning some of that in my class."

This could be a subtle insult, but I can't figure out why she would bother. Maybe she really is this nice. "Yeah, I've been taking a lot of classes," I agree.

"Ollie was impressed. He said that for a newcomer, you're doing really well."

Is that another insult? Or am I paranoid? "That's very sweet of him."

"Yeah. He's a really sweet guy." Her face puckers into a frown. "I'm just a little worried about him."

"Okay?" I prompt, when it becomes clear that she's waiting for me to speak.

"Well," she sighs, "I don't know if you know what happened with his ex-wife, but..."

I nod.

"I just worry that maybe he's trying to create some kind of replacement family for the one he didn't get to have."

Wait, what? I take a moment to reply, trying to make sure I'm not getting her wrong. "You mean, because I have a daughter?"

"I don't mean in a bad way. At all," she rushes to say, her voice warm and kind. "I just mean he's been kind of a lost soul the last couple of years. I've talked to him a lot."

I don't say anything. Did she really just imply that Ollie was dating me because I have a kid? And he wants to replace the one he lost when his wife left him?

Early-twenties Laura would have gone on the attack, but I decide to channel my passive-aggressive accountant. "Well, if you're worried about something you should definitely speak to him about it. Use the words 'replacement family,' too. That should go well."

Her eyes widen, like she is genuinely surprised that I've taken her words as anything but kindness. "I'm just warning you that I don't think he's in a healthy place. I don't want anyone to get hurt."

Her voice is so sincere that I'm a bit taken aback. Is she really trying to help me? It slowly dawns on me that she may be the most brilliant kind of manipulator, the kind who imputes such a purity to her own motives that she convinces herself that she has no underlying stake in what she's saying. I remember the way Ollie always talked about Eliana, emphasizing what a good person she is and how sorry she was for hurting him. She must have told him all of that herself, and now she believes her own press. She must be really certain that she should be judged by the supposed purity of her intentions, not the damage caused by her actions. Nick was like that, in his own way. He lied to me so well for so long because he had completely convinced himself that his motives were good.

"Sure. Thanks."

She blinks once. "I really did mean well," she persists, acting wounded. "Well, I should go compete."

"Have fun out there!" I say as brightly as I can.

If she is the person that Ollie wants, I think angrily, then they deserve each other. But there is something very strange about what she said, a tone I can't believe would exist if Ollie were dating her. Ironically, it is Eliana who has given me hope that Ollie still likes me. I'm not sure if I can forgive him, though.

I remember what I said to Ben about Paige coming back: I told Ben that he should be ready if Paige came back, that he should know what he wanted. I don't feel sure that I am capable of the same.

Jody shoots me a quick glance and raises her eyebrows.

"What was that about?"

"I think Eliana is the devil," I say.

"Well," Jody says as we take our seats in the audience, "looks like the devil is up first."

The 'Routines' event pits the top pairs against each other, taking turns with planned, choreographed dances. I am surprised to see that the atmosphere is still pretty relaxed: although there are costumes and pre-set music, West Coast Swing doesn't have the polished atmosphere of ballroom dancing. No tuxedos, plenty of cheering, and lots of people getting out their cell phones recording the routines.

Ollie and Eliana are first up, wearing matching dark outfits that cling to their bodies. He looks more polished and handsome than in any of their old videos together, and they dance to a blues rock song that I don't know very well, but it has a great rhythm and interesting tonal changes. Eliana looks charming and polished. Ollie looks sexy and focused. They work together as an elegant team.

I should feel intimidated, but I don't, and it takes almost their whole routine to figure out why. They aren't *magic* together. They are dancing well, but it doesn't seem like they are in love, or full of desire, or even full of humor and camaraderie. Maria once said in class that great dance always has emotional content, and here, there doesn't seem to be any. Ollie is doing everything perfectly, with his signature poise, but there is no underlying sense of joy.

Maybe that's why the Jack & Jill dances—the improvs—are usually my favorites. It's why they are more likely to go viral.

You are watching two people delight each other with the surprising choices they come up with. I don't feel surprised by anything Eliana and Ollie do. It is scripted. Careful. Polite.

Or else maybe I just want to think so, because as soon as they are done, Helen whispers, "That was *incredible*."

There is booming, worshipful applause. Next to me, someone says, "I am so excited that these two are back together. They were always my favorite pair." Eliana wraps her arm around Ollie's waist as they bow, then looks up at him with an affectionate smile.

Ben glances over at me. "Want to get a drink?"

"Yes, but I'm sober."

"Oh, damn. I forgot. Sorry. Want me to make out with you?" He is wearing a mischievous smile. "Make him jealous? I'm willing to take one for the team."

I laugh. "Very noble. I'll let you know."

Hugo Persson is up next with his new partner Sarah. Hugo is astonishingly skilled, a smooth, Fred-Astaire-like dancer who always appears to be gliding across the floor, and Sarah matches him step-for-step. Then comes Connor Yung and Jaana. I can feel the room buzzing. The dance gossips are right about one thing: Connor is hot. He is lean, polished, and incredibly skilled, with a smoldering connection with his partner.

"Look at Eliana's face," Jody whispers. Eliana sits to one side of the dance floor, glaring at Connor.

"The drama," I hear Helen whisper back.

I am entranced by Connor. I can't help it. In lots of dances, there is one half of the pair who is the more riveting one, and it is definitely Connor who shines. He has natural magnetism. I also wonder if he deliberately picks people he can outshine, subconsciously. There's a chivalrous tradition in social dancing for the leader to showcase the follower, never stealing too much thunder. The leader gets to decide the moves, so they make sure the moves make the follower look good; it's something that Ollie and Dion are instinctively good at. I don't think Connor does that well. He seems particularly good at making himself look particularly good.

Last among the heavy hitters are Dion and his partner Paula. To me, they are clearly the best: smooth, elegant, relaxed, adding humor to their choreography to a Beyonce song. I applaud along with the crowd at the end, feeling lucky that I got to dance with him even once.

"Connor just realized he's not winning this thing," Helen mutters. "Wonder how he's going to feel about that."

"We won't really know how anyone feels until we see them all forced to dance with each other in the Jack & Jill tomorrow," Ben replies. Apparently, Ben is caught up in the drama, too.

The final rankings make sense to me: Paula and Dion win, which means they will enter the nationals as the top-ranked couple yet again. Connor and Jaana place second, which means that Connor's machinations have sent him higher in the rankings, but not to the top. And Eliana and Ollie place third, right behind Connor. I expect Eliana to look disappointed, but she seems pleased with the results; and I remember that without Ollie, she would not have had a partner at all.

Eliana gets up and grabs Ollie's hand as the top competitors are named, and then she turns, throws her arms around his neck, and kisses him lightly on the lips.

I feel my feet carrying me out of the ballroom, through the lobby, and out the door. I don't so much as take another breath until I am outside the building, my back against a wall, my heart racing.

It is a steamy evening in July, hot and sticky, the air full of cooking smells from local restaurants and filthy trails of car exhaust. I stand alone in the evening light, wondering if I have the energy for any of this: for dating, for getting my heart broken, for trying to make new friends instead of hiding in my house watching Netflix. He kissed her, even if she initiated the kiss. That wasn't a peck; it was a claim.

I didn't want to fall in love with him. It would have been so much easier not to. And now I'm here, alone in the stultifying heat, my heart wrenching like someone's pulled it out with their bare hands. I told myself I could get over him, that I could watch the competition for sheer entertainment value, but the only person I was fooling is the one leaning against a hundred-year-old theater with sweat pooling beneath her bra and cheap dancing shoes on her swelling, overheated feet.

After a moment, Jody comes out and leans against the wall next to me.

"It is sickeningly hot out here," she observes.

"Yeah." I lean further against the heat of the wall, trying to dissolve my feelings into languid forgetfulness and instead just getting more sweaty.

"You have to let him go." Her voice is unexpectedly gentle. "Don't pick someone who didn't pick you. That's the most important thing I learned from my divorce."

I nod. "It's just—when he broke things off, he said a friend told him he wasn't ready to date yet. What if it was her? What if Eliana talked him into breaking things off with me because she wanted to sweep in and start seeing him again?"

"He's not a baby deer, Laura. He's a grown man. If he wants to let his ex-girlfriend make decisions about his dating life, he gets to do that." Jody shrugs, looking out into the street. "In my opinion, if he were worth having, he'd be out here on his knees, telling you he was an idiot and wanted you back." She glances back at the entrance, her tone withering. "Oh."

"What?"

I turn around and see Ollie approaching us.

"Hi," Ollie says to me. He glances over, looking nervous. "Hi. It's Jody, right?"

"I'm going inside." Jody pushes off the wall, irritated. I watch her leave and then turn to face him, my heart speeding up all over again. He looks hot and tired and very handsome. I am still getting used to him without the beard, and some unhelpful part of my mind wants to touch his face to see how it feels.

"Congratulations," I say, aiming for polite but probably sounding petty. "You guys did well."

"Laura, listen. I'm not trying to be confusing or—I want to explain. When we were together, I really liked you."

I want to turn and run again, but I just nod.

"I just kept thinking about..." he goes on, "I kept thinking that any second you were going to get back together with your ex, and then you didn't, and I just kept waiting for it. I thought that maybe if I broke things off, you would finally just pull the trigger and do it. I didn't want you to leave me two years into our relationship or something, so I guess I tried to find a way to make it happen sooner, so I'd be out of my misery."

"Your misery?" I don't even know where to start.

"Yes!" His green-brown eyes look earnest. "It was miserable. Knowing I was falling for you, and...My wife was still in love with my brother the whole time we were married. And your ex-husband...I saw him. You told me he couldn't be with you until he got successful, and now he is in a band that has dates at Madison Square Garden."

"I don't want him. I wanted you."

"I know that's what you said. It was just..." He looks frustrated. "With my history, that was really hard to believe. And you said yourself that you weren't attracted to me."

"I was trying to cover for how embarrassed I was that I didn't know how to talk to you."

"I know that's what you said." He grimaces. I can feel skepticism radiating off him.

"I told you I loved you!"

He nods. "And then you said you didn't mean it."

"Oh, come on. It's not me who rushed right back into a relationship with my ex as soon as we broke up."

"I'm not in a relationship with Eliana."

"She kissed you on the lips."

"In a friendly way!"

"Oh, right." I take a breath, trying not to blow up at him. "Quick question. When you broke things off with me, and you said that you were talking to one of your friends who didn't think you were ready for dating yet, did that friend happen to be Eliana?"

He looks down, which is as close as I'm going to get to confirmation. I almost laugh. "It was, wasn't it?"

"She didn't tell me to break up with you," he says, but he can't meet my eyes. "She just said that any reasonable person would know that you were still in love with your ex. That I was deluding myself if I didn't realize that."

My jaw drops open. A number of things are coming together in my mind: Ollie's question about Nick, Ollie's statement that he was 'giving me space.' He was expecting to be dumped, and a small part of me feels sympathy for him, but the larger part of me feels outrage at Eliana. "And you didn't think she had any kind of ulterior motive?"

"I didn't think she did, no."

"Oh, come on. Ollie, she tried warn me off you."

"She did?" He blinks in confusion.

"She told me you were only with me because you wanted a replacement family."

His eyes darken. "She said that?" It bothers me that he doesn't believe me, that he might think I'm the one lying.

"Clearly you've decided she's trustworthy, so I'm not going to convince you."

I see him visibly collect himself. "Well, it doesn't matter what she wants, because I still want to be with you, okay? I made a mistake, and I am trying to say... I'm trying to say that I want to try again. I want to apologize."

"No." The word comes out before I have time to think about it. I can't do this. "Listen, I know you have a difficult history. I know it's hard for you to trust," I say. "But I have a history, too. And I am not going to put up with another man who comes in and out of my life whenever he feels like it because he isn't sure what he wants. I deserve better than that."

His face falls. "I know that."

"You let your ex-girlfriend talk you out of dating me, and you accused me of being unreliable when it comes to my ex?"

"You let him stay in your apartment!"

"Yes, I did. I let Nick stay because my daughter wanted more time with him. And I helped him take his shirt off, several times. I helped him get undressed once for a shower. And you know what? I wasn't tempted to sleep with him—not once—and I didn't kiss him on the lips in a *friendly* way, not once. Because the whole time I was thinking about how much I wanted to be with you."

Ollie looks a little stunned, like I really have slapped him.

"So if you wanted to test me and my feelings about my ex," I say, "guess what? I passed the test. You didn't."

I turn and walk away.

WHEN I PUSH my way back into the cool air of the lobby, I see Jody leaning against the wall, waiting for me.

"You two getting married?"

"I told him off."

"Good." She nods, slowly, but doesn't move from the wall. "So, guess what happened while you were talking to Ollie?"

"What?"

"Téa broke up with me."

"What? Right now?"

"By text. To cancel our plans. She said I was a negative person who didn't seem excited about her." Jody looks miserable.

"Oh, no, Jody. I'm sorry."

"And the worst part is that she's right, isn't she?"

"You're not a negative person." She raises her eyebrows at me. "Okay, maybe on the surface. But beneath that, you're a loyal, caring person. You use sarcasm as a shield."

"Yeah, well, I guess she couldn't see the bitter interior under my bitter surface."

"You're not bitter."

Jody rolls her eyes, looking like the teenager she must once have been.

"I mean it," I say. "I mean, look at Ben—he pretty much stands for everything you hate. He's an investment banker living in a building with a 24-hour-gym. But it was you who noticed how sad he was. You kept in touch with him. You watched out for him. And you did the same for me, calling me when I was about to quit dance. Those are not the actions of a bitter person."

Jody shrugs. I am surprised to see tears in her eyes; she hides her vulnerability so well that I hadn't fully realized she had any. "I just get so pessimistic, you know? My divorce wrecked me. Allison...my wife? She was my first girlfriend, from when I was eighteen to twenty-seven. We were roommates in college. And then she fell for someone else. Out of nowhere, you know? But the more pessimistic I get, the more it's like a self-fulfilling prophecy. It's like—my dating pool is smaller, so I feel like I can't wait for a spark. I have to make it work. I want to put in the work with someone, and no one wants to put in the work for me." She wipes at her eyes. "And don't tell me I'll find my one special person. Because you know it's bullshit."

"Hey." I give her a hug. "I found my person. I found you, and you're a really good friend. I thought when my sister left there would be no one else I could rely on, but I know I can rely on you, because you're honest, and you tell me when I mess up. And that means a lot. And I know how special you are."

Jody pulls me tighter and then releases me. "Shut up, okay?"

"Okay." I look around. "Want to ditch the social tonight? I don't have the energy."

She laughs. "You got it. Let's tell Ben and Helen we're going home."

We don't go straight home, though. We stop for ice cream first.

"I won't still be able to do this as much when Hannah gets back," I tell Jody.

She shakes her head at me. "I'll keep dragging you out of the house. You can bring the kid if you want."

"Promise?"

She nods. "Dragging people out of the house to do stuff they don't want to do is my *gift*, Laura."

JACK & JILL

THE FINAL DAY of the swing festival includes Jack & Jill events that have the potential to pair up me and Ollie, or Eliana and Ollie, or Connor and any one of his ex-partners. From Helen's perspective, this is poised to be a very good day.

From my perspective, it is the day when—in my dream version of this weekend—I was supposed to prove myself to Ollie, getting paired up with him in the Novice/Champion Jack & Jill and showing him everything that he's been missing.

But I'm not excited about it anymore. There's no guarantee of which partner I'll get, for one thing. It could be Hugo. It could be Dion again. (Please, let it be Dion!) It could be Connor, destined to outshine me. It probably won't be Ollie, and even if it is, I am too frustrated with him to want to prove anything to him, and I'm pretty sure that Eliana won't see us and immediately realize how much we belong together and move back to California in shame.

I am here for my friends, at this point.

In the morning, Helen and I go get coffee and listen to other conference attendees theorizing about which couples might be the viral hits after the competition.

"If Connor gets to dance with Paula in the final Jack & Jill," one woman suggests at a table nearby, "that is my dream pair. They always seem like the perfect couple that never was."

"I would like to see Dion with Marianne," another person adds, referencing a Belgian woman who's been a hit in European festivals. "They have similar smooth styles, like they're floating."

Nobody is speculating about us Novices getting a turn around the floor with the big shots. The Novice/Champion event is no stakes and no drama, at least to outside observers. To my surprise, I notice Katy from Murano Accounting in the crowd when I get ready for the event; she must be here to watch Ollie. I have a brief, horrified thought that maybe his ex-wife will be here, too, but I don't see her anywhere.

Helen and Ben find seats as they watch me and Jody lining up in front of the room, and then our announcer, a young man I recognize from the Newcomers event, announces the rules: Novice Leaders and Novice Followers will each be matched up with an equivalent number of expert Champion dancers, and we will each take turns to show our stuff in front of the entire room of observers. So, you know, no pressure at all.

I look across at the leaders to see if I can spot Ollie, but he's nowhere near me. I do catch Jody's eye at the end of the leaders' line. She gives me a dryly amused smirk; too bad that she'll be matched up with an expert follower and we have no chance to dance together.

The first novice follower gets picked—a petite, nervous young woman—and her partner is revealed to be Dion. So that hope is dashed. He is, of course, smooth and delightful, and manages to make her look good despite her visible nerves.

The first novice leader gets picked...and it is Jody. She ends up dancing with the Finnish woman named Jaana, Connor Yung's new partner. To my delight, the two of them look incredible together. They click like pieces of a jigsaw puzzle—smooth, romantic, light on their feet. Jaana responds perfectly to every one of Jody's signals, and Jody is finally getting the attention she deserves as a terrific new leader. I am happy for Jody's chance to shine, but I am getting more nervous as my competition gets drawn out.

Then Ollie gets picked to dance with...another follower, a bouncy, eager young woman who seems like a recent transplant from East Coast Swing, with her crisp flourishes and little kicks. So my dream to dance with Ollie is dead. We may never dance again, I realize. As they finish their dance, Ollie shoots me a meaningful look, and I feel it again—that stupid invisible rope between our chests. Why does he have to be handsome, and act so mature and thoughtful, and then not know what he wants?

More dancers. More pairings. I manage to blow right past nervous into not caring anymore. Then I am up, and my partner ends up being...Connor, the heartbreaker. I am briefly terrified. I walk up and smile, and he gives me a half-friendly, half-smoldering look as the song begins, and he puts one hand into mine.

Oh, he's good. I can see why women keep agreeing to be his partner, in spite of his reputation for drama. Even in a small event like this, he is ready to dance like it's a seduction. When the music begins, I decide that the one thing I want, more than anything, is to enjoy this.

It feels like every lesson that I've learned comes back to me. Every move I've tried to master is there in my brain. There are little moments when we pause, exactly in sync, and then jump back into the dance. He starts smiling like he's proud of me even though we've never met before. I remember that Connor runs his own dance studio. He probably did a really accurate assessment of my capability during our first ten seconds and made sure not to throw me any curveballs, but it works. I land every suggestion he gives me, and he doesn't give me anything I can't land. Dancing with him is fantastic.

And if some tiny part of my brain is thinking, *Take that, Ollie*, then so much the better. The applause afterwards seems authentic, and Connor steps back to let me take my own little bow, which surprises me. In this event, he seems ready to share the limelight, like a gracious host giving the wobbly newcomer her flowers. My heart feels lighter when I finally sit down.

I am still in a state of confused delight when I hear that Connor and I have won the Novice/Champion Jack & Jill competition. We look at each other, amused, and he gestures again to give me credit. I laugh and shake my head and point back to him.

At the end, Helen runs up to give me a hug. "You were a star!"

Ben is steps behind her. "Are you kidding!" Ben puts an arm around me. "You were incredible!" He pulls me into a huge hug and spins me around twice. "You looked amazing, Laura!"

"That was entirely Connor," I say, waving one hand.

"No," Helen says. "A bunch of people were videotaping the whole thing. You are going to look back at yourself and be shocked."

"Oh no, there's video evidence?"

"Where's Jody?" Helen asks, looking around. "I think she was taping it."

We turn to see Jody chatting with Jaana. They are both smiling as they talk to each other, leaning in just a little bit. I make eye contact with Dion, who waves and gives a thumbs up. I wave back.

Jody approaches us after another few moments. "I got Jaana's number." She says it like this is a major event.

"That's great!"

Jody looks almost giddy, and her voice sounds younger than

usual. "She's only here for like, three more days, and then she flies back to L.A. because she's at Connor's studio until September, but she may come back to New York in the fall. She's not sure if she wants to go back to Helsinki, so I'm going to show her around. I'll convince her to stay."

"Wait a minute," I say. "Did our little cynic just experience the sparks she claims don't exist?"

"Ha, ha," Jody says, but she doesn't stop smiling.

I glance over to see Ollie chatting with Eliana and the young woman he danced with. Eliana glances at me and then keeps talking to him more urgently, leaning against his arm. Ollie looks over at me after a moment. It's hard to meet his gaze, and hard not to.

His own final competition is soon, I realize: the Champion Jack & Jill. That's the one the crowds seem the most excited for this whole weekend. It's the dance with the most surprises and unexpected pairings. We are already in the main ballroom where the Champion-level event will occur, so we find places to watch as more people begin to filter in.

Helen was right. The room is buzzing with excitement. This is the biggest drama of them all, with all its forced pairings and painful histories. Will Connor Yung have to dance with the partners he scorned? Will Dion and Paula claim a victory in not only the choreographed routine but also the Jack & Jill? Are Eliana and Ollie falling in love again?

I watch as Ollie and Eliana take their seats far from each other in the two separate rows of chairs. He gazes around the room until his eyes find me and stay there.

Why does he keep doing that? I remind myself that I'm the one who rejected him this time, but it doesn't feel any better.

Our pretty teacher Maria from Manhattan Swing has volunteered to help run the event, so it is she who is going to pick names out of a hat, putting together random couples and unexpected songs. The whole room vibrates with anticipation.

"First up," Maria says, "we have Dion...." Dion stands up grinning, "and Jaana!"

Jody grins next to me at Jaana's name. The room is abuzz. Dion and Jaana walk up to each other and hug, then face each other smiling, and their first song starts. It is a classic 1950s bluesy tune, and Dion clicks right into what I know is some solid East Coast Swing training, his footwork perfect. Jaana responds in kind, doing the moves with polish, grinning with delight.

As I watch them, I am reminded of what Hank told me in one of my training sessions with him: top-level competition dancing is different than social dancing because you get to shamelessly use large amounts of space. If you're in a crowded room, you need to stay in your little area so you don't knock into other couples by accident. But in competition, you can take advantage of the whole area, playing to the crowds on different sides of the room and extending your arms as far as they can go. Dion and Jaana are pros at this, and they end with a long slow slide that leaves Jaana doing a split on the floor.

When they finish, I turn to Helen and whisper, "How can anything beat that?"

She smiles. "Wait and see."

Soon Hugo is up—Yukka's former partner, paired with the Belgian woman Marianne who is also popular with the crowds. She has a mercurial flow and a bending quality that remind me of water being poured over rocks. Then a British man dances with Sarah, and I watch Connor's eyes as he watches his old partner: nothing but friendly support.

"Have we gotten Connor wrong?" I ask Helen. "Maybe he's just a nice guy who occasionally switches partners."

Helen looks him over. "Nah," Helen says. "There is ice in those veins."

Then the next couple is up. "Connor," cries Maria with enthusiasm in her voice. "And... Eliana!"

A murmur rushes through the crowds. This is drama. What will happen when Connor has to dance with the woman he just cast aside? They approach each other slowly as Connor gives her an amused, apologetic look, one that Nick has given me often enough that I can recognize it: *I know I let you down, but you forgive me, right?*

There is a determined look on Eliana's face as she takes his hand. *Oh,* I think. *She's going to kill this.* I don't even like Eliana, but I already know she's going to be great before the music begins. I glance at Ollie, whose face is impassive. Connor gently positions her close to his shoulder. They have been dancing together for years now, and it shows in every movement they make, every sexy turn, every little slide where he brings her close and then back again. When they finish, I genuinely wonder if they are going to kiss.

My eyes go back to Ollie, who has the same neutral expression on his face as he applauds politely. I look away from him toward the door, and that is when I see someone else staring at Ollie even more intensely than I am.

It is a man with red-brown hair, close to Ollie's coloring but more ruggedly handsome, his arms muscular and tattooed, his skin tanned. He could easily be a fashion model or a movie star in a 1960s Western. He is Ollie's brother. I know it at once.

It feels impossible. Coming here? Right when Ollie is about to perform in his first big competition in years and will be completely distracted if he notices his brother?

"Our next lead is...Oliver MacCormack!"

I am on my feet before I have time to think about it, crossing the room to him. To Sean. The name pops into my mind.

"Excuse me," I say. "Are you Sean? Ollie's brother?"

The man glances at me, then back at Ollie.

"Yeah, why?" he asks. His Australian accent is more noticeable than Ollie's, and I vaguely wonder if the older brother kept the accent on purpose. I suspect he must have, that it must be part of his charming, unruly auctioneer persona. Of course he's pulling the Crocodile Dundee thing, like he didn't grow up in a fancy suburb. His boots are artfully scuffed.

"Can I talk to you outside?" I ask.

"I want to watch him dance first."

"Well, this is a really big deal for him and if he sees you, it could distract him."

The man's eyes finally focus on me. "Who are you, love?"

"Just a friend of his, but I know he wouldn't appreciate you showing up without his permission."

"You're sure I don't have his permission?" Sean gives me a little smile. He is caught somewhere between trying to be charming and confrontational, and neither quite lands.

"*Do* you have his permission?"

"I'm just here to talk to him." He puts up his hands in an innocent gesture, and I'm tempted to leave so I don't make a scene, but there's a tension in his shoulders that I recognize from my bartending days. I know he is here to start something. The question is whether I can steer him away from doing it in public.

I hear the music starting. Hopefully nobody has noticed Sean and I whispering.

"Just come outside and talk to him afterwards," I say. "He'll be done in ten minutes, and you can speak to him then and have a proper conversation. Okay?"

Sean gives me a hard look, then pushes off the wall and follows me outside the doors and into the main lobby. I feel a wave of relief as he follows. When the doors shut, I lean against the lobby wall and look at him. For a moment, I consider going back in. This is none of my business. But I still care enough about Ollie to want his brother not to make a public scene, and that means I ought to keep Sean talking. It was a strategy I sometimes used with drunks. Just let them say whatever they want to say, and they don't notice that the bouncer is on his way.

He looks me up and down. "You the new girlfriend?"

"Well, I'm not the old wife."

Sean grins wolfishly. "Boy. He did a number on you, huh? Ollie the saint. You know Phoebe was with me before she dated him. Did he tell you that? He's the one who stole my girlfriend."

"I heard you dated her and then dumped her, yes."

Sean sighs. "And did he say that he only went after her to make a point? That he told me he was going to date her before he started? That he was doing it to get at me?"

I say nothing, and Sean continues.

"She was never the right person for him. If she had been, what happened between us would never have happened. I was just getting her out of a mess she got herself into."

"So you're the hero in this situation? That's quite a take."

"Look, I'm not here to defend myself, alright? I'm here to talk to my brother."

"And to distract him in the middle of a big competition?"

There is applause booming through the doors. We both glance toward the ballroom. Ollie's dance must be wrapping up.

Maria's voice can be heard faintly through the speaker system. "And the judges are just tallying up their scores..."

Sean gives me a look and then walks back to the doors, just as Ollie steps out. Ollie looks between us.

"What the hell is happening?" he asks.

Sean takes a step toward him, raising his hands in appeasement. "You can call off your girlfriend. I just want to talk."

Ollie's eyes flicker to me, filled with emotions. Ollie nods, once.

"Fine. Let's go outside."

"You should stay and hear who won first," I say.

He shakes his head. "It's not going to be me. I was a little bit distracted once I saw you two leave together." He glances at his brother.

"I'm sorry," I say, feeling chastened.

"I told her she was causing a scene," Sean says as they walk toward the doors.

Ollie looks furious. "She has absolutely nothing to do with it. What the hell are you doing here?"

Ollie's shoulders are stiff as he follows his brother out through the wide glass lobby doors of the theater. I stand there for a moment watching them. I should leave, but I've spent enough time around bad scenes to recognize when something might escalate. I step closer to the doors, just in case Sean tries to get into a physical fight. Not that it's any of my business.

"No," Ollie is saying. I can't see them, but I realize they must be right outside because I can hear their whole conversation. "You know what, fuck you, Sean. I have every right to be angry and you're going to have to deal with the consequence of your actions for once in your life!"

"She's leaving me."

There is silence, and I feel my own heartbeat pounding in my chest like a fist hitting a punching bag.

"She said she saw you the other day at some dance thing and realized she's still in love with you," Sean adds quietly.

Now it's me who stands frozen, waiting to hear what Ollie says next.

"Jesus," I hear Ollie mutter.

"What the hell did you say to my wife?" Sean demands. There it is. That's why Sean is really here.

"Nothing. Barely a sentence."

"Tell me the truth. What did you—"

"I said I hadn't forgiven her! That's all. Because it's true."

"Well, she took that as a sign that you're not over each

other." My cheeks blush red and hot. Is that what I'm here to listen to? Ollie getting back with Phoebe? The one thing that wasn't even on my radar...

"That's...no, Sean," comes Ollie's voice. "I'm not getting back together with Phoebe. You of all people should know that I would never do that."

"It would be a nice revenge if you broke us up, though, right?"

"I don't want to break you up. I just want to stay away from you until I've gotten past it."

"Stay away from us? You only went after her in the first place to mess with me. Out of all the women in New York, you chose the one woman I had ever gotten serious about. You just dated her to prove you were the better man."

"I was the better man."

Sean laughs loudly. "Exactly. You used her against me. And now you're doing it again. Just like Dad."

"I haven't tried to steal your goddamn wife. Which makes one of us!"

There is a scuffle and then Ollie backs into my field of vision, and I can guess that his brother has taken a swing at him and he's trying to avoid the battle. I'm glad he's not the type to launch into a fight, but I'm worried he won't have a choice.

I finally step outside. "Ollie," I say. "Are you okay?"

Ollie glances at me with worry in his eyes. He glances quickly between Sean and me.

"He's fine, love," Sean replies. "Go inside."

Sean advances again.

"Stop! I was a bartender," I say in my best no-bullshit voice, "and I will call the police on you if you start fighting, so you both better calm the hell down."

"Oh, I like her," Sean says.

At those words, something snaps inside Ollie like a broken

string, and he rushes forward and punches his brother in the face.

"No! Don't you dare!" I yell. I'm not even sure which of them I'm trying to stop.

Sean is grinning as Ollie breathes hard, and then they are grappling and shoving each other like teenage boys. Separating them seems impossible. "I'm calling the police!" I call.

"It's okay," Ollie says to me as he shoves Sean a few steps away and then staggers back, waving one hand vaguely without taking his eyes off his brother.

"We're fine, love," Sean replies. Sean rushes forward and hits Ollie hard, knocking him down, then backs up again.

"Ollie—" I begin.

"Just go," Ollie says to me from the ground, holding his jaw. "It's fine."

I have a strange thought, watching them glaring at each other. This whole time I've been worried about Ollie finding out about my trashy background, and here he is getting into a fist-fight with his brother. Maybe we're more alike than I realized: two people who chose steady careers because we have the same inner capacity for chaos. I've never been a fan of men getting into fights; it's one of those things that's idealized in movies but horrible and silly in real life. But a worry eases in me, just knowing Ollie can be this messy.

"You're sure you're okay?" I ask.

Ollie nods once, and I turn and head inside. They are grown men and can deal with the consequences on their own actions, as Jody would say.

Why did I even try to stop them? I probably made it worse.

I walk back inside the ballroom to hear the winners being announced. Ollie was right; he didn't win anything. The winners are Connor and Eliana.

I can't bring myself to care much, but sheer curiosity brings my attention to Eliana's expression. She smiles brightly at the room as everyone applauds. I wonder what Connor is thinking about his choice to break off their dance partnership.

Maria still has the microphone. "And I just want to say from a personal perspective how great it is to have Eliana back on the East Coast!"

Eliana takes the microphone. "Thank you." She seems ready to go full beauty queen, clutching the mic like she's about to make a drunken speech at a wedding. "And I just want to announce that I really hope Ollie and I continue to dance together, because he is really special. And we make a great team."

Boy, she's laying it on thick. I'm wondering how much of that is to rub Connor's nose in what he's missing.

Then Eliana glances around. "Ollie?" she says. "Where did he go?"

"He left the building," someone shouts. There's a ripple of mirth across the room.

"He left the building?" she says. "Oh." Her voice is small as she hands back the microphone to Maria with a downcast expression. In any other circumstance, I would feel terrible for her, but I can't help but feel a bit smug. I glance around the room. Someone is filming this, their camera on Eliana's uncertain face as she turns away.

The crowd eventually starts to disperse. When I look around for my things, I find Jody, Ben and Helen standing together, demanding to know what I was doing during Ollie's dance.

"What was that about?" Helen asks. "Who was that man?"

"Long story. How was Ollie's dance? I missed it."

Jody shakes her head. "Terrible. He was not on his game at all. I think that's probably why Eliana wanted to boost him up."

"Well, he had a family member show up, so he was distracted."

"The brother who stole his wife?" Helen asks, a sparkle in her eyes.

"How did you even know about that?"

Helen shrugs. "Dance gossip." I think about Katy from Murano being here, and wonder if she's the kind of person who posts on dance blogs. Maybe she *is* the dance blogger.

Jody sighs. "Alright. Let's go to dinner. And no more talking about terrible men. Let's talk about terrible women for a change."

"I've got one of those," Ben agrees.

On our way out, I see Ollie in the lobby, one eye slightly bruised. His brother seems to be gone now, and he looks shaken and a little unsteady. I want to give him a hug, but I don't. I step closer, though.

"Are you okay?" I ask quietly.

"Sorry. That was my brother," he says to me. He looks tired, I think. Tired and sad, though his body is shaking a little from the adrenaline.

"I know," I say quietly. "I'm sorry if I made it worse. I was trying to get him out of there before you saw him so you could focus on the competition. Are you sure you're okay?"

"Yeah, sorry, I just...I saw you go outside with him and I just..." Ollie shrugs, embarrassed.

"I didn't want him to mess with your head when you were competing," I offer as an apology. It was me who distracted Ollie, not Sean, in the end.

"Why?" he asks, staring at me. "Why did you care?"

"Because I care about you." I look away. "I wish I didn't sometimes, but I do."

Ollie has a curious expression on his face as he looks at me. I vaguely notice that Helen, Jody and Ben are still nearby.

"Look, if you want to get back together with your ex-wife…" I begin.

He looks at me like I'm insane. "What? No." He frowns. "We keep doing this, don't we? Doubting each other."

I nod slowly.

"And I'm sorry about the fighting. I promise it was out of character," he replies. "I only hit him once."

"Is that Australian for non-violence?"

Ollie gives a short bark of a laugh. "I just… Phoebe and I are done. Sean was blaming me for something I had nothing to do with."

"Okay."

"And I want to say something to you." He looks vulnerable in a way that instinctively makes me want to flee. "It can be right here, if you want. Just listen. Please."

I'm stuck now, frozen in place. I feel both grateful and embarrassed that my friends are listening.

"You know that I originally learned to dance for Eliana," he says quietly.

So this is going to be about her. "Yes, I know."

"And then you learned to dance for me. And nobody had ever done something like that for me before. Not even as a kid. I was always the one doing things for other people, learning to dance for Eliana, going into law for my dad. So when you did that, it was…intoxicating. I knew I was in love with you on our first date."

The words take my breath away. I don't know where to look. I notice Ben out of the corner of my eye, staring politely at the floor.

"When we danced on the street that time," Ollie continues, "I was scared about how much I felt. And then your ex showed up, and he's this handsome guitarist for the Big Lie, and I thought, *Of course.* Of course this is who she actually wants.

There was no way someone that beautiful wouldn't already have somebody."

I catch Ben out of the corner of my eye mouthing to Jody, "*The Big Lie?*"

"So I pulled away," Ollie says. "Because I was so sure you'd pick him. He had everything on his side, you know? Your kid, and the fucking motorcycle."

"That wasn't even his motorcycle."

Ollie holds up a hand. "And when you told me you loved me, I felt like as soon as I said it back, you were going to disappear. Like you were waiting for me to get vulnerable and then you'd go. And I knew you deserved better, so I broke it off. But the point is, I stopped fighting for you. Remember when you told me that I quit the field after my divorce? I did the same thing with you, didn't I? I let your ex-husband win because I couldn't handle getting my heart broken. But I don't want to do that. I want to fight for you." He grimaces, looking at his bruised hand. "Not literally, I hope. But I've spent the last twenty-four hours wracking my brain for how I was going to prove that to you. I had these ideas about flying you to Paris or Fiji for a weekend..."

"Norway is nice," Helen mutters behind me. It makes me laugh in spite of myself. Ollie throws her a glance and then continues.

"But I realized, that's not what you have been asking for. You haven't been asking me to take you on fancy weekends or to expensive restaurants."

"I mean, I wouldn't mind," I say softly.

Ollie looks serious. "Yes, but what you told me you wanted the most was for me to be there, consistently, and not change my mind. You wanted me to keep showing up, over and over, the way your ex never did. And the problem was, I couldn't figure out how to do that without acting like a stalker and showing up at your house all the time."

"Ollie," I begin.

"Let me finish. Here's what I'm proposing. What if I move to your neighborhood? So that I can be there if you want to get an early dinner before you put Hannah to bed? And so I can help if you need someone to pick her up because your work ran late? What if I could help you with little things, and errands, and give you more time to relax, and spend time with your kid... and hopefully spend time with me?"

My brain is struggling to compute what he is offering. He would move to my neighborhood so he can help pick up my drycleaning? Nick expected me to move to Atlanta when he wanted to try again.

Ollie continues softly. "I want to prove to you that I'm capable of doing something real, not just for one weekend but every day. For as long as you need me. And I want to prove it over and over again. Will you let me do that?"

"You'd give up your apartment?" As a New Yorker, that seems like the most improbable thing of all. He really must be madly in love to offer that.

"Well," he says shrugging. "I own it, so I would probably rent it out."

"Oh my God." I hear Jody's voice. I glance at her. "That's a really good offer," she grumbles. "Even I know that."

"It is," I agree, fully meeting his eyes at last with what is probably a huge, goofy smile. "It's a really good offer."

"You learned dance for me," he says. "Let me do something for you."

"I don't think those two things are equivalent," I say.

"Maybe not," he says, "but I'll catch up eventually."

I step forward to put my arms around him, and he grabs me very tight and gives me a squeeze that reaches my soul.

"I mean," I hear Helen say behind me, "you could still take her to Paris for the weekend."

"I love you," I whisper. It feels like a relief to say it this time.

"I love you, too," he says. "I'm sorry it took me this long to say it."

I wipe my tears away. "Come on," I say, wrapping my arm through his. "Come to dinner with us."

"Who won?" Ollie asks after a moment.

Jody answers. "Connor and Eliana. You didn't make top three."

He nods. "Was Eliana thrilled?"

Helen's eyes light up. "Oh, that's right, you missed it."

"Missed what?"

Helen tries to hide how much she's enjoying this, but it's audible in her tone. "You left Eliana standing up there when she was pouring out her heart about how much she wanted to keep dancing with you."

"Oh no." Ollie looks horrified. "I'll talk to her. That's terrible."

Helen shrugs. "You know how Connor Yung used to be considered the bad boy of West Coast Swing, the one who leaves his partners heartbroken? I think that just became you."

WE HAVE dinner at a fast-food style Korean barbecue place, our group shoved into a booth together as Ollie texts Eliana to apologize. I am right next to him for once, and it is the least fancy meal ever, but I feel happier than I can remember for a long time. He drapes one arm over my shoulder and kisses the top of my head. We're together, which means everything will be okay.

After dinner, Ollie decides to track down Eliana as soon as we get to the evening's social dance, but it turns out that we don't have to. She is standing by the door when we enter, talking to friends from Manhattan Swing, and she calls to Ollie as soon as she sees him, then glances between us as she notices that we are walking together.

"El," Ollie says. "I'm really sorry. My brother turned up, and I went out to talk to him."

Her blue eyes widen. "Sean? He was here?"

"I left so I didn't make a scene, but I didn't mean to leave you hanging up there. Congratulations on winning the Jack & Jill. That's fantastic."

Eliana bites her lip. "Yeah, so...I wanted to talk to you about that."

There's something odd about her manner. I feel myself tense up as Ollie nods.

"So Connor has asked me to come back. He says he thinks it was a mistake for us to stop dancing together. That what we needed was some time apart," Eliana says.

Ollie raises his eyebrows. "And you're okay with that?"

"Yeah, I thought—you were never that into dancing with me in the first place. So I think it's for the best." Eliana's eyes move to me and then away again, and I try to keep my expression neutral.

Ollie seems utterly unphased. "Well, if you want to get back with him, then that's good, I guess. If you're sure he'll treat you well."

She waves a hand. "Oh, it's not like we're dating." She glances at Connor across the room as he dances with Paula Reyes, doing one of his beautiful, long-lined moves. "He's an absolute nightmare as a boyfriend. I just want to be at a school where I can teach." She looks between us. "And are you two back together? That's great. I'm really happy for you guys."

"Thank you," Ollie says. Ollie wishes her well, smiling, but I can't quite bring myself to follow suit. I wear a facial expression that's the equivalent of my 'Cordially yours' email send-off.

And good luck to you, Eliana. May you fall off a pier into the Pacific Ocean.

As soon as we step away, Ollie pulls me onto the floor and spins me into his arms to dance with me. This time feels even better than before: I can finally keep up with most of his moves. I can enjoy myself rather than counting steps. I can be happy that we finally ended up here, both of us hopeful, and tired, and full of joy, coming back into each other's arms like there's a string between us that won't ever break.

He draws me closer and leans into my ear. "When you were dancing with Connor, I was so jealous. And then you were with that blond guy."

"Ben? We're just friends."

"He was here all weekend, talking to you. And then you left with my brother!"

"Is your brother really getting a divorce?" I ask.

Ollie shrugs. "I don't know. But it made me realize I should probably see my parents. I think Sean's been doing too good a job of getting them on his side, and it's my turn to defend myself a bit. Do you want to come along? See my nouveau riche origins?"

"As long as you won't be embarrassed by me."

Ollie looks appalled. "Embarrassed by you? I'm horrified by them. My father is the kind of man who owns three Porsches and will ask about your ethnicity within five minutes." He breaks into an imitation of his father's accent. "'Where ya from, Laura? With that dark hair, you have to be what, Italian? I slept with an Italian lady once. Nice girl.' And then watch my mother doing the math in her head, trying to figure out if the Italian woman was before or after they were married." Ollie wears a tight smile. "You'll have to be very tolerant not to want to dump me just for asking you to deal with them for an afternoon."

I squeeze his hand. "I'm not leaving you."

His eyes look soft. "I trust you," he says quietly.

We dance for a couple of songs and then split up to dance with other people... but only, as Ollie said in my very first lesson, so we can come back together again, all mistakes forgiven.

"Let's get out of here," I whisper into his ear when we are back in each other's arms.

I say goodbye to Ben, who is dancing with the cute woman with long braids who danced with him once at Manhattan Swing. I say goodbye to Helen, who is dancing with her Jack & Jill partner, and I say good-bye to Jody, who is gazing into Jaana's eyes as they spin around each other.

Jody just waves me off. "Yeah, yeah, get out of here."

This time, Ollie and I go to my place; Ollie insists. It is a Sunday, so if we spend the night together, one of us is going to have to have to get up at 6 a.m. to return to their apartment and get a proper set of work clothes, and Ollie doesn't want it to be me.

We decide to take a shower as soon as we get to my apartment, washing off the sweat from a July night in a crowded ballroom. When I am done, I wait for him in my bedroom, feeling giddy and embarrassed. I pull the curtains tight and throw on silk pajamas, unsure what to wear, unwilling to lie in bed naked. He comes into the bedroom wearing only a towel. My whole body reacts to the sight of him: he is so lean and strong, and even his bruised cheekbone adds to his appeal. But he looks different without his beard, younger and sharper. I have a moment of wondering whether I know him at all.

"If you have any emergency phone calls coming in," he says, "I'd like to request that they arrive in the next few seconds."

I smile. "Your beard is gone. Was that Eliana?"

He shakes his head. "That was me trying to turn over a new leaf."

"And did you?"

He sits on the end of my bed near me and hesitates for a moment. "I hope so." His voice is so quiet that I barely can hear him. I wonder if we are both nervous. Without looking at me, he starts massaging my feet. He is really good at it, probably the result of dating a lot of dancers. I feel a brief flash of insecurity about the women he's been with before, but I can't sustain it. There is love in his fingers, kindness in his hands. My whole body starts to melt.

"If that's your version of foreplay, it's working."

He laughs. "Why does it have to be foreplay? Can't I have a nice, old fashioned foot fetish?"

I laugh as he continues to massage up my calves, up around my knees, up to my lower thighs.

"Massage isn't your move with the ladies?"

He slides up the bed to look directly in my eyes, his expression so tender that it dazzles me. "I'm not putting the moves on you," he says. "I'm madly in love with you." He waits for it to sink in, watching my expression soften. "Okay, I'm madly in love with you *and* putting the moves on you."

I laugh and roll onto my side so I can press my entire body against his.

"Wait," he says, "I was not done with everything I wanted to do."

"I just…" I kiss him on the lips. "You know when you said you were relieved? That night?"

"I remember every single thing about that night."

"I am so relieved right now. That you're here. That we have time and space to just be together."

"Me too."

He kisses me again and then rolls me onto my back and gently slides my hands up and then behind my head. It reminds me of a dance move, smooth and certain.

"Hands up here, please," he says in his teacher voice. "I

am requesting to be the leader for a while." Then his mouth is on me. and he is better at this than Nick, I think distantly. He is more attuned to my reactions, more willing to observe exactly what is working, how much I am melting, what I need. Then he slides his hands down and I am so flooded with feeling that I'm not thinking anything at all. When I come, it is an echoing loop that leaves me wrung out. I can feel his head resting against my shoulder like he's done the same, though he hasn't.

I whisper in his ear. "This is where I should show you what I want to do, but I'm not sure I can move."

He gazes at me, full of affection. "You don't have to move."

"I want to," I murmur, and then I push him backwards. When I am on top of him, I get to watch his eyes as he starts to look as overcome as I am. I hold both his hands in mine.

"Keep your frame," I whisper.

THE NEXT MORNING, we get up very early and have our first morning dance around my coffee machine and toaster.

This could be every day, I think. *I could get used to the kisses over breakfast and the carefully washed dishes. I could get used to amazing sex with someone who puts me first.*

It isn't scary. I'm not caught up in the thrill of whether he's going to stay or go. I can just trust that he is going to be there.

When I go back to my bedroom to get ready for a shower, my phone buzzes, and I glance at it. I immediately relax when it isn't Abby. Hannah is fine. Everything is fine. Abby is going to be flying back to New York with Hannah in another day or two, and then Abby will stay on my sofa for a few days while she visits and writes her financial articles in her pajamas.

It is Helen texting me.

Guess who went viral? her text reads, and I click on the link, expecting to see Dion smoothly drifting across the floor with Paula.

But no. It is me and Connor, dancing together with the label: 'Newbie dancer with two months experience and Connor Yung. IMPROVISED DANCE!!!!'

Who even posted this? I scan the page, then quickly text back to Helen.

Dion Reyes posted this???

She replies, *He reposted someone else's video, but he added the label. He must like you!*

That is when I finally sit back and watch the video. It has over eight hundred views already, which is pretty astonishing. I look good, I can admit to myself. Not amazing, and nothing compared to someone like Paula or Yukka or Eliana. But I look good for a beginner. And more importantly, I look like I'm having fun.

I dare to read the comments, and most of them are about how hot Connor is, and how he can make any partner look good, which is fair. Then there are comments about how I could *not* have only been dancing for a couple of months, which I decide to take as a win. Finally, there is my favorite comment of all, the one that I've seen on dozens of my favorite videos: *There is no way this was improvised! That had to have been planned in advance.*

I know the feeling. It was exactly how I felt when I first saw an improvised dance: I felt like the dancers were so connected to the music that everything must have been choreographed ahead of time. Now I realize it's just about experience and being in the zone, like being in a jam band. It's something I could talk about with Nick, if we ever reach the place where we can talk about things like this. I hope we will.

I decide to 'like' the post on YouTube. Maybe I'll get a TikTok account now, too, just to follow whatever Dion is up to.

. . .

Two DAYS LATER, on Tuesday night, I meet Abby and Hannah at the airport after work.

By the time we're at baggage claim, it's clear that their patience with each other has grown thin. Three weeks is the longest that Hannah and I have ever been apart, and Abby has had to set some ground rules in order to get her work done. They are sniping at each other when I see them, and they never do that; Hannah has always worshipped the ground that Abby walks on, but now she is groaning the words "I knooooooooowww" when Abby guides her out of the path of someone's luggage cart.

Once we are tucked into a taxi, though, they start flipping through photos on Abby's phone, updating me on their trips and swimming holes and whale watches, and I sense that everything is going to be okay between them once I get Hannah tucked back into her own bed.

"It was a long trip for her," I say quietly when Hannah starts to nod off.

"It was good for the first two weeks," Abby replies with a shrug.

"That may be the limit next time, then," I say.

"Well, she's getting older. We'll see." Abby grins at me. "And how are you?"

I smile, too. I'm glad that she's not upset with me or Hannah. I've missed her so much it's like a physical wound.

Later that night, we sit on my sofa, the sounds of New York rumbling through the windows behind us. Hannah is passed out in her own bed, three stuffed animals back in her arms.

"It still feels like home whenever I come back to New York," she says. "Sometimes I talk about moving back here with Paul, but I don't know. Newfoundland is growing on me."

"It'll always be your home here."

"Technically, Troy is home, but I don't feel that when I go there." She gives a little shrug. "Home is the place you feel most like yourself."

"And the person you feel most like yourself with."

She looks thoughtful. "So what happened with your swing dancing event? You didn't tell me whether you won the whole thing or not."

"Oh! I went viral."

I hand her my phone, and she watches the video of me and Connor, then looks back at me. "You sassy bitch. Is the hot guy the one you were in love with?"

"No, that's Connor Yung. I didn't show you a video of Ollie dancing yet?"

"There are videos of him dancing?"

"Here's Ollie."

I click on a video. and she watches it for a long moment. "I mean, I get it. I can see why he managed to get you tangled up."

"We're actually back together."

"What? Wait, what? Why didn't you start with that?"

Abby swears a lot when she's excited. It's one of the things we have in common. I get a full twenty seconds that would be removed from network television before she shoves me. "Make him come over. Now."

"It's late, and he has work in the morning."

"Do I look like I care? I want to see him in person."

"It's after nine. You can meet him tomorrow."

"Just do it. For me. Please. It needs to be tonight. I'm dead serious. Right now, Laura. I'm not kidding."

"Okay, fine. I'll see if he's free."

Ollie arrives at a little after 10 p.m. She gives him a thorough looking over as he shakes her hand. His face is still a little bruised, but he has his usual polished appearance otherwise.

"How'd you get here so fast?" she asks. "You're on the Upper West Side, right? Did you drive? Taxi?"

"Taxi."

"How much was that?" Now I can tell Abby's planning on giving him a hard time. I want to ask her not to. This is too new.

"Well, she asked me to come right away," he says.

"This isn't a booty call for my sister, you know. You can't spend the night."

Ollie laughs. "I hadn't planned on it."

"So you were planning to just hook up with her and go home? Shameful."

Ollie still looks amused, which is a relief. "I was hoping to meet her sister, actually. The famous Abby."

I step in. "Okay. I think that's enough torturing him."

"No, no, no. I decide when he's had enough. So why'd you give her such a hard time? Dating, not dating, all that nonsense..."

Ollie sighs. "I was scared things weren't over with her ex."

"Nick?" Abby considers this. "Yeah, I could see that. But only because Nick is such a manipulative weasel. That's not Laura's fault."

Ollie grimaces. "Well, I'm glad she's not with him, then."

"So what are your intentions?" she asks. I try again to interrupt, but Ollie doesn't bat an eye.

"Serious ones."

"So you'll still be together in June?"

"I hope so."

Does she mean...? "Wait. Why?" I interrupt.

"Because that's when my wedding is. Hannah and I looked at locations together. We've got a date!"

"That's amazing." I give Abby a huge hug.

She looks at Ollie with a smile. "And now that I've decided that Oliver is acceptable, he can come, too."

Ollie grins. "What did I do to earn the acceptable label?"

"You dropped everything to show up here at ten at night just because she asked you to."

"Well, she wouldn't have asked if it wasn't important to her."

Abby smile slowly widens as she glances at me. "Yes, he'll do."

THERE ARE few things as terrifying as arriving at work to find a meeting invitation from someone who is not part of your department. Destiny has asked to see me, so I head up to her large corner office, which turns out to be as elegantly styled as she is: all cool whites and understated paneling.

"So," Destiny says. "Someone came into my office this morning to discuss something with me, and I think you need to be informed about it."

I sense that this is not good news, but I can't be sure. "Okay...?"

"Apparently people in the office have been following Ollie's swing dancing career?" Destiny says it with skepticism, like she's asking whether Ollie is part of a Dungeons and Dragons club or a hacky-sack tournament. "And I guess there was some story about Oliver confessing his love to you at an event? In the middle of a crowd? I didn't get all the details. But does that sound right? That you two are seeing each other?"

"Oh." My voice suddenly sounds like a teenage girl's.

"I gather there's video of you dancing at a party, as well?" Destiny asks it like it's a question, but I know that it is not. "My concern is this. Our committee is creating a report about how everyone in the company should act with regard to disclosing a relationship, and it will look extremely poorly if two members of the committee were getting together in the middle of it.

Which is why I asked that question at the beginning of the process."

"I'm sorry," I say. "Ollie and I were not in a monogamous relationship at that point. We didn't know what to report, and then we put things on hold for several weeks entirely, and then broke up, and last weekend, we did end up getting back together. But I thought our committee work was essentially done."

"Done but not presented. You should have told me about this immediately."

I take a breath. "The truth is, unless the people are reporting to each other as manager and employee, relationships are usually too complicated to define them in the early stages."

"I can respect that. But someone felt concerned enough about this to report this to me and your managers."

"Was it Brant?" I ask.

"I can't say who it was. I'm just giving you a heads-up. I want you to know that the information is out there. And I would like you and Ollie both to withdraw your names from the committee ASAP."

"I'll do so immediately."

"Thank you." Destiny sighs. "Well, I suppose this explains Ollie taking a dive off the side of a boat for you."

"Is that all you need me to do?"

She frowns. "Laura. I'm not interested in turning this into a big thing, but I can't predict how your managers might react if they feel like you weren't forthcoming. So I just want you to be prepared for that."

My heart sinks. "Just so you're aware," I say, "I think Brant was romantically interested in me and this was retaliation, if it was him who told you."

She looks at me, blinks, and then puts her head into her hands. "You three were supposed to be my grown-ups," she says wearily, and I have a flash of sympathy for anyone having to deal with the human resources side of office work, where all the human messes arrive sooner or later.

"The fact that you didn't know Ollie and I had gone on a date, broke up, and then got back together—the fact that none of that was visible in our work—means that we were being grown-ups," I say quietly.

When I leave her office, I briefly debate whether to talk to Ollie or Brant first, but my undiluted anger, mixed with a distant hope of improving the situation, sends me back to my own floor. I knock on Brant's office door, and he opens it for me, unsurprised. He closes the door behind me, walks over to his desk and leans back against it. It's only then that I register a vicious quality to his expression.

"Brant. Did you report to someone that Ollie and I were dating?"

"Well," he says, "if you've had some changes in your relationship status, as your manager I specifically asked you to tell me about it."

"Going after someone for their relationship status could create a lot of potential lawsuits, couldn't it?"

"It's the lying that concerns me," he replies, almost primly, but I can see anger below the surface.

"And if I get laid off because of it?"

Brant sighs. "That is not up to me."

"The situation was complicated. It was hard for me to know what was going on," I say. "We weren't together and then we were. It wasn't some kind of betrayal."

"Except it was. Because I fought for you. I was one of the people who pushed Murano to take you back. And the irony is..." Now Brant looks away. "I have been pushing for you to get a promotion." He takes a breath. "I didn't want you reporting to me."

I pretend not to understand his meaning. "Why didn't you want me reporting to you?"

He frowns. There is a long silence.

I stare at him. "So you were hoping to maybe ask me out yourself if I got a promotion? Because you'd be allowed to? And once that no longer seemed likely, you retaliated against me?"

He knows he is on thin legal ground, and I watch him backtrack. "That's not what I meant at all. You're putting a meaning to my words that I did not say."

"You were never a real friend to me. You wanted something from me. And when you couldn't get it, you put my job at risk."

"I just reported what happened. Your choices are yours."

"I hope you don't mind if I also report what you said in this meeting."

"I didn't say anything at this meeting that can be used against me." He smiles, and I can tell that he hates me. He probably hates women in general, but right now, that specifically extends to me.

I walk out of the room feeling physically ill.

I send the email to Destiny withdrawing from the committee. I wonder what would have happened if I'd sent it earlier, if I hadn't been so distracted by my new relationship and my sister's visit and forgotten about the potential blowback at work.

As soon as I hit send, I hear a buzz from my phone. There is a text from Ollie: *We should talk right away.*

OLLIE and I meet outside the building a few minutes later and walk to the courtyard across the street. I am still shaking and unsteady from the shock of my confrontation with Brant.

"Destiny spoke to me," he begins.

"Me, too. Brant is such an asshole."

"You're sure it was him?"

"Nearly positive."

Ollie nods, taking this in. "And what did you tell her? About us?"

I shrug. "As close as possible to the truth. That it was a confusing situation, that we weren't involved in a serious way until this weekend, and that we didn't mean to be misleading. What did you say?"

"More or less the same. I told her I would resign from the committee, which I did."

"Me, too. I'm so sorry." I feel so stupid that I didn't manage this better. I had felt like it was all under control, until it wasn't.

"No, don't say that. I should have waited to tell you how I felt about you until we were somewhere more private. I forgot about being careful, just—after my brother, I was so worked up that I felt like I had to say something. But I had no idea it would become public like this. It was all my fault."

I step closer to him. "This may blow over. In a few weeks, people will have forgotten about it."

"Unfortunately, I don't think so. I told you that I had to fight to come back to the New York office. They wanted me to stay in Toronto. My boss just called me in, and I think he's going to use this issue as an excuse to send me back to the Toronto office."

More layers of shock rush through me. Ollie is leaving New York?

"When?"

"He said he'd give me until October first. Apparently, my absence there has been an issue. I was more of a manager for the whole legal department, and they want me back in that role."

I feel ill. The sensation hits me in waves. This is why you don't trust the universe to give you good things. Of course this was too good to be true. Of course men don't stay. I want to weep or scream, but instead I feel dead inside. The utter predictability of it. Every single time. Even when it's not their fault, they go.

"So you're leaving." My voice is flat and empty.

He shakes his head. "No. No, Laura. I'm quitting." I look up at him. "I am not going to lose you over this."

It takes me a moment to register the words. "But... Are you sure?"

"I'm completely sure." He puts his arms around me and holds me for a long moment, long enough that I start to relax.

Something clears in my head, and I look up at him.

"You don't have to do that," I say. "I could come to Toronto. If you wanted. It would be easier to visit my sister in Newfoundland. And I don't have that much keeping me here anymore. I know you love New York, but..."

I am shocked by the words coming out of my mouth... shocked by how much I mean them. I swore I would never uproot my life for a man again. But this is different. Everything about this feels different, because I know that Ollie would also uproot his life for me.

He leans over and kisses me, then looks into my eyes steadily. "We'll figure it out. I promise. We'll figure something out, and it will be okay. If I have to quit my job, I'm okay with that. I can find another. If we have to leave the city, I want to take you with me. We'll figure it out, okay? I promise. Do you trust me?"

Strangely enough, I do.

EPILOGUE
ONE YEAR LATER

EARLY JUNE in Newfoundland is iceberg season. Abby has picked a wedding location on the coast near St. John's, and she has been insisting for months that she is going to order up an iceberg to float past her ceremony, 'in the background, for dramatic effect, like a massive white dildo.'

I arrive two days before the ceremony with Ollie and Hannah, and we rent a car to drive down the island to the hotel near where the ceremony will be held.

In the end, Brant wasn't able to get me fired or get Ollie moved to another office. Strangely enough, it was Ollie's friend Katy who helped the situation. At Vivi's request, Katy spoke up to back up my claims about Brant's retaliatory intentions; she was the one who told Brant about Ollie and me, not realizing there might be a problem until she saw how badly he reacted to the news. Rather than dragging us all through the legally messy nightmare that was brewing, Brant eventually agreed to look for a job outside the company.

Ollie and I still might move to Toronto together, though, since the company is still pushing for it...but Ollie has managed to push off the decision until this summer, after Hannah has finished her school year. He has been staying in a rental apartment two blocks from me for the last few months, but we have discussed renting somewhere together from now on, either in New York City or wherever our jobs might send us.

In the meantime, we have been doing a lot of traveling together. Ollie took me to New Orleans while Hannah was on tour with her dad last summer, and then at Christmas, Ollie and I flew with Hannah to London so that she could spend Christmas morning with her father while The Big Lie was on its European leg of their tour. Then in February, Ollie and I spent three days in Paris together while Hannah visited with Nick during his show dates in France.

This trip feels different, though. This time, it feels like the three of us are becoming a family.

It hasn't always been a smooth transition. When I finally told Hannah that Ollie was my boyfriend, she acquired a new hobby of testing his limits. She would be rude to him whenever I wasn't there to stop her; if I was getting dressed for a date, she would corner Ollie with skeptical questions, or she would spill salt and sugar on the table in restaurants if I left her alone with him. Ollie's unflappable calm diffused the worst of her behavior, but I knew that Hannah was acting out of loyalty to her father, a problem I didn't know how to fix.

Things took an unexpected turn once Nick got a girlfriend, though. Hannah met Leela, Nick's twenty-six-year-old publicist girlfriend, briefly at Christmas. Then they spent a lot of time together during her February visit. Hannah told me that Leela seemed 'fake.' Certainly parts of her were, I thought. But after that February trip, Hannah finally warmed up to Ollie. I suspected Leela tended to treat Hannah as a mild inconvenience, which annoyed me as a parent, but had the positive effect of making Hannah come around to appreciating Ollie's polite, amused attention.

It is now the night of the rehearsal dinner before Abby's wedding, and the whole guest list fits at four long tables that have been set up at a local seafood restaurant. Faint music is playing, and I know it must be Paul's playlist: Dire Straits, The Tragically Hip, Rush. As Hannah nods off on my lap, I look around and think about Ben and his search for the perfect rehearsal dinner that could satisfy his would-be in-laws. Ben is dating someone else, now, and very happy. Jaana and Jody have moved in together, and Helen has fallen in love, too...this time with tango dancing.

Weddings are so much simpler when they are just about the people that you love the most. Abby and Paul practically glow every time they look at each other. After the mess of our mother's love life, I sometimes feel like Abby and I are two princesses who have broken the family curse. The fact that we can be happily in love with kind men is a small miracle I am grateful for every day.

I slide the sleepy Hannah onto a soft bench next to the dessert table, then step out onto the balcony to look at the wide-open sky. The air is buffeted by cool gusts of wind, the sound of surf making a distant whisper.

"See an iceberg yet?" Ollie asks as he steps next to me, putting one arm around my shoulders. We stare out into the blue dusk, scanning the horizon for floating shapes. To my surprise, Hannah appears outside a moment later and wedges herself between us. Once again, she wasn't actually asleep.

"Did you ask her yet?" Hannah says to Ollie.

"Not yet," Ollie says, smiling. He glances at me, embarrassed.

"Ask me what?" I look between them.

"I gave him permission to ask you a question," Hannah says.

"I was going to ask her later in the weekend," Ollie tells her. "We don't want to distract from your aunt's big day."

"Fine," Hannah sighs, looking annoyed at the foolish rules of grown-ups, and heads back inside to approach one of the photographers.

"You asked Hannah for permission to ask me something?" I feel like my heart is so full that the whole sky can't contain all of it. My love is going to flood out across the night like the endless stretch of stars.

"Later this weekend." He smiles. "Unless you want me to ask you now."

I can feel the string between my heart and his, the tension that means that we are always going to come back together. "No," I say. "It can wait."

Ollie smiles, the familiar mischievous look back in his eyes. "Hey, can I ask you something?"

My heart flips in my chest. "Okay?"

He waits for a long moment, his eyes sparkling, then puts out one hand as the music drifts out the doors. "Would you like to dance?"

Arts and Lovers

Yes, And...

Jack and Jill

Long Exposure

Rachel Carey writes satirical plays, serious screenplays, and lighthearted books about characters falling into love or trouble. She grew up moving around between rural Vermont, suburban Massachusetts, and New York City, and currently lives in the Garden State.

A small press bound by the belief that every voice matters.

Sign up for our newsletter to learn about new releases and more.
https://oliver-heberbooks.com/subscribe/

Follow us on social media:

facebook.com/oliverheberbooks

instagram.com/oliverheberbooks

amazon.com/oliverheberbooks

youtube.com/@OliverHeberBooksPublisher